For Chico

.

ONE

Chico is a pleasant little farm town nestled along the northern edge of the Sacramento Valley. It's home to a medium-size state university, mom-and-pop bookstores, and ice-cream shops that are generations old. It's full of affable, friendly people, and has a big, beautiful municipal park running through its center that's a nice place to watch the leaves change in the fall. To the outside world, Chico might be known as the hometown of professional football quarterback Aaron Rodgers or as the birthplace of the world-famous craft beer company Sierra Nevada.

I was born in Chico in the middle of Reagan's first term. IBM had just rolled out their first computer, unemployment was falling, and the recession from a year earlier was starting to feel like only a blip on an otherwise upward economic trajectory. The country was generally feeling pretty pleased with itself. But if you were growing up in Chico at that time, it was easy to have the outside world exist on the fringes of your consciousness, since Chico is a very insular place.

I moved south for college and never thought I'd return home, and even though I spent those four years huddled around video games and accumulated more acquaintances than friends, I figured leaving Chico meant I was destined for bigger things. I spent college watching Aaron Rodgers throw touchdown passes on national TV, and admired Sierra Nevada as they grew to one of the largest independent breweries in the world. Aaron Rodgers, Sierra Nevada, and me. That was the plan.

My family flew down to Southern California for my graduation, and we interacted in the strained way we always did, as four strangers bound only by blood. My father has a way of gritting his teeth when he speaks, and he murmured something that sounded like "good job." My sister hugged me in a perfunctory gesture, and my mother looped her frail arms around my neck and offered her praise. She insisted we take pictures all over campus, and even though our familial relationship was mostly symbolic and honesty between us felt forced, appeasing her was important to me. She had always been sweet and gentle as a mother, and I could appreciate the arduous work of raising my sister and I. The least I could do was show her love and patience. So we took pictures all over campus.

No one looks happy in the photos.

After a late-afternoon dinner spent mostly in silence and a stressful ride through gridlock traffic to drop my family at the airport, I spent the rest of the evening in my apartment alone, watching the rays of the setting sun bounce off glass buildings in West LA. For a few days I was filled with hope and boundless optimism that my life was going to be special. But it was 2008 when I graduated college, and the only job I could find was cold-calling confused elderly people to hawk a new experimental drug designed to prevent dementia. That wonderful entry-level position barely covered rent, so I took another job delivering pizza. Inertia took over and months passed, until one night I was heading south on the 405 with two large pizzas in my back seat when I had the sudden urge to swerve into oncoming traffic. My life felt like a gross injustice. I didn't have any special talents, I didn't have family connections. I felt listless, and I didn't know how to change things. So I did what all risk-averse twenty-somethings with no unique talents do: I studied for the Law School Admission Test.

Law school was going to be my ticket to something bigger and better, and when I received a letter of acceptance to a bottom-tier school in Southern California, I felt the same euphoric rush as a newly released parolee. But law school turned out to be merely a deferral. Three years later, with graduation looming and my student debt insurmountably high, I panicked and decided that in spite of my apathy, I'd try to become a lawyer. I applied to corporate law firms, to district attorney offices up and down the state, to every public defender's office I knew of, to in-house jobs, to nonprofits ranging from the Environmental League to the American Indian Fellowship Council.

Rejection letters piled up in the corner of my apartment like the first stages of a hoarder collection. I couldn't fathom going home to Chico, and the option wouldn't be thrust on me just yet. But just as I started seriously considering selling everything I owned (not much) and living out of my car, I was accepted into the US Navy's Judge Advocate General Corps. It was a ray of hope, and basking in a glow of optimism, I felt like working as a US Navy JAG was my life's purpose. It felt like the job I was always meant to do but never knew existed. I loved it. Purpose, meaning, the honor of serving my country, the distinction of being a US service member, and perhaps most important, the feeling that my father was finally proud of me. We had a connection, and we could finally talk about something other than the weather or the front-page news.

But life is never that simple, is it? It's never just a job, a purpose, or any one thing that makes a person happy. I've learned that happiness is more like an effortless state of satisfaction with the present, and it seemed forever elusive.

It was toward the end of my second tour in south Florida when anxiety crept in. Silence became oppressive and unbearable. The cold, quiet nights alone were torture. Perhaps worst of all, I had no one to explain the feeling to. I started trolling Key West bars, suffering as the silent young man, staring into his drink, alone. I tried internet dating, and my clumsy invitations of flattery landed with the thuds of bodies flung from a high rooftop. Rejections exacerbated my shame.

* * *

When I think about what brought me back to Chico, it comes down to one event, one person, and the story that followed. How was it that three years after that event, I found myself defending a childhood friend from a charge of murder? It started with falling in love.

On a gloomy day in October, I was gazing out my office window at the low gray clouds rolling in over the ocean when a dark-haired, brown-eyed woman appeared in my doorway. Mascara-stained tears ran down her cheeks like rivers of blood. She could barely compose herself, and there was something both disturbing and moving about the way she shuffled softly into the chair across from me, asking for my help.

She was the catalyst for my return to the mom-and-pop bookstores and ice-cream shops. She was why I begrudgingly came back to Chico and the memories of my youth. She was why, three years later, I would be forced to reconcile the person I thought I was with the person I'd become, and it was in that moment when she walked into my office that everything started to go wrong.

TWO

She'd discovered text messages on her husband's phone, she told me through heaving sobs. Multiple messages. Multiple women. Dirty stuff. Going back years. She passed her phone across my desk and showed me. "See?" she said, as though asking for confirmation she wasn't dreaming. She'd moved three times already. She had two young kids and no job.

"I've never done this before," she said.

I'd seen a little bit of everything providing legal services in Florida, but mostly I saw a lot of divorces. A lot. Crazy people fall in love, and love makes normal people do crazy things.

I gathered the proper forms from a drawer in my desk and offered her what assurances I could. I nudged a tissue box closer to her so she could wipe away her tears. Despite the somber mood, something lifted in my heart. I felt a kindred spirit with her; perhaps we both harbored the pangs of shattered idealism.

"I never thought this could happen," she told me. *Could*, not *would*, as though she had never considered the possibility. "I'm so stupid," she said.

I assured her she wasn't stupid. "Trusting someone is an honest mistake," I said.

She thanked me in sobbing heaves, choking on her breath.

She had fine, dark features, like a delicate bird. I told her to come back if she had any more questions, hoping she would, and she did. She came back three more times over the next two months. Each time she was calmer, more poised. She'd look deep into my eyes as I answered questions about divorce law: kids, finances, what to do if things turned ugly. At the end of each meeting, I'd say with urgency, "Let me know if there's anything else you need." I stopped just short of begging her to return.

At the end of our fourth meeting, I shook her hand and caught something in her eye that told me there was something else between us. I walked her to the door and she thanked me, and we fell silent at the sad finality of our meeting. We'd covered all the issues. There was nothing more to discuss. I started reminding her once again to come back if she had any more questions, but she reached up, grabbed the lapels of my uniform, and pulled me close. She brought her lips to mine, and we kissed in a way that was all at once patient, gentle, and desperate. When she pulled away, she looked around like a frightened animal, mumbled something under her breath, and shuffled quickly out the door. We parted with an implicit, secret knowledge that we'd see each other again.

She'd visit my apartment late at night, two or three times a week, when her husband had the kids. We'd make love and talk about other lives we could be living, away from the obligations and pressures we faced. We'd laugh, enraptured in a schoolyard kind of love.

One night as we lay in bed together, I told her I'd been sad when I first saw her in my doorway. She thought it was sweet—I'd seen her crying, and I was sad because she was sad.

"No," I said. "I was sad because I knew we couldn't..." Here I paused, stammering over the words. I didn't want to say it out loud—that what we were doing was wrong, that what *I* was doing was wrong.

"Well, so much for that!" she said, deflecting my anxiety with a playful reassurance. It was sweet of her, and comforted by her legs intertwined with mine and warmed by the thought that this was the beginning of something special, I held her close. I kissed her forehead, and before I could edit my thoughts and filter my words, I said, "I've never been in love before. I think I deserve it for once. Rules be damned."

I felt a naked vulnerability once I realized what I said, but she looked at me in a way that told me she loved me back, and it felt like enough.

Yet sometimes I noticed her eyes shifting around the room when we talked. Her head jerked slightly in a spasmodic twitch when she was emphasizing a point, like she had a worm buried in her brain that she couldn't shake out. Perhaps learning of her husband's unfaithfulness had left a permanent scar on her mind. Whatever the case, I slowly realized her spasmodic twitch was worse than just an innocent oddity. Months passed, and her behavior became increasingly strange. She'd show up unannounced in the middle of the night and bang on my window. I'd let her inside so she could confirm her suspicions were misplaced. She'd cry in my arms after sex. She'd schedule appointments to be seen in my office despite my protests otherwise. I was confused. Hadn't I been the one to profess my love?

When the intensity of our interactions reached a manic level, I realized I had no choice. I had to end it.

On a quiet Friday evening, we sat on my couch and I held her hand. I was about to broach the subject when she pulled away. She told me she was sorry, but she'd reconciled with her husband. They weren't going through with the divorce, and she couldn't see me anymore. Blood rushed from my brain. My thoughts swarmed around a focal point of confusion. I had to remind myself, *This is a good thing. No more unannounced visits. No more sneaking around. No more worries.* But when we said goodbye, I did so with a mournful sadness.

The very next night, at a time when lovers consummate romantic evenings out and married couples tuck their kids into bed, I got a call from my commanding officer. She provided such meticulous details of the affair that I knew they could have come from only one place. My CO asked me to confirm the truth, knowing a denial would be both absurd and criminal. I had used a vulnerable woman, the narrative went. I'd preyed on a client going through a tough time in her marriage. I'd been the seducer, not the seduced. Even if the impressions weren't true, the basic facts were, and I had no choice but to admit to it all. The powers that be deliberated, and weeks later I received the verdict. "Submit your resignation, or we're kicking you out," my executive officer told me. If I resigned, the misconduct wouldn't be reported to the California bar, and the navy wouldn't prosecute. Technically I had had sex with a *former* client (not prohibited) rather than a *current* client (prohibited), and the offer to resign was an olive branch. It would save everyone a lot of embarrassment. That afternoon I sent my resignation letter, and my navy career was over.

Reeling from betrayal and bureaucratic indifference, I remembered that I still had student loans to pay, and I needed a job. I embellished my résumé, elevating myself from a utility player that had surface level experience about many areas of law to an expert in everything. For months I sent out résumés and cover letters, and as my final separation date loomed closer and closer, I still had no prospects. I walked the halls of Naval Air Station Key West with my eyes downcast, my new life as a pariah.

Is everyone's life punctuated so heavily by disappointment and failure?

Unreturned messages to former colleagues and fruitless internet job-board searches exacerbated my feeling of hopelessness. Then, one Saturday morning in July, I was on my laptop, scrolling through my Facebook news feed, and I came across a picture of a fit young man in a well-tailored suit standing behind a big mahogany desk. He looked about my age and stood next to a short gray-haired woman with an uncomfortable smile on her face. I looked closer. There was something familiar about the man in the suit, and then it registered. It was Will Norris, my childhood friend from Chico. I could immediately appreciate how the years had taken our lives down very different paths, and a glance at his profile showed that, other than his three years of law school, he'd never left Chico. But his photos were glossy, flattering snapshots of an enviable life. He sparkled with confidence. I'd forgotten about Will since we grew apart in high school, but seeing his picture became a reminder of what I'd left behind in Chico all those years ago, and it was the first time I considered that maybe moving home wouldn't be such a bad thing.

THREE

The Facebook post was sponsored by the law firm of Norris and Rivelli. Below the photo was a note celebrating victory in a recent case.

> Friends,
> I am so pleased to announce that we have just secured a TWO MILLION DOLLAR settlement for an indigent client in a personal injury case.
> $2,000,000!
> This is the quality of service and aggressive litigation experience you will get EVERY TIME from Norris and Rivelli, P.F.C.!

The gray-haired woman looked none too pleased in her role as human prop, but she couldn't have been too disappointed: she'd just collected a $2,000,000 settlement. I opened an internet browser and searched for "Norris and Rivelli Chico." Streams of local periodicals and legal journals noting numerous Norris and Rivelli million-dollar victories populated the search results. Most were from catastrophic personal-injury or wrongful-death cases, but it looked as though the firm would take anything that made money. Scrolling through the massive awards and even deducting for trial costs, overhead, and payments to clients, I estimated Will was worth millions. He must have paid off his loans years ago. I knew my balance was still in the hundreds of thousands, but I didn't dare look.

Will and I had been close growing up. We were neighbors. We snuck into movies, had sleepovers, and stayed up late playing *Legend of Zelda* and *Tecmo Bowl* on Nintendo. We played soccer on weekends. We spent school recess together. Bullies picked on Will because he had bad acne. They picked on me because I had a concave chest and the twiggy arms of a snowman. We bonded over the cruel ostracism of high school. Then, just before our sophomore year, Will's dad sold their house and moved his insurance business across town. However, geography wasn't the only reason we grew apart; we both changed. Will started talking incessantly about sex, even for a teenager. Will gossiped about who was getting laid and who wasn't and agonized over when he might be able to lose his virginity. The prospect of even approaching a member of the opposite sex terrified me, while Will used puberty as a springboard to pursue it with a fresh vigorousness. His acne cleared up. He started dressing better, and a fearless courage I'd never seen before started to seem natural. When he quit the basketball team, I started hanging out with the other benchwarmers, and I remember standing on the periphery of an in-game time-out huddle watching Will strut across the baseline toward his seat with Liz Templeton like he was parading around a new prize he'd just won at the county fair. He whispered something in Liz's ear, and she laughed. My face felt hot, and I cursed myself, wondering if I should have quit the basketball team too. Maybe there were moments I was missing out on.

But it was a fleeting moment of regret, and over the next two years, Will and I crossed paths so infrequently that we started to operate in different worlds. When we did talk, we'd chat in the strange but familiar way old friends do. By the time we were seniors, the inertia of our dwindling friendship made goodbye easier, and we never had to say the words. That was well over a decade ago, and the person I saw on my computer screen in Key West seemed to be the inevitable result of Will's sophomore transformation. I scrolled through his photos, one of which was him standing with his arms spread wide between two parked cars: a gleaming cobalt-blue Tesla Model X SUV and a silver Porsche 911 Carrera 4. The picture had some stupid caption about treating himself and hashtags about hard work and motivation. In another picture he was in a nightclub with his arm around two buxom vixens, looking like a wannabee Hugh Hefner. His lifestyle was of opulence and hedonism. He wore skintight shirts that accentuated bulging muscles, and I felt a strange mix of nostalgia and resentment. But I had to swallow my pride. I needed a job. I wrote Will a message, apologizing for messaging him out of the blue and explaining the situation (omitting details, of course). I asked if he knew of anything back home. His reply was predictable: over punctuated and rife with all-caps, like he was shouting over the background noise of a loud bar after our fourth beer. But he told me to send my résumé and he would circulate it among the local attorneys in Butte County. I did.

We corresponded over the next two weeks, and soon I had a phone interview with a local Chico attorney named John Hodgkinson.

"I understand you're a Chico guy?" was how John started the conversation.

We talked about Chico High ("Right across from my office!" John said.), about Will ("Good guy," John said. "A little crazy, but a good guy."), and about how little Chico had changed since I'd left ("Love this place," John said.).

"Yes, me too." *Doesn't everybody?* I thought.

John admired all the experience I had and noted that there was nothing like the pride and honor of serving your country *and* getting great experience. I failed to mention that I knew very little about a lot and that I was actually getting kicked out of the navy. John never served, he told me, but had a lot of respect for those who did. After chatting for twenty minutes, he offered me the job. Just like that. He wanted to know how long before I could be in Chico. Before I could think about what that meant or whether I could stomach the return home, I told him I could be there in a month, as soon as I was discharged.

When I hung up the phone, I picked up a copy of my résumé and examined all the stupid embellishments I'd made. A few unpopulated scenes of Chico rushed back to me. A basketball gym. An outdoor ball field. A stuffy classroom. Lake Oroville. Wheat fields. Crowded pine-tree forests high above the brown weeds of the valley. I imagined conversations I'd get trapped in with people I'd rather remain forgotten. I got the sick sensation that returning home would feel like returning to a lover I'd broken up with years ago, knowing somehow she'd take me back.

FOUR

Chico is in Butte County, located just east of Interstate 5, the highway running north and south through the middle of California, bisecting the state. A butte is an isolated hill with steep vertical sides and a small relatively flat top, like a little peg forming out of the earth or the male part of a button. A lot of landmarks in and around Butte County are named for the little flat topped mountain, like the Sutter Buttes, Butte Meadows, Butte Junior College, and Black Butte Mountain. The population of Chico hovers around one hundred thousand, which is a little less than half the population of Butte County. There aren't enough indigent defendants in Butte County to justify a public defender's office, so Butte County uses the "panel attorney" system, whereby a group of criminal-defense attorneys divvy up cases between them. John Hodgkinson was one of these panel attorneys, and he was my first real mentor.

At 7:30 a.m. on a hot August day, I got out of my aging Honda Accord and straightened the lapels of the hundred-dollar suit I'd purchased the day before. John's office off Vallombrosa Avenue was next to the largest flower shop in town, and after standing outside for a few minutes waiting, I took a seat on a cement planter housing various dying cacti. The dry late-summer air was already starting to thicken, and a dank, musty fog from the surrounding crop fields hung low in the sky. A half hour later, the cement planter was starting to make my butt go numb, and I wondered if anyone was going to show up. Then a tall slender brunette woman in a pencil skirt got out of her white Lexus and introduced herself.

"Hi, I'm Shelly," she said. She shook my hand, smiled pleasantly, and unlocked the office door. "John should be here soon." The sing-song chime of an automatic doorbell rang out and we went inside. I sat in the waiting room listening to Shelly's manicured nails clacking away on her keyboard, and an hour later, John showed up wearing gym clothes and open-toed sandals, with bloodshot eyes and carrying a duffel bag. He was slim, with wavy black hair trimmed neatly around his ears and a narrow, thin nose. He struck me as a very handsome, distinguished man.

He asked how long I'd been waiting, and when I told him, he chuckled. "Military man. You need to relax a little. You're back in Butte County now."

"I guess so," I said.

"Come on," he said and gestured to indicate the beginning of a quick office tour. "And don't say, 'I guess,'" he added.

"What?"

"Don't equivocate," he clarified. "If you say 'I guess,' Juries will think you lack conviction, and they'll hang your client because of it."

"Okay."

"Not that we're still hanging people these days, but you know what I mean."

"Right."

"We're frying them in the electric chair."

"Right."

My office was first off the hallway. John's was at the end of the hall. The office across from John's was mostly empty except for a few boxes of case files. The low ceilings and buzzing fluorescent lights made me claustrophobic, an impression exacerbated by one of the lights always blinking maddeningly.

I regarded the bare walls of my new workspace while John changed out of his gym clothes. Minutes later he walked in, dressed in a perfectly tailored blue three-piece suit and holding a stack of files. He dropped one on my desk.

"Work up the case," he said. "This one's yours." He dropped another file. "This one next." He dropped another. "Then this one." By the time he was done, there were half a dozen files piled on my desk. We were not wasting time.

By the time I met him, the business part of lawyering had left John long ago. Being a panel attorney suited him well. He wanted only to show up to court for trial, collect his paycheck, and go home. He was eager to delegate and did so often. There was no formal training, no learning curve, and no junior associate peers to learn from. One day I'd draft a motion, and the next day I'd argue it in court. I'd stand in front of his desk while he attacked an assertion I'd made. He'd poke holes in my logic until my argument crumbled. I'd give in and he'd shout, "No! My argument wasn't any better than yours. I was just better at arguing it! You gave up too easily!"

We'd do a postmortem. He'd evaluate my use of case law, explain points I should have argued, and offer suggestions. He'd double-book court proceedings so that I'd be forced to go it alone. Trial by fire. He'd pop his head into court only to make sure I hadn't lost the case entirely, and my first few appearances were shaky. Sometimes he'd launch into frustrated rants that would morph into surprise tutorials. Late one afternoon we had a motions hearing in front of Judge Sandra Gold, a tough judge in her late sixties and built like a bowling ball with short curly hair. She proceeded to eviscerate opposing counsel because he'd asked for more time on a case when it had already been delayed multiple times before. The man's pale neck turned a splotchy red as he took the verbal beating. He mumbled barely audible responses to Judge Gold's questions; she denied his motion; and after court had recessed, she brought him back into her chambers for a further ass-chewing.

As John and I walked down the courthouse steps, embarrassed for the poor old man on the other side, John said,

"Any good attorney possesses three essential characteristics." He counted them each on his tanned slender fingers. "Organization, competence, and emotional dispassion." We tossed our briefcases in the back seat of his Lexus and got in the car. "Early in my career, I made organization a habit," he explained. "Organization usually means good preparation, and most attorneys do poorly in court because they fail to prepare. Competence comes with experience, but you'll have all the experience you'll need in the first year."

I laughed. *The first year?* I had figured it'd take about a decade.

"What's funny?"

I shrugged.

"I'm serious," he said. "You just wait and see."

I nodded and smiled.

"Finally, emotional dispassion," he said as he flicked out a long index finger in no particular direction, emphasizing his point. We zoomed along, away from the courthouse and back toward town. "Once you get emotional, you stop thinking clearly. You lose your grip on reality. Plus, appealing to emotion or theatrics usually means your legal argument sucks."

The navy had given me experience, but John Hodgkinson taught me to be a lawyer. When he stopped talking, I put my pen down and listened to the dull hum of the wheels on the road. I looked out over the countryside and cracked my window, thinking that maybe moving home wasn't such a bad thing. As the wind blew across my brow, I felt a sense of calm and marveled at the sun setting over the horizon above the golden wheat fields stretching across the valley floor.

FIVE

Like many lawyers I'd met, John never wanted to be a lawyer. He had wanted to be an actor. But after five years of waiting tables in Los Angeles and more failed auditions than he could remember, he'd had enough. He wanted something more stable, so he applied to law school. He barely studied for the LSAT—"I looked at a couple of books," he said—and scored in the ninety-ninth percentile. He earned a B average at UCLA without ever really going to class, and he moved to Butte County after graduation because being a country lawyer sounded romantic. "There's also good fly-fishing up here," he said.

From John's perspective, the most important attribute any lawyer could have was to be reasonable. "Just because we have an adversarial system of justice doesn't mean you have to be adversarial," he'd say. "It's important to keep zealous representation of your client at the forefront of your mind and not to be guided by passion." He scoffed at defense attorneys who were "blindly convicted" to "The Cause" like they were intentionally spreading a virus. John believed that if an attorney wanted to accomplish something on a meta level, "they should have gone into politics." Facts were all that mattered. "Judges don't fall for emotion. They've seen too much, and they'll cut through the bullshit." The one exception was the jury trial, since a jury trial was the one time you could really put on a show and it counted. If a jury thought you believed what you were saying, they would too. And John was one hell of a showman. He had the presence of a veteran stage actor and the bombast of a throwback politician. Juries would fixate on his every move, and even judges would be entertained by his oratory.

John was not without his vices, some of which I knew about and some of which I only guessed at. He was a childless bachelor. The only family I knew of was a sister who lived far away, and without anyone to worry about him, John had little regard for his safety. He would duck in and out of the office at odd hours. He sipped relentlessly from paper coffee cups that never betrayed their contents. Although slim and fit for a man his age, his eyes were perpetually bloodshot. He liked driving his red Porsche 911 at high speeds around the winding country roads on the outskirts of town or along the flat straightaways by the municipal airport. I went with him one time. It was well after work, during the dusk of a long summer day. We were on the north side of town, and once John saw no other cars around, he slammed the gas pedal to the floor. I lurched back in my seat as the Porsche engine roared alive. We picked up speed, and I peered over at the speedometer—100 mph. John eased off the gas, and for a moment we glided along as though we were in flight. Then he slammed the pedal to the floor once more and shifted gears, lurching us forward once again. When I looked over at him I saw a wide-eyed euphoria on his face I hadn't seen before. It was the expression of a man alive, and he looked back at me and howled into the night. It was the one and only time I saw an expression of true happiness on his face.

* * *

During that first year home, the hours I spent outside work were hard to account for. Without anyone to share experiences with, moments evaporated into the ether, memories got distorted into something more like dreams. There's no one to check on you when you're alone, and I started drinking a lot, going on long drives, and I'd only later have vague recollections of how I spent my time. I thought about my navy career, and I thought about the one and only time I'd been in love. Sometimes I'd exercise. I'd go for long runs up Honey Run Road and through the canyon. My life was becoming more and more solitary, and I didn't exactly remember all of it, at the time.

My family was in town, and I'm sure old friends were too, but keeping my distance felt more natural. Only my mother's protests brought us together since I didn't want to disappoint her. Will was in Chico, of course, since he was the whole reason I'd moved back. But we didn't take to each other right away. He'd invite me out for drinks, to the shooting range, or to parties with college coeds, but time and status had wedged something permanently between us, and I'd make an excuse at every invitation. Each time he called, I'd hear the clatter of cocktail glasses or the laughter of young women in the background, sounds I associated with lonely nights at a bar looking for someone to talk to, and something inside me would burn.

* * *

John started making daily references to some vague master plan that he refused to elaborate on. "Any day now!" he'd say as he strode past my office.

"Any day *what?*" I'd call back.

"Very soon!" he'd say.

I'd throw up my hands in exasperation. "Very soon *what?*"

I went from carrying John's briefcase and soaking up what I could to acting as lead counsel on two jury trials. John introduced me to members of the bar. He'd exaggerate my credentials and talk me up to the judges, remarking to anyone who would listen that I was the best young attorney in town. I would sit quietly like a son embarrassed by his proud father.

I'd heard rumors that John wanted to retire, so eventually it became clear what all his vague allusions meant. A lifetime of unruly clients, obstinate judges, and incompetent clerks had worn him down, and I was his ticket away from it all. He'd get that wish very soon, but not in the way he might have hoped.

Almost a full year had passed since I moved home. A little after 2:00 a.m. on a Thursday night in July, three teenagers were riding their bikes north of town when they came across John's cherry-red Porsche 911 wrapped around a solitary light pole beside the road near the airport. Shards of glass, plastic, aluminum, and the metal alloy of the vehicle's red exterior were scattered all over the road, illuminated by the streetlamp's still-burning orange glow. Crickets chirped in the distance. The three boys on bikes looped a few circles around the wreckage in silent disbelief, looking to see if there was a body inside. There wasn't. Then one of the boys pedaled fifty yards down the road and spotted something just outside the periphery of the streetlight. He gazed through the dark, out into the adjacent field.

"Hey!" he shouted to his friends. They pedaled over, got off their bikes, and stood on the side of the road looking out into the field, like passengers on the balcony of a cruise ship, gazing out to sea. Together they took a few steps toward what they soon realized was a crumpled mess of skin and bone tangled in the vast lot of brown weeds. The pile of clothing, skin, and bone only vaguely resembled a human form, and the boys stood with mouths agape, silently agreeing that no one wanted to go any closer. One of them called an ambulance, and they all hopped on their bikes and fled for home before the police arrived.

SIX

On Monday, I waited until 9:00 a.m. before I started worrying.

I texted him, "You coming in today?"

Ten minutes later, I texted, "John?"

At nine thirty, I called him.

No answer.

I called again.

No answer.

Two more minutes passed. I walked to the front of the office.

"Shelly, where's John?"

She shrugged.

It took me until lunchtime to start thinking the worst, and I googled his name. The gruesome pictures of his crumpled Porsche immediately popped up on a news article describing the accident. I couldn't help but imagine his body slamming headfirst through the windshield, tumbling silently through the air, then skidding over rocks and dirt for an incomprehensible distance before coming to rest in that field. I imagined all the Chico business professionals reading that news article, shaking their heads. "We knew something was up," they were probably saying. "John was always a risk-taker," they'd tell one another. A wave of guilt washed over me when I realized I could have possibly done something to prevent it. I'd ignored his paper cup, his bloodshot eyes, the reckless driving on the country roads, the howling into the night. I could have intervened. I could have saved him.

I comforted myself with clichés people use to avoid the truth: *I'd only known him a year. I never actually saw him do drugs. He always seemed so assured, so in control, so unflappable.* I told myself the things I needed to in order to ease the pain of guilt. Investigators had ruled out foul play after finding a cocktail of drugs in his system, including oxycodone, Vicodin, Adderall, and a BAC just north of 0.18.

I walked out of my office to our waiting room. Shelly's head was in her hands, and she was bawling. "He was really a good person," she said between sobs. She said it over and over while I rubbed her back.

"I know," I said. "He sure was."

It'd be another year before we knew just how good John was. In his will, he'd left both of Shelly's children $100,000 in trust, earmarked for their college education. I wasn't around to see it, but I could picture her crying tears of joy.

I wish I could say John's funeral was a well-attended affair where countless friends and family stood up to offer fond memories. Instead, it was a small memorial service at Chico Christian Church, the eulogists' remarks came off as perfunctory, and the few family members who'd flown in from far away seemed more concerned about the division of John's assets than mourning his loss. I leaned over to Shelly during the service and reminded her that John was an atheist. She nodded and laughed. Then she choked back more tears of grief, crying even harder into her handkerchief.

The handful of local lawyers who attended the funeral seemed to be there only out of a sense of duty, and I felt sorry to be a part of the whole melancholy affair. After the service, Shelly and I went downtown to Fifth Street Saloon for a drink. Even though I'd known him barely a year, I'd learned more about the practice of law from John than anyone else. He was the best boss I'd ever had and seemed like so much more. I owed him everything, and now he was gone.

In the days after John's death, I kept his cases afloat and contemplated my own fate. We had obligations to clients, but I also had to get a new job. Without my professional mentor and biggest cheerleader, I thought seriously of quitting the practice of law. I reached out to Will for advice. He offered his condolences and apologized that he couldn't make the funeral. As I listened, I scrolled through Will's Instagram feed to pictures of him partying in Vegas. The pictures were dated the same day as John's funeral. "It's all right," I told him, and explained my plight. I asked him if his firm needed any help since they'd certainly appoint someone other than me to John's now vacant position. The grooming had been cut short. The handoff would not be smooth.

"Sorry, bro. We're really firing on all cylinders now," Will said. "We don't have the need. I'll let you know if anything changes, though."

I went back to trolling job boards and handing out résumés. Shelly and I propped up John's practice until his replacement could be found. Weeks passed.

A couple weeks later, Shelly transferred a call from the most senior member of the Butte County defense bar. I'd met him at a cocktail mixer while trailing John around town, and we'd exchanged pleasantries while passing in the courthouse hallways. He was a grumpy old man with a watermelon belly who shared John's indifference about practicing law, but instead of recreational drug use or drag racing his Porsche, Watermelon Belly took out his grievances on everyone around him. He was perpetually dissatisfied with the world.

"How would you feel taking over John's cases permanently?" he barked over the phone.

I mumbled something, both shocked and confused by the question.

"We're considering you for the position," he said.

I wondered why or how they couldn't find someone better.

"John spoke very highly of you," Watermelon Belly shouted, as though it were an indictment.

"Are you sure I'm prepared to do this?" I asked.

"Didn't you grow any nuts in the last year and a half? Jesus Christ, son. Do you want the job or not?"

Only later did Shelly share her inside knowledge that she had seen it coming. The defense attorneys on the panel had reached their conclusion to select me specifically because of my "extensive experience prosecuting serious felony trials during my five years in the military."

The résumé embellishment had come back to haunt me.

"No one had prosecuted a murder case before," Shelly said. Before I could correct her to explain that neither had I, she started organizing my calendar for court appearances.

* * *

By the summer of 2015, I was running my own defense law practice, juggling dozens of clients. I think only my neurotic fear kept disaster at bay. I'd remind myself often of John's three main principles: organization, competence, and emotional dispassion. The nervous panic I felt during court appearances started to fade. My confidence increased, and routine kept me distracted. I'd wake at 6:00 a.m. and spend the day drafting motions, assigning pleadings to Shelly, and meeting new clients. Watermelon Belly provided gruff encouragement. So gruff, in fact, that I stopped asking for it. Will provided levity and optimism to alleviate my concerns of malpractice. At 4:00 p.m. each day, Shelly would leave to pick up her kids from school. I would stay late into the evening, some nights not returning home until eight or nine. I started eating a weekly dinner with my family, and every Thursday I'd drive to their two-bedroom house on the west side of town. But soon the pace of justice in Butte County couldn't keep up with my appetite for it, and work slowed down. Attorneys, judges, and court staff took winter holidays. They went skiing in Tahoe and the Chico State students returned home for winter break. Five o'clock would hit, and I'd shuffle papers around my desk, searching for a case I hadn't reviewed or a motion I hadn't written. I never liked idle time, and I'd sit alone on my old beige couch with my solitary TV dinner, and the darkness outside would haunt me. I started having one or two cocktails with dinner, usually a straight whiskey, and eventually I was finishing half a bottle of bourbon. I'd have to make frequent runs to the liquor store down the street.

Three more months passed, and I started hanging out with Will. He was an occasional companion, but I had to deal with comments like "There are so many fuckable chicks in this town," or some accusation like "How have you not been laid since you've been back?" He had the unpredictable energy of a heavily caffeinated teenager that constantly teetered on annoyance. If anything, I wanted to find a date so I didn't have to listen to his perverted rants.

In early 2016, hope arrived in the form of Emily, a thirty-one-year-old "freelance journalist" who'd recently moved back to Chico from Los Angeles. My mother set up the date. Emily was the daughter of my mother's friend. Emily had graduated from USC, and her work had been published in some major media outlets. She was funny and engaging, and at the end of the date I told her I'd love to see her again.

"That'd be great," she said.

But when I texted her two days later, she didn't reply. I wondered if something was wrong with my phone. "Hey," I wrote. "Not sure if you got my last text, but I just wanted to say I had a great time with you. Hope to see you again." Two days went by. I texted, "Is everything okay?" Finally, a week later I texted, "You must be dead. I'll be sure to notify your family you've passed away."

It had rained earlier that day. That's a fact I'd be reminded of much later. The wind was howling hard that night, but not as much as it was above the tree line, above the base of the canyon. That was another fact I'd come to recall. I drove to the liquor store down the street, bought a bottle of whiskey, and sat on my back porch drinking it, looking up at the stars—shiny points of light in the pitch-black night sky spinning around my head in orbit. The cool, crisp night air numbed my face, and after finishing the bottle of whiskey, I looked up at the sky and imagined myself an astronaut, untethered from my ship in deep space, drifting out into nothing.

SEVEN

Before I got assigned the only murder case I would ever try, my mother's condition declined. It happened over a few months. Her hearing got so bad, we'd have to shout at her. She refused to wear glasses despite barely being able to read the giant font size on her phone. We begged her to stop driving and she angrily protested. She was rude and dismissive to the housekeeper we hired for her. She forgot names of good friends, then my sister's and my names. Then she started forgetting our father's name. My sister and I started exchanging daily phone calls about the plan of action moving forward, like military strategists preparing for battle against an unknown and unknowable enemy. Whenever we talked to our father about it, he would shrug his shoulders in resignation. It seemed like he'd rather not be bothered.

But there were incidents too shocking to ignore. First, my mother ran her car into a telephone pole in a grocery store parking lot. The following Sunday, she removed her blouse during church, looped it through one of her arms, and ran howling for the exit while it billowed behind her like a kite. Three weeks later, she tried to bake one of her shoes into a casserole. She put her shoe in the casserole, put the casserole in the oven, and sat on the couch to take a nap while the rubber, plastic, and cheese melted together. Our father walked in to smoke rising out of the cracked windows of the house, like steam from an industrial power plant. He doused the flames, called 911, and rushed over to the couch to wake her up. The family meeting to discuss what was next didn't last long. When I visited her, she refused to speak to me. She sat in the corner of the room and cried. I cried too.

* * *

On March 17, 2016, Shelly walked into my office and set a file on my desk.

"New client," she said. "They're emailing over the rest of the discovery. Looks like you're going to be busy for the next few months."

She turned on her heels and glided out of the room. It was a notice of appointment from the district attorney's office. There was the appointment letter, the sheriff detective's police report, and the charging document. Without looking at the name, I read the charges: "Violation of California Penal Code 187: An open count of murder."

Blood rushed to my face. The room felt hotter. I stood and took off my suit jacket. Distant sounds became amplified. I heard the faint cackling of a group of women passing by the office, the roar of a skateboard rolling across the asphalt parking lot outside, Shelly's nails clacking against her keyboard. I smelled the sweet scent of potted jasmine Shelly had placed on the filing cabinet behind my desk. I rubbed my eyes and looked at the charges again. *Murder.* I read through the file.

The client was a thirty-three-year-old white male, born in 1983, with brown hair and hazel eyes. He had two prior convictions stemming from the same incident-one for possession of an unlicensed firearm with a discharge enhancement, and one for burglary. He'd been arrested for simple assault and possession of methamphetamine but never charged. He weighed one hundred and eighty-two pounds, and he was born in Chico.

I went over the report, scanning through the facts. I glanced back at the charging document. There was a familiarity to the facts, and as though I was scanning through a scrapbook of old photographs, images started popping into my mind. A basketball gym packed with roaring fans. A teenage couple talking at a party. Suddenly I was part of the scene, holding a red cup, standing on the periphery of the party, alone in a crowded room. I saw a boy holding a baseball mitt high above his head with a triumphant smile on his face. A cabin in the woods.

I shut the file and said two words out loud. When they came out, they shocked me, like a stranger had whispered a terrible secret in my ear. Having read the client's name one more time, and without thinking or looking up, I said, "Oh God."

EIGHT

When you're raised in Chico, you have old-school values. You marry your high school sweetheart. You start a family. You drive a Chevy pickup truck. You go to church. You have a sense of community. You're good to your neighbor. You work hard. These are the things you can count on, and values aren't the only things that have stayed the same. The suburban homes, the downtown storefronts, the local schools, the parks, and the people—nothing's changed much in the last fifty years. It's the kind of place where strangers say hello on the street, hold doors open for one another, and don't fight over parking spots in the local Walmart. If you flip someone the bird because you don't like their driving, you should be prepared to explain yourself when you see them the next day in the cereal aisle. Chico is big enough that there's no way to know everyone, but small enough that being kind is a good insurance policy.

I'd moved into a small house at the southeast edge of town off Honey Run Road, on a little street running parallel to a Little Chico Creek. Most of the homes on this edge of town were two-story ranch-style, complete with swimming pools and space to roam. I felt lucky to find my decrepit little two-bedroom house, and the large lot provided a feeling of remoteness. It had old hardwood floors, aging appliances, and retro light fixtures. Perfect for just me. When I moved back, I constantly fretted over potential encounters with ghosts from my past, and it was part of the reason why I moved to this edge of town. The neighborhood was foreign to me. No one knew where I was from.

* * *

Scotty was one year older than Will and me. He was in my sister's class. He was the star point guard of the basketball team, and before we left for college, his athletic prowess was so legendary that he was better known among Chico sports fans than Aaron Rodgers. He would boisterously hold court after school, spitting out one-liners that would have kids doubled over in laughter, holding their stomachs. He was a natural politician and the resident stand-up comic.

We hadn't quite been friends, not like Will and me, but by junior year, Scotty would nod hello when I passed him in the hallway since, by then, we were teammates. Will and I got to admire Scotty's basketball skills from up close. Will was in the stands, and I got a front-row seat to Scotty's athletic wizardry from my spot on the bench. He would float around the court, dominating the game in an effortless way that made the opposing players shake their heads in disbelief. He never practiced, so he wasn't a great shooter, but he'd outsmart opponents, using his quickness and speed to manufacture points with creative drives to the basket.

He was smart, and not just socially. He was book smart too. He earned As and Bs while feigning nonchalance. He partied hard, and all the prettiest girls adored him. My sister always gritted her teeth when she talked about Scotty, expressing a mix of jealousy, admiration, and desire. Every other kid in school aspired to be him, especially Will. When Will quit the basketball team that winter, I think it was partly because he knew he could never be Scotty Watts. Will was the first person I called when I got the file.

"Guess whose case I just got assigned?"

"I'm busy," he growled.

"Scotty Watts."

The reaction on the other end was not what I had been expecting. Will laughed. I didn't know if it was vindictive, callous, or indifferent, but I didn't think it was funny at all. Will laughing just struck me as strange.

"What's funny?" I asked.

"That's not exactly a shocker," he said. "Dude, you remember high school. By sophomore year, Scotty was popping two Oxys in the morning and two after lunch. He was a drug addict before sixteen. No surprise they're locking him up now. What's the charge?"

"Murder one," I said.

The line went quiet for a moment. "Geez," he said.

"Yeah," I said. He wasn't laughing now.

"Well, he already did some time, didn't he?" Will asked.

There was a rumor that after high school, Scotty had got so addicted to opioids that he tried to rob his drug dealer. He brought a gun. There was a struggle, and shots were fired. The dealer called the cops. No one was injured in the robbery, but discharging the gun carried with it a sentence enhancement, I think by a number of years. Yet I heard he had served two years of his five-year sentence because of good behavior and jail overcrowding. Like I said, it was a rumor, so I didn't know if it was true. In Chico, rumors and gossip count as news, and news travels fast. Last I heard, Scotty was working as a plumber for his dad. But that was years ago. I was in the navy then.

"I guess he never got clean," Will said.

"I guess not."

Will changed the subject and started talking about his weekend plans. My thoughts drifted to one of those images that had flashed in my head when I first saw Scotty's name in the DA's file. It was the boy holding the baseball glove above his head. I saw clearer now that it was twelve-year-old Scotty celebrating after a miraculous diving catch. I had thrown the ball, and I remembered how during the summer before high school, he'd come over sometimes, and we'd play catch in my parents' backyard. My mom would call us in for dinner, and we'd come inside and scarf down food. Were we friends? Or was he just trying to get to first base with my sister? I don't know.

"So do you want to go?" Will asked. I hadn't been paying attention.

"I don't know. Let me think about it," I said.

"All right," he said. "Scotty Watts…Good luck with that one."

I thanked him and hung up.

My first thought was that I wanted off the case. It was all uncomfortably familiar, and I hoped there was a conflict of interest. That would be an easy out. *This has to be a conflict of interest,* I thought. *I can't be appointed counsel for someone I know— someone I grew up with.* I went online and scanned through the professional responsibility rules, looking for an escape. Rule no. 3-110…no. 3-300…no. 3-310? No. I couldn't find anything. I called Watermelon Belly.

"I need off a case."

"Why?"

"Conflict of interest."

"Is this the Watts case?"

"I know the client."

"So what?" Watermelon Belly chortled.

"I know him. I grew up with him."

"What's the rule say?"

He knew I'd already looked it up. He knew that I didn't have an out. He was just being an asshole, taking pleasure in my squirming. He jumped on my silence. "I know it's a murder charge, but we assigned it to you because you have to cut your teeth sometime, and everyone else is swamped."

"I'm not prepared."

"It's not that confusing factually and will probably end in a plea. If you need hand-holding or a diaper change, you can call."

I sighed.

"There's no conflict," he said. "Next time check the rule first. Don't call me with stupid questions." He hung up.

I walked up to the front desk and explained the situation to Shelly, who offered no help. "The panel is really understaffed right now," she said. "If you ask to be removed, the other attorneys are going to be pretty upset."

I walked back to my office and eyed the file as if it were a maggot-filled sandwich. I heard the ticktock of the wall clock above the door. I looked at the clock and then back at the file. Finally I opened it up and went over the detective's report.

Just after midnight on Sunday, March 13, 2016, the Butte County sheriff's deputies Haskins and Sanchez responded to a call of shots fired. The caller reported hearing gunshots on a residential street of Forest Ranch, a tiny mountain town a thirty-minute drive northeast of Chico. Deputies Haskins and Sanchez were in the area and arrived at the scene. They ascended the stairs leading to the front door and found it ajar. They knocked and announced their presence. Hearing nothing, they drew their weapons and went inside. As soon as they pushed open the door, they found Scotty on his hands and knees in the middle of his kitchen, "frantically wiping up a large pool of blood." That's how Sanchez and Haskins had both reported it.

"There was a lot of blood," Deputy Haskins specifically noted.

When Scotty saw the deputies, he froze. With their service weapons pointed at Scotty, Sanchez asked Scotty if anyone else was in the house. Scotty said no. They asked what he was doing. Scotty said he didn't know. Haskins asked if there was a gun in the house. Scotty said no. Haskins and Sanchez sat Scotty at the kitchen table. They radioed for an ambulance and backup, and shortly thereafter, practically the entire Butte County public safety and services arrived.

Scotty sat and waited while detectives and forensic crews canvassed the scene.

Detectives found a half-eaten bowl of cereal rested on the

edge of the old wood dining room table. A bloody knife was on the kitchen counter. A white Nissan Titan truck identified as belonging to a twenty-four-year-old former Chico State student named Josh Anderson was parked in the driveway of Scotty's Forest Ranch cabin.

Investigators went next door and woke Scotty's eighty-five-year-old neighbor, Eleanor Jackson, who told them she had seen the white Nissan truck, "around seven thirty or eight p.m.," pull up and park. She described a man fitting Josh Anderson's description going inside the house.

Hours passed. Josh Anderson was declared missing. Detectives notified Scotty he was suspected of the assault and kidnapping of Josh Anderson. They read him his Miranda rights and drove him to the sheriff's station. At the station, Scotty was treated for minor injuries—bumps and bruises—including minor blunt force trauma to the head. He waived his right to an attorney and started talking, but investigators didn't get much. "I don't know" and "I don't remember," Scotty answered over and over.

Scotty explained that his girlfriend, Kelly, had left for work early in the evening. He did "a couple of hours" of work in his garage and sat to a bowl of cereal "around 7:30 p.m." The next thing he remembered was waking up face down in a pool of sticky, viscous blood. He panicked. He grabbed kitchen towels, paper towels, and whatever else he could find and started wiping up the blood. Not a minute later, deputies arrived.

Investigators interviewed Scotty's girlfriend. They talked to Eleanor Jackson again. They asked the other neighbors if they had seen anything. They wrote up their reports and filed them. The reports were forwarded to the district attorney's office, forensic tests were completed, DNA tests were gathered, fingerprints were taken, charges were drafted, an arraignment was scheduled, the file was delivered to my office, and there I was reading it. When I finished, my throat swelled and my head felt hot. For a long moment, I sat in silence, thinking about that twelve-year-old boy with the baseball mitt above his head.

* * *

I hadn't litigated a murder trial before I was assigned Scotty's case, but I'd met murderers. Unsurprisingly, the look in their eyes left a deadening impression that there was little behind them except a black pit of darkness. There was a navy second-class petty officer who had stabbed his wife to death after discovering text messages from her lover. There was a chief petty officer who had beaten someone to death in a bar fight. What had prompted the brawl got lost in the tragedy. It was a spilled drink, an errant comment, or some other pointless exchange of machismo. The chief kept slugging the victim long after his face had been reduced to a pulp and his body had gone limp. In law school I had worked on an appellate case that involved two sixteen-year-old gang members involved in a gang turf war. One summer night at 2:00 a.m., one of them had emptied a magazine into the other. He saved a few rounds to shoot his rival's defenseless girlfriend. Scotty wasn't recognizable to me as any of these characters. I remembered Scotty fondly, even admirably. He seemed too human to kill another person. Too gentle. Too normal.

There was something familiar about the facts of Scotty's case, and I wondered if it was just that I knew Scotty from years ago or if there was something more to it. Then again, everything had started feeling familiar since Scotty's file landed on my desk. Perhaps because it was another reminder of home, or maybe it was something else. It took me a while to figure that out.

NINE

If you drive south from Chico on Highway 99 and turn onto Highway 70, eventually you'll see the beige-colored compound of the Butte County Courthouse off to the left. The drab building is technically located in the city of Oroville, but feels like the middle of nowhere. It takes about thirty minutes from downtown Chico to get there. The land is dry and flat, covered in golden-brown thickets of weed stubbornly refusing to allow something more fruitful to grow, as if in angry protest to the summer heat. The drive is hardly scenic. The color and makeup of the land are reminders that Butte County is in the heart of water-starved Sacramento Valley, and that California is perpetually drought prone. The worry over dry conditions is never too far from the minds of Butte County residents since, despite the prominence of celebrities like Aaron Rodgers and Sierra Nevada beer in Chico, agriculture is the true linchpin of the local economy.

When I first moved home, the drive to the courthouse was therapeutic. It was a comforting reminder of how liberating it is to be surrounded by open space. The feeling wore off, just as the magic of anything dulls with exposure, and by the time John died, I stopped considering the landscape. I'd focus instead on things like preparation for court or my dinner plans. But as I drove to the courthouse for my first meeting with Scotty, the feeling came back. I watched as the golden-brown fields of dry brush became a blur in all directions. Gray boulders seemed to grow out of the earth. A plush green square acre of trees appeared in neat rows. I saw bright splotches of red and orange that, when I looked closer, I realized were fallen fruit rotting in the dirt. I marveled at the Sutter Buttes jutting out of the earth above the valley floor. I drove past more farmland and saw a John Deere combine lumbering through the field. The faceless driver wore blue jeans, a plaid shirt, and a baseball cap. As the combine kicked up dust behind the driver, I wondered if he too was an old classmate.

When I arrived at the entrance to the Butte County jail, a bald, stocky guard met me at the gate and led me through a series of cement-tunnel corridors until we reached an interview room. Scotty sat with his hands folded on a metal table. He stared straight ahead with a vacant expression of hopelessness.

I expected a shock of recognition when he saw me since there was no way of him knowing I'd been assigned as his counsel. I figured he'd at least recognize me in the same way I'd recognized his name on the file. Instead, when he saw my face, he reacted as if I'd offered up some mildly interesting sports trivia in a barroom conversation. He saw a familiar face but didn't light up in the way I had expected. He looked at me with a tired, hangdog expression, like he was fighting the effects of a heavy sedative. The guard shut the door. I set my briefcase down.

"Hey," he said.

"Hi."

"I didn't know you were back in town."

"I wasn't sure you'd remember me. I've been back almost two years now."

"You're a lawyer," he said.

"Yeah."

His brown hair was buzzed short. What had used to be bright and mischievous eyes seemed lifeless. Sinewy tendons of muscle danced on his forearms. He wore a baggy orange jumpsuit. We sat for a moment in silence, each taking stock of changes from the years gone by.

"Well?" he asked.

"Don't talk to anyone. Don't say anything to the guards, the other inmates—"

"I know, I know," he said. "I've been here before."

"I'm just reminding you," I told him. "I read the file. DNA reports indicated that the blood they found on your floor..." I paused.

"Okay."

"It's the victim's. Almost all of it anyway."

He shook his head in disbelief. He started to speak, but I raised my hand to stop him.

"I don't want to know yet, okay?" I pointed to the file in front of me. "For now, everything I need to know is in the report."

"I don't remember," he said.

"I understand that's what you told them—"

"I swear to God, I don't remember."

"Okay. That's fine, but I don't want to hear anything until I get more information from the prosecutor."

"Okay."

That was all we said about the case that day. We regarded each other for a long moment, then talked about other things. He wanted to know what had happened to me after high school—where I'd been and about my path to becoming a lawyer. I told him, leaving out the part about my affair with a client and getting kicked out of the navy, of course.

"Huh" was all he said when I finished.

I ended the meeting by giving him more reminders. I knew he'd heard them before, but it was the same speech I'd heard John give every criminal-defense client, and by that point, delivering it was automatic.

"Say nothing, to no one," I told him. "I don't want to know your side of the story until I ask for it. This is only so I can provide you with the best defense. Let's see what the government's case is before we do anything or you commit to any statements. You're innocent until proven guilty. There's always hope. We can always negotiate a plea if it doesn't look promising. Remember to contact me and me only."

Scotty furrowed his brow. "You think I did this?"

"It doesn't matter what I think."

He crossed his arms and sat back, scowling. "You? Of all people, you think I did this? Are you serious?"

"It doesn't make a difference. It doesn't matter what I believe. All that matters is what the jury is going to believe. We are so far away from that point right now. Right now we gather facts. That's it."

"Have you ever even tried a murder case before?"

"Yes, of course," I lied.

"What now?"

"I interview witnesses, I review the case file some more, and we prepare a strategy."

"All right."

"Is there anything you need?"

"Anything I need?"

"Is there anything I can get for you?"

"How about a key so I can get the hell out of here?"

I chuckled nervously. I told him to reach out to me if there was anything he needed, but as I got up to leave, he put his hand on my arm and leaned forward.

"I would never do something like this," he said, looking me in the eyes.

"Sure."

"You know me," he said.

I nodded. "I know. I know."

The corrections officer opened the door and escorted me back down the hallway and out to my car. I tried to reconcile the gregarious high school celebrity I had admired with the desperate criminal defendant in the orange jumpsuit. I'd just told Scotty I knew him, but as I walked back out into the sunlight, I thought, *Do I?*

* * *

Part of the reason I didn't want to hear Scotty's side of the story was because I knew there was a very good chance he was lying. He was lying to investigators, and he was lying to me. It wasn't personal, but I'd been lied to so many times by clients. They were often bald-faced lies that contradicted irrefutable facts. I had to assume Scotty would be no different. Until I could cross-check Scotty's version of the facts, I didn't want to hear a nonsensical story that I couldn't even attempt to corroborate. I also knew that if I ever wanted the truth out of him, I would first need to earn his trust.

The other reason why I didn't want Scotty's version of the story was because I knew that no matter how guilty he was, he was going to say he was innocent. Every client did this. Even if multiple eyewitnesses could pin them at the scene and had given investigators a signed confession, clients would say they hadn't done it. Especially when a client's lawyer showed up, they thought it was their last chance to rewind the clock. They would say the words as though saying them out loud might make them true. Criminal-defense attorneys are used to reserving judgment, and I'm no different. They make an assessment of the merits of their case only when it's time. Eventually I would figure out what had happened that March night. It would just take time.

As I drove back to Chico from Oroville, I thought about how even though Scotty was a grown man with the physique of a professional athlete, he was also somehow much smaller than the Scotty I remembered. In high school he seemed to be giant. Now his features seemed more angular, and the magnetic energy he had exuded when we were younger was completely gone. I wondered whether my perception of Scotty's guilt or innocence was clouded by our history together. It must have been. We'd grown up together, after all. So when he had looked me in the eyes and told me he hadn't done it, did I believe him just because we'd once played catch in the backyard? Maybe.

I always prided myself on having a healthy skepticism of my clients' stories. But sitting in that interview room on that old metal chair, with my hands resting on that glossy metal table, with Scotty's deadened eyes bearing down into my soul, there was something about the way he had said it that made me believe him.

TEN

I sat in the cavernous living room of my parents' two-bedroom house. The room's high ceilings and recessed lighting gave the impression of a tomb for the living. It'd only been two months since we admitted my mom to the assisted living facility, and we were all dealing with the fallout of that decision. For the past thirty years, my father hadn't cooked so much as a frozen pizza, so the steaks he cooked had the coating of recently extinguished campfire logs.

A week earlier, the facility had called to alert us that Mom had stopped eating. I poked at the overcooked meat before trying a bite, but all I could think about was her lying on a twin mattress with scratchy wool blankets draped over her skeletal frame. The nurses had asked us what we wanted to do about the eating situation. A man with short black hair and a thin mustache seemed to be the point person for our mother's care, and every time I visited Mom, he reminded me about the need to make a decision soon.

"She's going to lose weight rapidly," Thin Mustache would say, as if this were not obvious, like I needed his clinical opinion on it. "We're going to need some guidance from the family," he'd say to me, as though I were just a messenger and not her son. No one wanted to decide, so we punted on the issue. But Thin Mustache was right; we did need to do something soon. But what kind of choice is that, really? Let your mother die or force-feed her? It was all new territory. Hoping to avoid more plodding and awkward conversation, I brought up Scotty Watts. I wondered if my sister and father remembered him. Of course, they did.

"He's charged with murder," I told them.

"Geez…murder," my sister whispered, and then said "geez" one more time.

I described the facts for them, like how Scotty had been found mopping up blood, how the victim's truck was found outside his cabin, how Scotty's neighbor saw the victim go in, how the knife on the counter had Scotty's fingerprints, and how Josh's blood was found all over the cabin.

"Did Scotty talk?" my father asked.

"He told them he didn't remember," I said.

My father frowned. "Maybe you can get him a good deal." For all the unspoken tension between us, my father knew how juries worked. Before taking his seat on the county Board of Supervisors, he had practiced civil law in Chico for more than two decades.

"You think he did it?" I asked.

"Based on those facts? Yes."

There certainly was a lot of circumstantial evidence pointing to his guilt, but I still wasn't sure.

"Poor Scotty," my sister said. "He was always so smart."

"Couldn't have been that smart," my father said. "Didn't he just get out of jail?"

It didn't take long, but I didn't want to talk about the case anymore. I looked down at my sister's belly. She was pregnant and showing even more now. She must have been about four months along, and I asked her how the pregnancy was going. She said it was fine and asked me when I was going to come see her preach. She'd recently taken over as the associate pastor of Northgate Community Church, and I hadn't been to one single service since moving home. *Church. That would be good for me,* I thought. I had always viewed church as motivational speaking for the desperate and pious, but my sister was family, so I told her I'd go. We spent the next few minutes listening to the din of one another's silverware clinking against the plates before I couldn't take it anymore.

"I'm gonna put on some music," I said. And I got up.

Later that night, after I arrived back at my two-bedroom off Honey Run Road, I sat at my dining room table with my back to the kitchen and looked over Scotty's file again. I had another daydream of twelve-year-old Scotty—me throwing a baseball to the heavens in my backyard, him running under it to snag it in his glove. That night, sitting alone at my kitchen table, I wished John were still alive, and I imagined his counsel if he were advising on Scotty's case. "Emotional dispassion," he would say.

I looked out the window into the dark night. I heard a dog's bark. I heard the sound of a door closing far away. Crickets chirped in the distance. For a moment there was nothing but the still, quiet darkness of the summer night closing in. Trees outside my kitchen window stood like sentries surrounding the house on the edge of the yard. Then a gust of wind blew in through the window and brought my attention back inside. John was there, sitting at the table across from me. He was freshly shaven and in his dark-blue three-piece suit, his shiny wave of black hair parted neatly to the side. He looked tan and healthy. He leaned over the old folding table, his face shrouded in the shadowy glow of the dull kitchen light. He looked at me and smiled.

"How're you doing?" he asked.

"Fine," I replied.

"Having trouble with the Watts case?"

I nodded.

He sat back and took in a big breath. He pursed his lips. "The facts aren't good," he said. He looked out the window into the dark. "The facts are not good," he repeated.

"No."

"There's a lot I didn't have time to teach you," he said. "I'm sorry about that."

"It's all right."

"The thing is," he said, "a lot of times there's not an easy answer."

"It seems that way."

"That's being an attorney. Isn't it?" He smiled.

"John," I said, not questioning my belief. "You should have seen the look in his eyes. I'm telling you. He just seems like he's telling the truth."

John scoffed at the suggestion. "How many liars have you met?"

"You think he's lying?"

He got up from his chair and placed his hand on my shoulder. "Let me ask you this," he said, then passed by me into the kitchen. "Whether he's lying or telling the truth…does it make a difference?"

I stared at the file on the table, forgetting John was with me, and wondered, *Does it matter? Do I even need to know if Scotty's version of what happened is the truth?* I had a lot of questions for John, and I was glad he was there. I spun in my chair, but when I turned to the kitchen, he was gone. The fridge hummed. The microwave clock blinked 12:00, as though the power had gone out. I stood and peaked over the kitchen counter, looking at my dirty tile floor.

* * *

Later that night, after I readied for bed, I switched off my bedside light and tried to distance my mind from Scotty's case. Crickets rang out in a sweet vibrato chorus. *Crickets,* I thought. *Most crickets don't live longer than a year.* I'd read that in high school. Generations of crickets had come and gone between the time Scotty Watts, Aaron Rodgers, and I had graduated high school and that moment. I remembered listening to that same sweet vibrato of crickets in summertime almost two decades ago. I shut my eyes and brought the bedsheets to my chin. The crickets stopped chirping, and the stillness of the night surrounded me. When I closed my eyes, I realized I'd forgotten to tell my father and sister the most important fact about Scotty's case: the victim, Josh Anderson, was still missing. The sheriffs hadn't found his body.

ELEVEN

If you asked a random person to describe the land north of San Francisco, he or she would probably look at you like you had just asked them to sketch out Einstein's theory of relativity. "It's like there's a gap in the map," a Navy JAG Corps colleague had said when I asked that question. The only major city north of San Francisco is Sacramento, and Northern California is surrounded by eight different federally or state-recognized forests: Humboldt, Plumas, Lassen, Modoc, Klamath, Six Rivers, Shasta-Trinity, and Mendocino. While these forests are visited by hundreds of thousands of people per year, their defining characteristic is untrammeled land—thousands of acres of vast uninhabited area that naturalists like John Muir marveled over. Chico is situated in the center of it all, and after realizing I had failed to tell my father the most critical fact of Scotty's case, all I could think about was all that forest, and the army of Butte County law enforcement personnel combing through it to find Josh Anderson.

* * *

Will and I met for lunch. He wore a perfectly tailored gray suit with oak-colored dress shoes. He went out of his way to emphasize that the shoes were Sutor Mantellassi, which meant nothing to me, but I nodded and told him they were nice. I didn't care about what he was wearing; I wanted to talk about the case. I asked him what he thought Scotty's chances were if we took the case to trial.

"Your dad is right. Scotty is screwed," he said.

"What about the body?" I asked. "How're they going to move forward on a murder charge without a body?"

"They'll find it."

"Butte County law enforcement can't cover all that ground. No way."

"Maybe not. But Butte, Lassen, Plumas, Yuba, *and* Tehama County law enforcement—they can."

He must have seen that I looked confused.

"Yeah. Everyone is pitching in. Multicounty effort. They even have the coroner's office looking. It's insane. It's an election year, and Sullivan is getting a lot of heat from Mr. and Mrs. Anderson. Apparently they're none too pleased with how us country folk do business. With the Andersons putting the pressure on, Sullivan called in some favors."

"Why does he care?" I asked. "Isn't he running unopposed?"

Will shrugged. "Not sure yet. But you know him. He's conservative. He doesn't want to take the chance."

Apparently Josh Anderson's father was one of Southern California's biggest real estate developers. Even though he and Josh had been semi-estranged, it appeared he was going to leverage resources into a full-on media campaign to find his son. Will seemed to know more facts about the case than I did, which struck me as strange. The Southern California news media were already running stories about Scotty's case.

"The *OC Register* ran something," Will said. "They're calling us country bumpkins, and Sullivan a bumbling idiot. I guess a reporter from the *LA Times* was up here talking with Detective Cruz the other day. It's crazy."

"So what?" I said. "We're losing in the court of public opinion. Who cares?"

"Lose there, and you lose at trial. I guarantee it. People don't like to be embarrassed, but especially here."

I knew he was right. Unless it's a fantastic Aaron Rodgers box score or a delicious new seasonal beer, the constituents of Chico do not like a spotlight shown on their quaint existence. Mishandling a murder investigation would not go over well anywhere, but especially in a law-and-order county like Butte, and especially on a high-profile case like this one. There were already rumors that a forty-five-year-old medical-malpractice attorney named Bill Dubois had ambitions to challenge Sullivan's district attorney seat, and if Sullivan couldn't find Josh Anderson's killer, the mishandling of the Watts case could give Dubois enough juice to make him a legitimate challenger.

"Has Sullivan assigned it?" I asked.

Will nodded, and when he told me who the prosecutor was, I wasn't so much surprised as I was concerned. Emma Numair was far and away the best prosecutor in Butte County. She had brains and savvy, but perhaps more importantly, she understood small-town politics. After escaping the crime-ridden Central California town of Modesto, she had done her undergrad and law at Stanford. After a few years of private practice at a large San Francisco law firm, she followed her husband to Butte County when he got a sales job at a local lumber company. Her legal ambitions were stifled by an appeasing personality and her unwavering affection for a lazy man. She may have had bad taste in men, but she was a hell of an attorney, and whenever I saw her name on the docket, it gave me a flutter of panic.

"Well, shit…" I said, watching Will take a big bite of his salad.

"Let's get drinks this weekend," he said with a mouthful of food. I rolled my eyes and signaled to the waiter that I wanted the bill.

* * *

Two days later, I was walking out of the grocery store with

bags in each hand when I saw a stout woman with dark hair leaning into the open passenger's-side door of a decrepit old sedan. She was bent at the waist, trying to lift a man's limp body out of the car. A wheelchair was parked beside her, and as I approached, I recognized the woman as Eileen Watts, Scotty's mom. Her hands were looped under the man's armpits, and she stumbled back a little under his weight. The man was halfway out of the car, and I saw Eileen stumble again. I dropped my grocery bags and rushed over.

"Just grab that arm…" she said, as though she had been expecting me. I did.

"And the leg there…"

We lifted simultaneously. I put together what should have been obvious: the man with bones made of jelly was Scotty's father, Ray. His eyes were glassy and darted back and forth. He groaned as we jostled him out of the car.

"Here. Yes. Good," Eileen said.

We swung Ray's limp body into the waiting wheelchair stirrups, plopping him down like a sack of rice. I stood up, stretching my back.

"Thank you," she said. She looked up at me and smiled. She had always been pretty, but her dark hair had gray streaks now. Her eyes that had once been soft and kind had narrowed a little, but she still had the youthful, mischievous smirk that had made her alluring to us as teenage boys. She carried at least twenty more pounds on her frame, undoubtedly muscle built up from lifting her husband's lifeless body in and out of family vehicles, yet she also seemed less confident now. Her eyes jittered nervously behind large-frame glasses. She took my hand and shook it.

"Thanks," she said again. She was slightly out of breath. When we shook, I realized she didn't remember me. The skin on her hand was rough. Ray groaned again. His mouth was open, and his lip was contorted as though it were snagged in a fishhook. Eileen bent to check on him. She wiped a drop of saliva from his mouth.

"You okay, Ray?" she asked him.

"Hello, Ray," I said. None of it seemed to register. Eileen turned back to me.

"I can usually get it myself. I guess I'm just feeling a bit weak today," she said.

"No problem," I said.

I hadn't recognized Ray at first because the man in the wheelchair was so different from the man I remembered. The ravages of MS had made Ray a completely different person. I remembered seeing him wait in the high school gym parking lot to pick up Scotty after basketball practice. He'd be standing by his white pickup truck with his overalls unbuttoned at the waist and his hands jammed into his pockets. His plumbing equipment would be piled in the truck bed, and when Scotty walked out, he'd flash a broad pearly-white smile that contrasted with his thick black mustache. I always thought that smile had contained a hint of sardonic bitterness, like he had a dark secret he swore he'd never share. Maybe the secret was that MS was coming for him, and he knew he'd eventually be reduced to a shapeless, rubbery mass. As I looked down at him, I noticed for the first time that his eyes were a mesmerizing blue gray. They were almost clear, like the distant horizon on a cloudless day.

"Ready for some shopping?" Eileen asked Ray. She looked at me. "Thanks again," she said, and she grabbed Ray's wheelchair by the handles and turned it.

"Don't mention it," I said quietly and watched her push Ray's chair through the parking lot toward the grocery store.

TWELVE

It was both good and bad that Scotty told detectives he couldn't remember anything from the night Josh Anderson went missing. It was good since nothing he told the police implicated him in Josh's disappearance. But it was bad in that he said anything at all. I wasn't sure if Scotty was telling the truth, but the narrative of his defense had already started to be written the moment he opened his mouth. I thought Scotty was smart enough to know that talking to the police is never a good idea, but I was wrong. Telling detectives "I don't remember" didn't implicate Scotty, but it left me with little room to be creative. If he pled not guilty and took the case to trial, I knew we would have to explain *why* he didn't remember. We'd get there eventually, but that day there were other matters to address.

I was in the jailhouse interview room sitting across from him. He sat with his arms folded across his chest.

"I ran into your parents at the grocery store," I said.

"Oh?"

"I don't think they remembered me."

"My dad can't speak."

"Right."

"You were gone a long time."

"I guess so. Well, your mom didn't remember me, at least." I paused. "Do they know you're in here?"

"No, they don't," he said. "We haven't spoken in years."

We started from the beginning. The rumors about what had happened after high school were true. He did go to jail after an altercation with his drug dealer. There was a struggle with the clerk, and five years were added to his sentence when a gun accidentally discharged. He was released three years early thanks to a combination of good behavior and jail overcrowding. Ray was a plumber, Scotty reminded me, and when Scotty got out, he had started working for his dad, fixing leaky faucets and unclogging toilets. He was learning the plumbing trade during the day and attending night classes at Butte College. He was working toward a degree in kinesiology. He wanted to be a personal trainer. One day, Ray was working on a kitchen sink, and his hands started tingling. Then they went numb, and Ray told Scotty to step in. He needed a break.

"I'd never seen my old man take a break in his life," Scotty said. "Figured it was pretty serious."

Over the next few weeks, the pain in Ray's hands would come and go. Scotty kept pleading with him to see a doctor. Finally, one day they were going down the freeway, and Ray's vision blurred so bad, he could barely drive. His old white pickup truck started to swerve off the road. Scotty grabbed the wheel and hit the brakes. "Damn old man almost killed us both," Scotty said.

Scotty and Eileen forced Ray to see a doctor. Ray was diagnosed with progressive multiple sclerosis, and his insurance had lapsed. "Stubborn old bastard hadn't seen a doctor in thirty years. Figured he'd never need it," Scotty said. Eileen was already working full-time, so Scotty had to help with Ray's care, driving him to physical therapy and making sure he took his meds. Scotty also had to complete the plumbing jobs Ray's company had contracted for. The work was too much for Scotty, and he eventually stopped going to his night classes. He had to drop out of the kinesiology program at Butte.

Money was tight, so Scotty started tending bar at

O'Haras, a downtown college bar. When he got to this part in the story, his face lit up. He gazed off at a fond memory. "That's how I met Kelly," he said. The memory was like a passing ray of sunshine across his face. His brow furrowed, and a shadow came over him again. He explained how even with the plumbing jobs and bartending, he couldn't afford Ray's treatment. "Goddamn medical bills," he said. He had to do something else.

So he went back to the same people who had got him addicted to drugs in high school and asked if he could sell for them.

"I started selling all kinds of pills—opioids, oxys, Vicodin, Percocet, Xanax. Whatever I could."

MS doesn't usually get better, and Ray's condition got worse and worse. Scotty thought about drugrunning but concluded it was too dangerous. By that point, he and Kelly were in love, so while he needed money to care for Ray, he also didn't want to lose Kelly or put her in danger. He started brainstorming other ideas. He thought about legitimate businesses that could keep his family afloat. Scotty's grandfather had left him the Forest Ranch cabin years ago, and after Scotty quickly realized a convicted felon was going to have a tough time getting a business loan, he decided to put the property on the market. Months went by. He met with his realtor, who told him the market was down. The cabin was a tear-down project that would require a very specific and unique buyer to come along. It could be years before it sold. Scotty got another idea. He and Kelly moved into the cabin, and after looking over the plot with the realtor, Scotty knew his ownership stretched far back from the main road. There was a large open field at the back of the property. It was an area perfect for marijuana cultivation.

"About that time I met Josh," he explained. "We were at that party. Josh knew how to grow, and I had the land, so we went into business."

"Weed?"

"No. Alfalfa plants. Yes, weed." It seemed both legitimate

and safe. Marijuana would be legal soon anyway, they thought, and they decided to go into business together. "Took us six months to get to harvest, but we got there, and I started sending checks home every month."

I asked why he was estranged from his parents then, since everything seemed fine.

"One day the check I sent was returned. I kept sending them, and they never got cashed. I think my mom knew where the money was coming from. I showed up at the house over and over, but they stopped talking to me. Wouldn't take my calls. Wouldn't take my texts. My mom threatened to call the police. Locked me out of the house. Everything."

"Just because of your business?"

"To them it was drug money," Scotty said. "Stubborn, I guess."

I sat for a long moment thinking about the cast of characters in my orbit since I'd been back. I thought about Eileen and Ray, my own parents, my sister. I thought about Will, and then I thought about John. I pictured the scene of his death, and of his body lying all alone in that vacant field north of town after having flown through the Porsche windshield. I wished he was there with me. I wished he could help me with Scotty's case.

I drifted off in that very moment until I heard a muffled voice, like I was submerged in water and someone was calling me from the surface. The snap of Scotty's fingers roused me from the daydream. "Kelly, my girlfriend," he said. "Have you talked with her?"

"No," I said. *Kelly. A familiar name, of course. Have I talked to Kelly? Do I know her?* I had told Scotty no, but I wasn't sure.

"What about Arthur?" he asked.

"Who?"

"My dog, Arthur. Did they find him?"

"Sorry"—I shuffled papers from the file in front of me—"I didn't know there was a dog. It wasn't in the report."

"The cops never asked about him. Maybe that's why," he said. "Could you just check with the neighbors? He's probably still up there. Someone must have found him by now."

"Okay," I said, then told him I'd check on it.

He nodded and asked about my sister.

"She's good. Pregnant, actually," I told him.

"That's good. Sweet girl. Always was a sweet girl."

Scotty and I sat for a moment listening to the dim buzz of the fluorescent light overhead. The guard knocked on the glass window and pointed to his watch. I got up and told Scotty we would talk again soon. I figured next time I'd bring up the idea of pleading guilty. I had to check with Emma first anyway. Who knew what she was willing to offer.

As I packed my things, I could feel Scotty's eyes on me, like a silent judgment. Suddenly I had a nightmarish vision of Scotty stabbing Josh to death in that cabin, wrapping up his body, throwing it in his truck, driving into the forest, burying it, and mopping up the bloody mess. The vision pictured him doing it all with a calculated alertness of someone who knew exactly what they were doing, with meticulous care to clean up the mess. But those weren't the facts. Scotty was found in a puddle of blood in the middle of his living room floor. When detectives asked him what had happened, he told them he didn't remember. I wondered why my vision of what had happened departed from the facts I knew. Scotty must have noticed a change in my face.

"What?" he asked.

"Nothing," I said. "We'll talk again soon." But as I turned to go, I had a sudden sinking sensation in my stomach. It was a sick feeling of losing control. But over what? The case? Scotty's plea? I wasn't sure. It was vague and unquantifiable, a feeling of confusion more than anything else.

The guard opened the door. Before I crossed the threshold, Scotty called out, "Hey." I turned and looked at him, sitting on that metal chair with his hands on that metal table, that tired, hangdog expression on his face. "Thanks," he said.

I nodded and walked out.

THIRTEEN

Chico always felt like a place frozen in amber. Residents of Chico grow older, but the fabric of the place doesn't change. I've always thought this, and perhaps it's why I felt like if I never left, I wouldn't feel the passage of time. It's why I went south for college and never planned on coming back. It's why I joined the navy and happily moved when I received orders to Virginia and then Florida. It's why coming home was so hard. Because I hadn't found much out there except bitter disappointment. I thought adulthood would be filled with love, success, adventure, romance, riches, and comfort. Instead, I was doing a job I didn't want for a friend I no longer revered and who was possibly even a murderer. Before I moved back home, I had secretly hoped that Chico had changed. But it had been two years since I moved back, and I knew that my hope was at best misplaced and at worst silly. Chico hadn't changed, and I felt like the world around me was disintegrating. Ray Watts had MS, Eileen Watts had become jittery and nervous, Scotty was facing a life sentence, and my mother no longer resembled herself. My world was crumbling.

* * *

Lakeside Assisted Living Facility is a two-story stucco building on the east side of town that looks like a small apartment complex. The awfully uninspiring sign out front reads, "Lakeside, A great place to call home." Visiting my mother there might have been more depressing than visiting Scotty. Each time I visited, the Lakeside residents would watch me come and go with expressions of hopeless longing. Standing above my mother's bed, I regarded the outline of her frail skeletal frame silhouetted by a thin white bedsheet and scratchy wool blanket. She stirred softly in her sleep. I studied her dinner-tray meal of potatoes, ham, peas, and a scoop of red Jell-O. Judging from the meal next to her, it must have been Wednesday. My mother hated ham, or at least she used to back when she was able to tell what it was. Suddenly she jolted awake. She must have woken from a nightmare.

"Hello?" she called out, as if there had been a knock at the door. She turned her eyes toward me with a confused look on her face. Then she looked to the doorway where the nurse with the thin mustache stood. He smiled and nodded at us both and shut the door.

"Hi, Mom," I said and pulled my chair close to her. I saw the faintest hint of a smile on her gaunt face. Her eyes flittered back and forth like a scared, wounded animal. She must have weighed no more than a hundred pounds. Only a few white wisps of her once sandy-blonde hair remained. She was always so beautiful, and it pained me to see her mind betray her and body wither away. I remembered my college graduation when she looped her arms around my neck and congratulated me. She had been a constant presence of cheeriness and joy in my life, and now she was a shell of herself.

She jerked her head to the side. "No! No! No!" she shouted. I looked back at the closed door, thinking maybe I should get someone. "No! Please!" she screamed.

I touched her shoulder. "Mom. It's okay. It's me," I said.

"No…no…no…" she mumbled. Her voice fell to a murmur.

Thin Mustache appeared in the doorway again, and I waved

him away. I turned back to her. "It's okay, Mom. I'm here," I said. I rubbed her shoulder again, bending down close to her. She started talking about someone named Lawrence.

"Lawrence? Are you there?" she asked. My father's name is not Lawrence. I told her it was just me, and she rambled on about Lawrence until she rolled her head toward me. Suddenly a kind of clearness came over her. Her gaze sharpened.

"Oh, hi, honey," she said. She smiled at me.

"Hi, Mom." I felt so happy, like I had her back for a moment. I leaned in and kissed her on the forehead.

"Are you dating anyone?" she asked, barely lifting her head.

"No, Mom. I'm not."

"Oh…"

I held her hand. She shut her eyes slowly, like the brief recognition of someone she knew had tired her brain. I stared at the drab pink-and-beige walls of her room and waited a few minutes until she started snoring. I let go of her hand and wiped the tears from my cheek. I stroked her hair gently, kissed her on the forehead, and walked out.

* * *

O'Haras Bar was famous for lax ID policies and epic nights of binge drinking for Chico State students. It hadn't changed much. The stale scent of body odor and the pungent stench of urine emanated from the wood floorboards. It was early evening, and the place was empty. I was there to see Kelly. Scotty had told me she was still bartending there.

Something about O'Haras felt more familiar than just a memory from a long time ago, and I wondered if I'd been there during one of my epic nights binge drinking with Will. *Had I been there recently?* Maybe it was just another place frozen in amber that I'd never truly forget.

Kelly appeared from the kitchen. She wore a skintight spaghetti-strap T-shirt with the O'Haras logo on it and Daisy Duke shorts. Her beauty was familiar and striking. She attracted the male gaze like a moth to light. I could picture her deftly flirting with hordes of drunk college boys obsessing over her body. I walked up to her and introduced myself as Scotty's attorney. She gave me a strange look, like I'd said something offensive. She was wiping down beer glasses, getting ready for her shift. A colorful tattoo sleeve covered her left arm, and her hair was pulled back in a ponytail. She softened when she realized I was on Scotty's side. We went over the events of Saturday, March 12, the day Josh Anderson and Scotty Watts had met in a cabin in the woods.

It was a regular day, she said. She had spent the day with Scotty. They went for a walk in the morning. They made love in the early afternoon. She drove into town for groceries. Scotty worked on a project in the garage—something about reframing a window—while she did homework upstairs. "I'm studying to be a nurse," she said. "Been working on that degree for the last decade now." She had left at around 6:00 p.m. for her evening shift at O'Haras. That was the last time she saw Scotty before visiting him in jail. By the time she arrived home from work, the cabin had already been declared a crime scene. The sheriffs wouldn't let her past the yellow tape. She had a phone message from Scotty, and she rushed to the jail to see him.

"I don't really have much to add that I didn't already tell the detective."

"Was there anything strange about that night?" I asked.

She shook her head. "No. Nothing I can think of."

"Scotty mentioned something about a dog."

Kelly's face lit up. "They found him?"

"I was hoping you could help me with that. The dog wasn't in the report."

"They didn't ask me about Arthur, so I never said anything," she said.

"What kind of dog is he?"

"A big friendly black lab," she said, "with a blue collar and a red San Francisco 49ers bandanna tied around his neck."

"The Niners?"

"I know, it's weird. Aaron Rodgers. Green Bay Packers.

You'd think we were in Wisconsin with how many Packers fans are around here. I'm from Yreka, and even there Aaron Rodgers is a god. But the Niners are Scotty's team. Scotty never let Arthur go anywhere without that bandanna. I think he took a certain pride in being the only person in town not rooting for the Packers." She smiled at the thought. Her bright-blue eyes sparkled like sunlight rippling across a flat lake. She finished wiping down the glass she was holding and set it on the counter. She tossed the dish rag aside and crossed her arms. I started to gather my things.

"You know he didn't do this, right?" Kelly said.

"Sure."

"I just feel like no one believes him."

I wondered if I should explain that it only matters what a jury believes, but it seemed inadequate. Kelly didn't want the party line. She wanted someone who trusted in Scotty's innocence. So after we stood in silence for a long moment, I nodded and said, "I know. I know he's innocent." I got up to go. "Thanks for your help." But Kelly must have felt like she hadn't yet made her case.

"You know why I liked him so much?" she asked. I stopped and turned to let her continue. "He never wanted anything from me."

I wasn't quite sure what she meant, but I feigned understanding.

"He was so sweet...the sweetest man I'd ever met in my life, and he was nothing but good to me." Tears welled in her eyes. She caught her breath, choking back a sob.

"Please help him," she said. She grabbed a tissue from behind the bar and wiped her eyes. "This is stupid," she said and laughed. "I shouldn't cry."

"It's fine," I said.

"I just know he didn't do this," she said. "I don't know what happened, but I know he couldn't do something like this."

"I'm going to do the best I can," I told her. "I promise."

She nodded. "Okay."

FOURTEEN

Northgate Community Church is in downtown Chico. It shares the same beautiful redbrick facade of the state college next door, and the inside is even more gorgeous. Large stained-glass windows decorate the walls. The old wood pews remind congregants that Northgate is a country church in a way that invokes nostalgia rather than decrepitude, since there's plenty of ornate woodworking behind the lectern to dissuade any false perception the church is behind the times. Yet standing in the back listening to my sister deliver the weekly sermon, I couldn't appreciate how pretty it was, since being in a police lineup would have been more enjoyable than being in that church, in Chico, on a Sunday. The idea of running into someone from my past caused the same anxiety-inducing paranoia one might get from imagining themselves delivering a commencement address naked. Looking out at the familiar faces—or rather the backs of their heads—my fears were confirmed.

My father sat in the section to my left, three rows from the front. Next to him was Ralph Morrison, the elder statesman of Morrison Family Farms. I picked out Ralph's boys—Paul, Cole, Jack, and John—with each of their families in tow. Only Paul was unaccompanied, and rumor had it that his divorce was amicable and should be finalized soon. Two rows back from lonely Paul was Gene Hammond, my old high school basketball coach, with his wife, Sue. On the right side near the middle was the Sterling family. Their son, Alec, was Chico's first football superstar. He had set the high school football rushing record at Chico High by over two hundred yards. He had gone off on a full-ride scholarship to San Jose State, until he realized he'd never be fast enough to earn a starting position at the Division I level and quit after his sophomore year. Five years later, Aaron Rodgers had been offered a full ride to Berkeley, and his career hockey-sticked to superstardom. Last I heard, Alec was a manager at Best Buy.

Ashley Davis and her husband, Tim, sat next to the Sterlings. In the fifth grade, I had passed Ashley a love poem during class. She waited until we were dismissed for PE to read it. She gathered her friends around the back fence of the playfield to read it aloud to them. Ashley and her audience giggled and pointed at me while I stood alone on the blacktop basketball courts. They mocked me for every last minute of the recess period while I burned with shame. My audacious hope that her friends would be impressed by and jealous of the flattery was rewarded with months of ridicule. Ashley developed into a gorgeous woman, and Tim courted her when they were both students at Chico State, where he was a star pitcher on the baseball team. By "courted," I mean Tim had drunken sex with her one night, and they hooked up for a few weeks before making it "official." A few years later, they married. One Thanksgiving while I was home from law school, Tim made a point to embarrass me about my elementary school love poem once again. He introduced me to Ashley as if we hadn't met and said, "If you ever write my wife another poem, I'll kill you." He smiled and laughed, clapping me on the shoulder with his palm. They seemed perfect for each other.

I listened to my sister preach about David and Bathsheba when the silhouette of a woman's face caught my eye. My soul stirred. Golden-brown hair cascaded down her back. Her top exposed a tiny square of bare olive skin of her shoulder, and a vague memory of junior high school bubbled to the surface. She was sitting alone on the right-hand side of the church, three rows from the front. It was Lacey Price.

One day in the seventh grade, a group of football players circled around Tex, a pale, beefy autistic kid. They'd taken Tex's football. "Give it back!" he shouted. Kids letting out of class started gathering in the courtyard to watch the spectacle. The bullies mocked Tex's nasal, slurred speech. They tossed his football around the circle, keeping their own football opposite him. Tex would reach out with his clumsy hands, following the football around the circle, while the bullies bounced their own football off the back of his head, laughing demonically each time.

"Hey!" Tex would shout. He'd spin around in an attempt to locate the mysterious culprit. He'd rub his head and return to the single-minded mission of retrieving the football, and thump, the other ball would jolt his head forward again. As I watched this happen over and over, my cowardice paralyzed me and I grimaced.

Suddenly Lacey's voice reverberated off the courtyard walls. "What's the matter with you?" From far off across the courtyard, she came storming over and ripped Tex's football out of a big linebacker's hands. "You guys think this is funny?" She held the football up to their faces. The bullies stood at attention. "You like picking on him?" Lacey gave each of them a long moment to appreciate their cruelty. They were frozen. She turned to the big linebacker. "You like picking on a defenseless kid?" she asked. She bounced the fat side of the football off his forehead. He stumbled back. Kids laughed. She turned to the rest of the bullies while Tex smiled at her with wide eyes. She paced around the circle, waiting for one of the bullies to say something. She let them stew in the silence. Finally she handed Tex his football back, and he said thank you.

"You guys are pathetic," she said to the bullies. She ripped the other football away from one of the block heads and stepped to the side. She turned and heaved the ball high into the air. It flew end over end in an awkward lame-duck spiral, hanging impossibly high in the blue sky. For the first half of the ball's flight, I don't think anyone thought anything of it. But the ball kept sailing, and we all started to wonder. A lonely trash can sat across the courtyard a good twenty yards away.

Did she aim for...

No way. It's not...

Is it going to?

The ball kept traveling.

Thud.

It disappeared into the trash can. Mouths gaped. Someone cheered. Two girls walking by giggled at the bullies. "Morons," one of them said. The bullies looked at one another in disbelief, trying to deflect blame.

I looked back to Lacey's, but she was already leading Tex by the arm to the other side of the courtyard. She walked him to the spot where he waited each day for his mother to pick him up. I don't think she ever looked back to see that ball go in the trash can. I wondered if she had even done it on purpose, but I doubt she cared.

"Thank you!" Tex said loudly, as though he were being led to his bed after a night of heavy drinking.

"Sure thing," Lacey said quietly.

Tex stared at her in awe. She smiled politely back at him and stood by his side. She scanned the sea of cars with the same resolute expression on her face. Tex never took his eyes off her, and Lacey waited there with him until his mother pulled up to take him home.

* * *

When the pews started to empty, I snapped out of my daydream. My sister wished everyone a nice rest of their Sunday, and I slipped out the back of the room before anyone saw me.

FIFTEEN

Drive east of Chico on Highway 32 (a.k.a. Deer Creek Highway), and you'll run right into Forest Ranch. If you keep going, you'll eventually hit Butte Meadows, Lake Almanor, and Lassen National Forest. Highway 32 is the only road in and out of Forest Ranch, and it's the only road connecting the residents of Chico to the Southwest. Most of Forest Ranch residents are farmers, retirees, or hippies, but all of them value the privacy of living in a place where your only neighbors are pine trees.

I left Chico heading east and drove up Deer Creek Highway to Forest Ranch. I made two phone calls on the way. The first was to Emma Numair.

"Still haven't found a body?" I asked.

"You read the news just like I do."

"Sullivan really wanted you to charge this as an open count of murder?"

"It's always an open count," she said. "You know that. Are you calling about a plea?"

"Are you offering one?"

"If Scotty tells us where Josh's body is, we'll agree to second-degree and cap the punishment at fifteen years."

Second-degree murder and a fifteen-year cap on

confinement seemed like a pretty damn good deal to me, but there was one obvious problem. "You're assuming he knows where the body is," I said.

"Oh, please. DNA matches the blood on the floor and the knife on the counter. Victim's truck is out front. The neighbor saw him go in the cabin. The doctor will testify no one could survive that blood loss. There's motive. And let's not forget that your client was found frantically cleaning up a crime scene. That's a mountain of circumstantial evidence." She didn't stop there. "I'm pretty sure a jury will put the pieces together. Just let me know if he's willing to plead. We don't need to find that body. We will, but we don't need to."

"I'll get back to you" was all I said, and I hung up.

My next call was to my defense investigator, Ricardo "Rick" Martinez. Rick was the most senior defense investigator in Butte County. A former marine, Rick had spent nearly a decade at the San Bernardino County Public Defender's Office before moving to Chico. I didn't need any assurances from Watermelon Belly that Rick, imposing but affable, would do the best job. He was the most well-regarded public defender in the county, and I was grateful he was on the case.

"I know the case," Rick said when I started describing it. "It's going to plea, right?"

"I haven't talked to the client about that just yet," I told him.

"Let's do that before we start chasing our tails."

"I need some ammo for the negotiations."

"You know how strapped for resources I am. If your guy had a shot at trial, I'd interview Ms. Jackson, I'd contact the medical examiner, and I'd monitor the search for the victim's body. But unless you absolutely think those things are going to get us anywhere, I think you should talk to the client first."

"I just want to do our due diligence,"   I   said.   Rick sighed. "Please, Rick. Something tells me he didn't do it. I haven't had the chance to talk about the plea, but there's something else going on here. I'm sure of it."

There was a long silence. "Fine. But please talk to the client first."

"I will," I said. The phone connection started to break up. "I'm losing you," I said, and shortly thereafter, the line disconnected.

High up in the mountains, I turned left off the highway onto a narrow gravel road. I navigated my rusty green Honda under a tunnel of pine trees until I arrived at Forest Rim Lane, Scotty's street. I drove to the end of another even narrower gravel road that opened up into a clearing where I could turn the car around. Scotty's driveway forked off to the right. I parked, grabbed the case file, and walked down Scotty's driveway. Pine needles crunched under my tennis shoes. I looked back at my car. Across the street through the pine trees, I saw a large white cabin propped up on a small hill. Eleanor Jackson's house, I presumed. The farther I made it down Scotty's driveway, the more Ms. Jackson's house was obscured by the thick pine-tree forest.

Scotty's cabin was a squat brown-and-green building. A decrepit RV and a rusted-out beige Chevy Impala were parked on the side. I ducked under the yellow caution tape cordoning off the crime scene and approached the front door. I could see why Scotty couldn't sell the place. More than a few tile roof shingles were missing or had been pulled loose. The front window pane had a baseball-size hole where someone might have tossed a rock through. Glass shards spider-webbed around it. The home garden out front had been overrun by weeds. Once again I looked up the hill toward Eleanor Jackson's house. The row of trees lining Scotty's property obstructed the view enough that it was hard to see her house. I wondered how she'd been so confident that she saw Josh Anderson's white Nissan Titan truck parked out front, or how she'd seen him walk inside. Unless she had X-ray vision, her description was remarkably detailed for an eighty-five-year-old woman observing something just before dusk.

Scotty's cabin was two stories. The garage and basement were on the ground floor. The living room, kitchen, and bedrooms were upstairs, accessible by ascending a wooden set of stairs. A wood deck surrounded the top story. I walked up the steps and went inside. The kitchen and living room were separated only by a "U"-shaped counter demarcating where one ended and the other began. A large sliding-glass door led out to the back deck, where a matching set of back stairs led to the backyard. Decaying outdoor furniture sat on the deck. One chair was overturned, and the other looked like it would collapse under the weight of a house cat. I opened the case file and thumbed through the pictures taken during the investigation. I imagined investigators pacing the scene, snapping pictures, and collecting evidence. I walked over to the kitchen table and stood in front of it with my back to the sliding-glass door. I looked down at where Scotty's half-eaten bowl of cereal had been found on the table. I turned to the sliding-glass door behind me. When I looked outside, I saw what appeared to be a man standing on the edge of the property, just where the forest began. It was like a picture flashing in my mind. I did a double-take, and when I moved closer to the door, the person was gone. I looked back to the file. I walked into the living room where the large pool of blood had been found. The dull-red outline of the stain had discolored the floor. I had a vision of Scotty waking up in that pool, and (if he had actually been unconscious) the panic he must have felt. I walked to the kitchen where the knife had been found on the kitchen counter, its blade covered in blood. I matched each of these locations to the photographs.

A lot of things bothered me about the case. Deputies had responded to the scene after receiving a call of shots fired, but had guns been found? I flipped through the file. Yes, a standard-issue .45-caliber Beretta and a Remington 870 shotgun had been found. But they were disassembled and in the basement. There was no gunshot residue indicating that either had been fired that night. The 911 caller had been identified as male, but he hadn't provided his name or information. He just reported the situation and hung up. Why?

I walked to Scotty's bedroom. Other than a few articles of clothing strewn about, the room was mostly empty. The rest of

Scotty's clothes still hung in the closet. The bed was unmade. I walked back to the front door and surveyed the cabin one last time. I looked back down at the outline of the red bloodstain that had seeped into the old wood. Questions raced through my mind: *What the hell happened here? And where is Josh Anderson's body?*

SIXTEEN

Standing in Scotty's cabin in the middle of the woods, I felt like visiting the crime scene aroused more questions than answers. Suddenly I felt stupid and naive. Scotty probably had killed that poor kid. It's not that hard to get rid of a dead body with thousands of acres of forest land surrounding you. Josh Anderson was gone. This was a waste of time. I started wishing I'd recused myself and had Watermelon Belly take me off this case. He couldn't have forced me to be Scotty's attorney. I could have protested. Instead, I acceded to it. A gust of wind howled against the house. I wished I would've never become a stupid public defender in the first place. I wished I would've never moved home. I wished John were still alive. What the hell am I even doing here? I asked myself. This was Rick's job. I'd been too impatient to visit Scotty's cabin without him.

I opened the sliding-glass door leading to the back deck and walked outside. Tall pines loomed above me. Acorns were scattered on the pine-needle ground. Birds chirped. I was admiring the white clouds passing in the clear blue sky when suddenly I heard the affable familiarity of a man's voice.

"It's a good question." I knew right away it was John. He stood next to me wearing his perfectly tailored blue three-piece suit, smiling.

"What?" I'd heard what he said, but I was too shocked to manage anything else.

"I said, 'It's a good question,'" he repeated. "You asked, 'What am I even doing here?' And I'm telling you it's a good question." He clapped me on the shoulder and laughed. "It's the weekend! You should be out having fun!"

I sighed.

"What did you expect to find?" he asked. He pointed at the file in my hand. "It's all in the report."

"I don't know." I was frustrated. "Isn't this case a little strange to you?"

"Not really." He patted my shoulder. "Come on. Follow me." He walked down the stairs and through the backyard across the dead pine needles. He led me to the edge of the property and into the thicket of trees. We walked through the woods for what seemed like too long. Just when I ducked branches and swatted away spiderwebs, just when I started to ask where we were going, the trees became sparse, and light started to break through. Suddenly the forest opened into a clearing. A flat expanse of land opened up before us, probably half an acre, covered mostly in weeds. It was the remnants of a large marijuana field.

"It stretches back almost to Ponderosa Lane and Big Chico Creek." John waved his hand over the land. "Pretty amazing, isn't it?"

"You could grow a lot of pot here," I said.

John led me through the flattened, vacant field. We reached the back of the property and stopped. Before us, the land gradually sloped away and dipped into a ravine. John and I breathed in the crisp morning air and marveled at the canyon's beauty. We stood at the edge of the property where the ground dipped sharply down, undulated back up toward a high cliff, and fell back down into the Big Chico Creek riverbed. No one was in sight for miles, but across the ravine I could make out a few cabins on the other side. They were tiny specks in the distance.

"Nice country up here, isn't it?" John said.

He could see from my furrowed brow that my mind was not on the scenery but on the case. "Seems like an awful lot of trouble to frame a guy just because he's growing a bunch of pot," I said.

He ignored me.

"John, why are you here?" I asked him. But his eyes were closed, and his head was tilted slightly upward toward the sky. He held a finger to his lips and shushed me.

"Quiet," he said. He opened his eyes for a moment to look out over the ravine and smiled. He shut his eyes again and breathed deeply through his nose like he was meditating. "Stop talking about the case," he said. "Just enjoy this for a moment."

He looked over at me. "Come on. Do it," he said. He shut his eyes and breathed deep again, tilting his head back to let the air fill his lungs. I followed suit. I breathed in deep through my nose, filling my lungs with the mountain air, and held it for a long moment. I exhaled and let the air seep from my body. For a moment I wasn't thinking about Eleanor Jackson's testimony or the shots-fired report, or the knife, or the pool of blood, or the truck in front of the house, or Scotty's DNA all over the crime scene. I wasn't thinking about my mother, my father, or Eileen and Ray Watts. I wasn't thinking about anything. I just breathed in and out and smiled. My mind was empty. Something washed over me.

"Thanks," I said to John, opening my eyes. "I needed that." I turned to face him, but when I did, I was alone again. I looked around. A squirrel scampered off into the woods at the edge of the property. A blue jay chirped high up in a tree. I could hear the faint knocking of a woodpecker far off. *Where'd he go?* I was alone again.

* * *

When I got back to my car, I figured since I was already up there, I should do a quick survey of the other neighbors on Scotty's street. I walked along the gravel road of Forest Rim

Lane back out to Highway 32. Next to Scotty's cabin was an empty lot. On Eleanor Jackson's side of the street, there were only two more homes, spaced generously apart. When I reached Deer Creek Highway, I looked in each direction, but it was nothing but empty asphalt curving and bending around the mountain until the road was out of sight. Just as I started to turn back toward my car, I heard a rumble in the distance. It grew louder and louder until I saw an old blue pickup truck come whipping around the bend, groaning up the hill toward me. The truck must have been going ten or fifteen miles per hour over the speed limit. Just as it was about to pass, time seemed to slow down almost to a stop. The windows were rolled down. Lacey was in the passenger's seat. Her long golden-brown hair was tied up in a ponytail, blowing behind her in the wind. Ralph Morrison's son Paul was driving. He wore a camouflage baseball cap over short dark hair, his thin lips shaded by five-o'clock stubble. It was Paul Morrison of the "amicable" divorce, of Morrison Family Farms. His eyes were locked on the road. With the truck frozen as a snapshot in front of me, Lacey slowly turned her head in my direction and looked over Paul's shoulder. She looked right at me and smiled. The fleeting moment passed just as quickly as it had come. Time sped up again. The truck lurched past, and a small cloud of dust and exhaust blew up in its wake. I watched the truck shrink in the distance until, just before it was out of sight, I saw its brake lights activate, then the faint flicker of a blinking left-hand-turn signal. A blue speck now, it turned left and disappeared down a side road.

* * *

When I got back to my car, I got in and shut the door. I looked down Scotty's driveway at the old green cabin with its decaying roof and smashed-out window.

Where did John go off to?

I suppose he was just trying to be helpful, but it was more annoying than anything. "Some help you were," I said out loud and put the key in the ignition. I heard a deep, muted murmur from somewhere outside and listened more carefully. The sound got louder and louder, as though it was approaching. I couldn't quite make it out at first, but I started to recognize it as the barking of a dog.

SEVENTEEN

I got out of my car. A big black Labrador retriever came bounding out of the woods, running toward me, and we met in the middle of the driveway. When he saw me, he growled and coiled his body as if he were going to attack.

"It's okay, buddy," I said and reached out my hand. He barked and growled.

Arthur. I could see he didn't have a collar, but it must have been him.

"Arthur?"

He took a couple of cautious steps backward and put his canine teeth away. I bent closer to the gravel road and reached my arm out. No doubt he was a little on edge after spending all that time in the woods alone, but he eventually started to calm. He eased over to me and sniffed my hand. He looked up at me with his sad, tired eyes and let me pat his head. He nodded his head up and down as if to say hello. I scratched his ear, and he licked my fingers with his big sandpaper tongue. He was a very sweet dog. He must have just been scared.

"Hey, Arthur," I said. He sat. "Do you know Scotty?" He twitched his head again and barked. I scanned the surrounding woods. We were alone. I waited for a few moments with him, listening to the birds chirping in the trees while he paced around me some more, getting comfortable. The midday summer sun beamed down on us. I sat on the gravel road and eventually asked him, "Well, do you want a ride home?" He was a big-boned Labrador with a belly the size of an oak barrel. "What'dya say?" I suggested. He stood up, and I saw that his black coat was a little dusty. "Come on," I said, motioning toward my car. "Let's clean you off." I took a couple of steps up the driveway, and he followed. It took a while for him to work up the courage, but eventually he jumped inside my car and lay in the back seat. As we cruised down the highway, I looked in my rearview mirror at him and smiled. He lifted his head slightly as if to ask, "What's up?" then dropped it back on his paws and let out a big sigh.

* * *

Arthur and I stood on the porch of the downtown Chico house where Kelly was staying. I rang the doorbell. A small mousy girl answered the door and looked me up and down.

"Who're you?" she asked.

"Is Kelly here?"

She called out over her shoulder, "Kelly! Some weirdo is here to see you!"

Kelly appeared around a corner, and when she saw Arthur sitting obediently by my side, she shouted his name and jogged through the living room toward us. "Arthur!" To which Arthur bolted through the door and into the living room to meet her. Kelly bent and let Arthur nuzzle his head into her cheek. He licked her face and wagged his tail.

"Where'd you find him?"

"I was up at the cabin looking over Scotty's file. He just came running up the driveway out of nowhere."

"Where's his collar?"

"He wasn't wearing it. He didn't have his bandanna either."

"That's weird. Was he hurt?"

"I don't think so. This is exactly how I found him."

Arthur bounced happily on his hind legs.

"Oh, Arthur!" Kelly said, hugging him close. She patted his head and scratched behind his ears. "I'm just glad he's okay."

Kelly set a big bowl of water on the floor, and we watched Arthur slurp it up.

"Kelly?" I asked her, turning our focus back to Scotty's case—the real reason I was there. "Is there anyone you can think of who might've had a problem with Scotty? Who might be pleased something like this has happened?"

"No one in particular. I mean, a lot of people didn't like Josh and him growing on his property. But he wasn't getting death threats or anything."

"What happened to the house next door? Looks like there was a fire there."

"Yeah," she said. She told me the cabin next door had burned down years ago. Apparently a mother and her children had died in the fire. The grief-stricken father moved to the Midwest, and the lot had been on the market ever since. Arthur finished slurping up the water in his bowl and regarded Kelly and me. Arthur walked over to her, and she brought his face close to hers.

"You want more?" Kelly asked. Arthur licked her face again and nuzzled his head close. "I love you, Arthur."

I asked her if she knew Eleanor Jackson, the neighbor across the road.

"She keeps to herself mostly. She doesn't do much except sit on her porch and bird-watch. Her husband died a while back, I guess. She's a nice lady, as far as I know."

As Kelly scratched behind Arthur's ears, she gave me a look I recognized. Doe-eyed, she batted her long pretty eyelashes and held my gaze with a knowing smirk. It reminded me of the look girls gave right before they asked me to buy them a drink. Usually when I did, they'd disappear before I signed the check.

"Would you mind looking after him?" she asked. "Until I get a more permanent place? One of my roommates is allergic."

"I don't think that's a good idea," I said. I wasn't exactly sure on the messy lawyer ethics of dogsitting for a client.

"But he's such a sweetheart."

Arthur brought his head under my hand on cue, jostling my hand with his nose until I patted his head. He was a pretty cool dog. Very well behaved.

"What about Scotty's parents?" I said without thinking. "Stupid question. Okay. I'll look after him and talk with Scotty to see where he should go."

"Thank you," she said.

Ten minutes later, Arthur and I were at the pet store looking at varieties of dog food. I felt bad for him, stuck in the woods all that time, so I bought a five-pound bag of dog food, a doggy bed, three chew toys, two tennis balls, a new collar, and a new leash. I even thought about buying him a 49ers bandanna, but that seemed like overkill.

* * *

The next Tuesday after work, I went to hang out with Will. He lived high up on a hill above the Canyon Oaks golf course. We were sitting on his plush cream couch inside his Tuscany-style mini-mansion when I was reminded that the bounds of his vulgarity knew no limits. He started talking about his sexual escapades.

"Oh my god," he said. "You should've seen this one girl I banged last weekend. Her pussy got so wet."

I cringed. "C'mon, man. That's disgusting."

"Body was a ten."

"Congratulations," I said. *What a cretin.*

"You love it!" he said.

"No, I don't. Keep that shit to yourself."

"Don't be a little bitch," he said.

Will had convinced me to join a basketball league, and our first game was in an hour. He filled up water bottles in the kitchen while I watched SportsCenter.

"How's Scotty's case going?" he asked.

I told him about the deal Emma had offered—for Scotty to plead guilty to second-degree murder in exchange for a sentencing recommendation of no more than fifteen years.

"Nice!" Will said.

But then I told him the contingency. "Only if Scotty helps them find the body."

"I can't believe they haven't found it yet…" Will said. "Whatever. That's great news. So you guys are gonna take it, right?"

"I haven't talked to Scotty yet. Plus, I don't know if he knows where the body is."

"Bullshit. You're not serious, are you?"

I shrugged.

"You think he's innocent?"

"I don't know," I told him.

"Think about the evidence."

"I've thought about it. I'm seriously not sure he did this."

"They found the victim's truck down the road?"

"Yes."

"The neighbor saw him go inside?"

"Yes."

"There's the knife with Scotty's prints?"

"Yes."

"The blood on the floor?"

"Yeah, I know."

"Motive?"

"Maybe."

"What exculpates him?"

"I don't know," I said. "Let's go. We're gonna be late."

"You're crazy if you don't *force* him to plea."

* * *

We drove to the game in Will's shining cobalt-blue Model X Tesla SUV.

"What about the bump on Scotty's head?" I asked.

"Maybe there was a struggle. So what? That might get it reduced to manslaughter, but second-degree with a fifteen-year cap keeps him from getting life, and if this case goes to trial, he's getting life."

I disagreed. There were too many questions in my mind. "What about the gun?" I asked. "Deputies arrived after a shots-fired call, but the guns found in the cabin hadn't been fired."

"Hunters," Will said.

"Two hours after midnight? *In the dead of morning?*" The quiet hum of the Tesla motor punctuated the silence.

"Okay, that fact is a little weird, but it doesn't exculpate him."

"What about the body? How is Emma going to prove murder without a body?"

I suppose at this point Will had had enough because then he said, "You wanna roll the dice in Butte County with all that circumstantial evidence? Go ahead."

We rode the rest of the way without speaking.

* * *

Will staffed our men's-league team with elite young professionals who took as much pride in their recreational sports accomplishments as they did in their professional careers. I was the lowly government employee and the lone player not in private practice raking in fistfuls of cash. I mostly just ran around and set screens. I rebounded, passed, and played tough defense. I hustled. Will was aggressive. He was a bruiser. He'd attack the basket off the dribble. He'd throw his weight around to take full advantage of the twenty-five pounds of muscle he'd put on since high school. He always looked for opportunities to score.

With two minutes left in the third quarter, a shot went up. Will jostled his way under the hoop. A wiry opponent with freak athleticism and sharp elbows came charging in for the rebound. The wiry opponent grabbed the ball out of the air and descended back toward earth. Will lurched up to grab it from him, and there was an audible crack when the wiry opponent's elbow came down across Will's nose.

"Fuck!" he shouted. Blood gushed from his nostrils and dripped onto the gym floor. "I'm fine! I'm fine!" he said.

He didn't look fine. He was bleeding all over the place. I ran over to the bench and grabbed some old Chico State Basketball shirt I'd used for warm-ups. It was white with red lettering, with the Chico State Wildcat logo superimposed on a basketball. Will pinched his nose with the shirt until the bleeding stopped.

Will came back in the fourth quarter and was reckless. He lurched his hips into opponents, swung his elbows wildly, and ran across the lane with elbows pointed. Thanks to Will's dirty play and some hot shooting late, we won the game by ten.

Listening to Will's Tesla purr as we cruised down the road with the cool spring air on my face calmed me, and as I was thinking about Scotty's case, I wondered if Will was right. Perhaps it was time to have the come-to-Jesus talk with Scotty and suggest that he plead guilty.

"Don't forget your shirt," Will said. We'd arrived back at his house. He pointed to the crumpled-up, bloody rag at my feet.

"Dude. That's gross. You take it."

"I don't want it!" he said. "Just take it outta here and throw it away."

"Fine." When I got home, I tossed it in the trash can in the corner of my garage. *Fucking Will. Spoiled brat.* When I got inside, I found Arthur lounging on my couch.

"Want to go for a walk, buddy?" I asked him.

His ears perked up. He slid off the couch and galloped over to me.

"Okay," I told him. "Let's go."

EIGHTEEN

A prosecutor will generally always charge an open count of murder. By not charging degree—first, second, or manslaughter—he or she allows for the jury to decide what degree is appropriate. That's the standard practice in Butte County at least.

A conviction for first-degree murder requires the prosecution to prove the killer had the intent to do it and something resembling a plan. As you might imagine, first-degree murder is difficult to prove because it requires knowing what the perpetrator was thinking. It's not impossible, however, since evidence of a person's thoughts can be deduced from how they acted in the moments leading up to the act of killing. For instance, if Scotty had driven to the local Home Depot on March 10 and purchased a shovel, a giant tarp, and twenty feet of rope; told Kelly (or someone else) he was going to kill Josh on March 11; set a death trap on the morning of March 12; and lured Josh to the cabin later that night, a jury could reasonably conclude premeditation and intent. But there wasn't any evidence of Scotty doing that, so I figured Emma was holding out for some more favorable facts to emerge, like the discovery of an execution-style gunshot wound in Josh's decomposing skull. For that to happen, they'd have to find

Josh's body first, which they hadn't. If Scotty was convicted of first-degree murder, he would face life without the possibility of parole.

Second-degree requires proving intent but not a plan. A jury could arrive at second-degree murder through a lot of different kinds of circumstantial evidence. The more the better—like DNA evidence, witnesses testifying that Scotty was the last person to see Josh alive, testimony from a medical expert that the amount of Josh's blood found would almost certainly have resulted in his death. If convicted of second-degree murder at trial, Scotty would face fifteen years to life. If he pled guilty, Emma would recommend the minimum, and Scotty wouldn't face the risk of a first-degree murder conviction and life.

The last option was voluntary manslaughter. Voluntary manslaughter is the intentional killing of another person but either "in the heat of passion" or "after a sudden quarrel." If Josh had shown up to the cabin that night and started arguing with Scotty, the argument turned into a fight, and Scotty killed Josh, that would be manslaughter. If convicted of manslaughter, Scotty would face only three, six, or eleven years in jail. To a certain degree, the decision as to whether to accept a plea depends on the accused's and the defense attorney's appetite for risk. For me, I didn't much like the idea of Scotty Watts spending the rest of his life in jail because I lost at trial. Even if he had killed Josh Anderson, I thought Scotty deserved a second chance. I also knew a Butte County jury was likely to convict.

* * *

The next time I saw him, Scotty had dark circles under his eyes, and his hangdog expression was especially dour, like he'd been getting his ass kicked. He said he was just tired, but I knew better.

"Thanks for looking after Arthur," he said.

"Kelly told you?"

He nodded.

"You're sure there's nowhere else he could go?" I asked.

"The pound."

"That's what I figured."

We talked about the particulars of Arthur's care, like how he loved playing fetch but was oddly indifferent to exercise, how he could eat until his stomach exploded if left unchecked, and how he was very affectionate and needed a lot of attention. "He might come across like he's dumb, but he's actually very smart." Scotty said that last part as though he were defending a friend against a familiar indictment. I listened to the Arthur-care instructions, but I was really just building the courage to bring up the real issue that had brought me to visit him. Finally I leaned in and told him I needed his version of what had happened that night. "The truth," I said. "Not what you told investigators, not what you want it to be. I need to know what happened. *Everything.*"

Scotty scowled at me. He leaned back in his chair and folded his arms. The harsh fluorescent light cast shadows across his face.

"You think I'm lying?" he asked.

"I didn't say that. I just need you to tell me the truth."

He shook his head.

"I need every detail. None of this 'I don't remember' stuff. I need the truth."

He frowned. "I was sorta happy to see you when you walked in, you know?"

I nodded. "Okay."

"You remember when we were younger?"

"Of course." Sort of.

"We'd play catch in your backyard. Your mom would cook us dinner. We'd ride bikes down your street in the summertime."

Yes, I remembered.

"I had hope when I saw you first walk in the door. I figured you'd understand."

"Scotty—"

"I thought, 'Finally someone who will believe me. Someone on my side.'"

"Facts are facts," I said.

"You think I don't know that! You think I don't know how bad it looks! You think I want to be sitting in here? You know, you got to leave this town. You got to go to college and law school. You got to have a future. You got to try and make a life. I was stuck here. You know what got me sent away?"

"You told me."

"Yeah, but people just think I went in there like a crook, guns blazing. I went in there *without* a gun. I wasn't robbing him. The dealer stiffed me, and I wanted my money back. *He* pulled a gun on *me*. He freaked out. I thought I was gonna die. Damn thing went off right by my ear. I could have died. But the DA said *I* brought the gun. My attorney didn't care. Told me I had no chance at trial. Told me I got the best deal I could hope for. So I pled. But how does that seem fair? Pleading to something I didn't do?"

"Sometimes it's not," I told him, and I asked him why he hadn't told me those details the first time we met.

"Cuz you would just think I was lying. Like everyone else. I already pled to something I didn't do, and I ain't doing it again."

I didn't have anything to say to that. Scotty was not just probably right; he was right. I would have thought he was lying. He didn't wait for me to apologize or comment.

"I know I screwed up," he said. "But I paid for it. It wasn't just the time I spent in here; when I got out, I had nothing. Just when I thought I was going to get my second chance, right when I thought, 'Life's not gonna screw me again,' my dad got sick, and I was back to struggling. I thought I might finally have a chance. Instead, I was driving my old man to physical therapy appointments, watching him fall apart, and spending nights rubbing my mom's back while she sobbed over it all until she had nothing left. All because she didn't want my dad to see how hard it was on her."

"I'm not calling you a liar."

"Yes you are. That's exactly what you're calling me."

"It's just that I've had clients—"

"You want to know what happened?" I said nothing. He went on. "I'm telling you, exactly what's in that report"—he stabbed the file on the table with an index finger—"that's what happened. That's all I know. That's all I remember. If you want a different version, I can't give it to you."

"I'm only bringing this up because the prosecutor offered a plea deal."

"I ain't pleading guilty," he said.

"I have to tell you what it is. It's my job."

He pursed his lips and said nothing.

"If you disclose where Josh's body is, they'll reduce the charge to second-degree murder and recommend a fifteen-year cap on confinement."

Scotty dropped his head in his hands. "I think you should leave," he said.

I got up and started putting my things away. "Fine. But you should know, it doesn't matter if you're telling the truth. A jury will convict you, and you'll go to prison for life."

He watched and waited as I packed my things, boring a hole through me with his eyes. I could barely glance in his direction before walking out the door.

NINETEEN

Three weeks went by.

Three weeks of Thursday-night family dinners. Three weeks of visiting my mother at Lakeside. "Are you dating anyone?" she would ask me from her bed.

Thin Mustache would pop his head in. "It's nap time," he'd say.

She'd shout at the blank wall next to her. She'd murmur about Lawrence. She'd nod off again. I'd watch her sleep. I'd leave.

Three church services passed. My sister looked more and more comfortable up in front of the congregation, standing with her shoulders arched back and her head high. I would stare at the back of Lacey Price's head—her beautiful hair cascading down her back. It would make me feel light-headed and empty inside. I'd look from Lacey to Paul Morrison, back to Lacey, wondering why their relationship was clandestinely hidden from the public eye. Three weeks of men's-league basketball games, listening to Will yammer on about the hot chick he was screwing, was grating on my nerves. I was starting to hate him, with his fancy cars, his harem of women, and his juvenile humor. *Asshole.*

Three weeks of work. On other cases, other clients, other

problems. Thank God for Shelly. She kept me on track. "Maybe as trial gets closer you can talk some sense into him," she'd say when Scotty's name came up.

"Maybe," I'd say back.

It was nice to have Arthur. He'd sit with me at night, and I'd talk to him about the case. At the end of a long day, after the sun went down, I'd throw a tennis ball across the room for him to fetch. He'd scamper after it, sliding across the old wood floors. He'd grip the ball in his jaws and bring it back in his mouth. He'd set it in my lap and look up at me, waiting for me to throw it again.

"Do you think Scotty's telling the truth?" I'd ask him.

He would nod his head at the ball in my lap.

"Okay," I'd tell him and throw it toward the front door.

My house off Honey Run Road had a small shaded backyard surrounded by a white picket fence where Arthur could run and play while I was at work. The fence was high enough that he couldn't get out. I installed a doggy door so he could come and go as he pleased, but something told me he wouldn't escape even if he could. Arthur was a good dog. He didn't bark much, and my neighbors all seemed to enjoy having him around. They would smile and wave when they saw me walking with him. In the evenings after work, we'd hike through Bidwell Park together. On Saturday mornings we'd go on long runs before the afternoon sun was high in the sky and the sweltering valley heat baked the land. I like to think he enjoyed his new life with me.

* * *

The school year came to an end. Downtown frat houses placed decrepit furniture on their porches with homemade For Sale signs draping off them. U-Hauls appeared in the streets to collect Ikea furniture frugal parents didn't want thrown away. Summer arrived. Court staff went on vacations. *The People of Butte County v. Scotty Watts* got pushed back on the court's docket. I talked to Emma about the case every few days, but nothing really changed. The search for Josh Anderson's body had dwindled into hopelessness. The Andersons even momentarily suspended their media campaign. Each time I spoke with Emma, I'd remind her of the missing-victim problem she had.

"There's no better defense to a murder charge than having no victim," I'd remind her.

"There is a victim," she'd say matter-of-factly. "Do we need to go over the circumstantial evidence again?"

We could go back and forth all day and get nowhere. Perhaps in a more liberal county, the missing victim would be a huge prosecutorial problem, but deep down I knew Emma was probably right. There was a lot of circumstantial evidence pointing to Scotty's guilt.

Election season started ramping up. Political signs dotted the front lawns of residential homes. Chico is a place where people have strong political opinions and vote them. Most everyone engaged in politics was focused on the 2016 presidential election since that whole mess resembled a Dumpster fire. But the normally bland politics of Butte County also took a dramatic turn. On my way to the office one morning, I passed an enormous billboard on the side of the road. There was a large picture of Josh Anderson with the word "Missing above the photo. "Justice for Josh?" it read below the picture. Mike Sullivan had been the district attorney in Butte County for the last twenty years, and while finding Josh's body was a top priority for the district attorney's office, with each passing day, it seemed less and less likely it was going to happen. This must be why Emma was unwilling to negotiate. Incumbent elected officials are rarely opposed in Butte County and almost never lose. If Sullivan lost, then it would be devastating for more than just the obvious reasons.

"Have you seen that billboard?" I asked Shelly one day in the office. I didn't need to specify. She knew exactly what I was talking about.

"Oh yeah," she said with a nod. "Have you seen the website?"

I googled "Justice for Josh," and a large timer popped up on the front web page. The counter ticked upward—"8 weeks, 3 days, 13 hours, 43 seconds…44…45…46…47"—clocking the time passed since Josh Anderson had gone missing. The site featured an assemblage of facts about Josh that read like a personal ad on a dating website.

"Josh enjoyed pickup basketball with his friends, snow-skiing, mountain biking, and soaking up the sun on long summer days at Big Bear Lake."

Scotty's mug shot was prominently displayed. He looked even more tired and disheveled than usual. It's amazing how consistently unflattering those mug shots are. In big bold letters, the site emphasized how "District Attorney Sullivan engaged in extensive delay in bringing Josh's killer to justice." I scrolled to the bottom. In tiny gray font, it read, "Paid for by Bill Dubois for Butte County DA" Sullivan had a challenger. Emma had more pressure to get a conviction.

Over dinner one Thursday night, my father filled me in on the political gossip. He explained that Bill Dubois was a medical-malpractice attorney from Sacramento. "Just some guy with a bunch of money," he said. Regardless that finding Josh's body was not under the responsibility of the district attorney (the sheriff had jurisdiction), Bill Dubois's ad placed blame at the feet of the public officials the voters *would think* were responsible. Irrational outrage, not truth, reigns in American politics. Dubois's campaign was genius.

* * *

In early June, I met Rick in his office. It was a one-room storefront next to a laundromat, but the decor was meticulously organized. Once a marine, always a marine. He had a big oak desk with a mahogany bookcase. A shadowbox with ribbons and medals celebrating his twenty years of service in the Marine Corps, certificates of achievement, degrees he had earned while serving, and letters of appreciation from supervisors hung on the walls. As I sat across from him, I could hear the churning of rotating dryers. I told him about my meetings with Scotty and how he wasn't going to take the deal. Rick was incredulous.

"I've tried everything I can," I told him.

"You're sure?" Rick asked.

"I've been visiting him twice a week for the last three weeks. Emma won't negotiate for anything more lenient because Sullivan's feeling the heat on the election. There's nothing more I can do."

Rick sat back and sighed.

There were facts about the investigation that we needed to explore, I told him. First, the bump on Scotty's head. Had he been struck with an object or a fist? Could we tell? How hard was the blow? Could it have knocked him out? I had to come up with a theory that Scotty was either attacked, or it was self-defense. I had to come up with *some* theory. "I also want to interview Eleanor Jackson," I said. Rick frowned. "I went to Scotty's cabin," I told him. "It's not a clear line of sight. Her testimony seems overconfident to me. I mean, she's eighty-five years old. There's no way she can be that certain." Rick crossed his arms. "At the very least, we need to visit the scene again," I said. "You need to see what I saw. The row of trees separating Scotty's cabin from the road. The obscured view Ms. Jackson almost certainly had of the scene." Rick nodded and then smiled.

"What?" I asked. "Why do you have that look on your face?"

"He's a lucky guy."

"Who?"

"Watts. He's a lucky guy."

"He's not that lucky. He's sitting in jail accused of murder."

"To have you as his attorney. He's lucky."

My face burned. "Thanks," I said.

"I'll run down these leads," Rick said. "I'll interview the neighbor and talk to the doctors. I'm still not sure it's anywhere near enough to prove his innocence, but I'll do it."

"I appreciate it," I said.

"I just don't want us wasting our time."

"We won't."

"I don't want you wasting your time," he said.

"I'm not. I promise. I have to go into court with *something*."

* * *

That Saturday, Arthur and I returned home from a long run. The dreaded valley heat was already smothering the land. I was drenched in sweat. I walked inside and filled Arthur's water bowl. He lapped it up. After I showered and changed clothes, I came back out into the kitchen. I grabbed a gallon of milk from the fridge and a box of cereal from my kitchen cupboard and set them on the counter. Arthur stopped slurping water for a moment and looked at me. I looked at him and then back to the milk and cereal sitting on the counter. I grabbed my wallet, keys, and phone and walked toward the door. Arthur followed me a few steps.

"You stay here, buddy," I told him.

He shuffled a few steps closer. "What are you doing?" he asked.

"I gotta go talk to Scotty," I said and walked out the door.

TWENTY

I called Rick from the car.

"Are you in a tunnel?" he asked. My phone was on speaker and resting on the dashboard of my rusty green sedan, so I could understand the confusion.

"No. I'm driving to the courthouse. The milk and cereal," I said.

"What about it?" Rick asked.

"There should have been a toxicology report done on the milk and cereal. It wasn't listed in the investigator's report."

"Okay," Rick said. "I'll look into it." He paused, which immediately made me nervous. I hated it when Rick paused because I knew he was thinking. If he was thinking, it meant he was probably about to ask a question I didn't have an answer to. "But even if there was something in Scotty's milk and cereal, who put it in there? His loving girlfriend?"

Yup. I was right. I didn't have an answer to that. I didn't know who had a motive to frame Scotty. "Just see if they tested it," I said. "It's better than nothing. Also, can you ask around for a list of substances that would knock someone out for a few hours?"

Rick groaned. "Remember what I asked of you?"

"We're not wasting time."

"Okay…"

"Rick, if I'm going to take this case to trial, I have to believe Scotty, and he told Detective Cruz the last thing he remembered was being midbite into a bowl of Honey Bunches of Oats before waking up in a pool of blood. There was either something in that milk, something in that cereal, or both. We have to look into this."

Rick mumbled something and hung up.

I passed the golden tableau of dry weeds, the Sutter Buttes, and the lush green trees in neat rows. I didn't see the faceless man atop the combine today. The land I passed on my drive to the courthouse was empty. But just before I merged onto Highway 70, I saw something in the distance. It was a blue speck of color the size of a small tree. *John? Is that John? Standing in the middle of a barren field?* But after looking at the road to make sure I didn't crash, when I looked back to the blue speck, it was gone.

When I arrived at the jail, the guards met me at the gate and escorted me inside. Given how our last meeting had ended, I shouldn't have been too surprised that Scotty was not happy to see me. I walked in, and we didn't exchange greetings. I just sat. "How's everything going in here?" I asked him.

"Fine."

"We need to talk about the case."

"Okay."

I wondered if I should apologize. But for what? For trying to convince him of what's best? That was just fine if he was angry. So was I. I was angry at how stubborn he had been. About how he'd lost perspective and hadn't listened to what I was saying.

"I don't know if you want a new lawyer or if you're still mad at me or what, but I'm your lawyer until I'm officially not your lawyer, so I'm going to do everything I can while I'm still here." Not my most elegant pitch, but I've never been one for eloquent speeches.

He sat up a little in his chair. "Okay," and that was the end of it.

We went over the events leading up to that night. Scotty's account didn't diverge much from Kelly's. He described the day—Kelly doing homework in the morning while he worked on a project in the garage. He took Arthur for a walk. He made love with Kelly in the afternoon. Kelly left for her shift at O'Haras, and he waited around for his planned meeting with Josh. Kelly had told me she left at 6:00 p.m.; Scotty thought it was more like 7:00 or 7:30 p.m. It didn't matter too much. People could never recall time exactly, nor should anyone expect them to.

"What happened next?" I asked. "After Kelly left, you told investigators you spent a half hour or an hour working in the garage. Are you sure that's right?"

He nodded.

"Then you went upstairs?"

"Yes."

"And poured a bowl of Honey Bunches of Oats?"

"Yes."

"For dinner?"

"Yes."

"Strange dinner choice."

"Well, I'm not exactly Anthony Bourdain, all right?"

"Okay, fine. What time was Josh supposed to arrive?"

"Like between seven thirty and eight o'clock."

"Was it seven thirty or eight? Or in between?"

"I'd told Josh, 'Let's meet between seven thirty and eight p.m.'"

"When did you talk to him?"

"Earlier that day."

"On the phone?"

"Yes."

"You didn't text?"

"No. We called. We didn't want to get in trouble with texts, so we called usually. I told him I'd be home in the evening and that he should come by."

"Do you remember what time it was when you sat down to eat?"

"I don't know. Between seven thirty and eight o'clock. How many times I got to say that?"

"Fine. Sorry. Then what happened?"

"Like I told the detective, I was sitting there eating, and the last thing I remember is eating the cereal. When I wake up, it's dark outside, and I'm lying in a sticky goo. I lift up my face, and I realize it's blood. I freak out."

"Do you remember what woke you up?"

"No. I don't know. I just woke up. Maybe it was the blood I was practically drowning in."

"Okay," I said.

"I heard sounds of voices outside, but they sounded really far away. My head hurt and my vision was blurry."

"What then?"

"I panicked. I grabbed towels—"

"Paper towels?"

"Paper towels, regular towels. Every kind of towel I could find. I mean, what do you want from me? I was freaked out. What difference does it make? I just woke up in a pool of blood."

"You never saw Josh?"

"No."

"Okay."

I looked over my notes, trying to think of more questions. "That's the truth?" I asked.

"Yes. That's the truth."

"Okay, okay. I just have to be sure."

Scotty looked into my eyes, and I could see he felt betrayed by me and by the rest of the world. He had the same sad eyes as Arthur, and there was something so sympathetic about his face. I suppose years of constantly being questioned, second-guessed, and judged had left him feeling lonely. I understood. Yet I also needed Scotty to fully understand the realities of his case, especially if he wasn't going to accept a plea. I reminded him that there was a lot to explain about the case. He nodded.

"Do you have any idea how your prints might have gotten on Josh's truck?"

"No."

"Had you ever been in the truck before?"

"Yes."

"When was the last time?"

"About a week ago."

I knew he couldn't account for Josh's blood or the knife, but I thought maybe the truck could be explained. I was wrong.

"Scotty," I said, lowering my voice, "I want to tell you two things."

"Okay."

"First of all, I'm going to try everything I possibly can to corroborate your story. I have my investigator working on your case right now. He's the best investigator in the county, so if there's something to find, he'll find it."

"Okay."

"I hope we can explain what happened. I'm working hard for you. I want you to know that."

He nodded. His lip quivered and his eyes looked glassy. He shook off whatever he was feeling and composed himself. I didn't want to say the next part, but I felt compelled. I *had to*. I half expected him to blow up at me, pound his fists on the table, and ask me to leave. I half expected him to tell me to go to hell. But there's no other way to go about saying something unpleasant than just doing it.

"Second," I said, "and I don't think this will be the last time you hear this from me, but there are some cases where it makes sense to take a plea deal even when you're totally innocent. Ultimately it's up to you, but taking a plea deal in this case might be in your best interest."

"I'm not taking a plea. I didn't kill anybody."

I sighed and leaned back in my chair. "Okay," I said. "I understand. But you just said you were eating cereal and don't remember anything after."

"That's right."

"The next thing you remember is waking up in a pool of blood."

"Yeah."

"So when you say you didn't kill anyone, my question to you is, If you don't remember, how do you know for sure?"

He scowled back at me and said nothing.

TWENTY-ONE

It was a dirty trick, and I felt guilty for doing it. If Scotty had ingested drugs without knowing and killed Josh Anderson in some crazy drug-induced rage, he could not be found guilty of murder. Involuntary intoxication is an absolute defense, so questioning his memory had little legal effect other than trying to get him to plead guilty. The problem, and why I did that to him, was that I couldn't prove involuntary intoxication because I had absolutely nothing to go on. Until I had toxicology evidence, I had no idea what had happened, and a jury wasn't going to believe the involuntary intoxication defense theory without corroborating evidence. As Rick pointed out, even assuming there was some crazy drug in the bowl of cereal, who drugged him? Why would someone do that?

As a defense attorney, you're forced to choose a certain path. Among the choices you have to make, you must ignore or disregard some evidence that might be valid and hone in on the facts that will convince a jury your client didn't do it. The toxicology defense seemed like our best bet, even if it didn't quite make sense just yet.

* * *

That Sunday, Arthur and I were hiking along a dirt trail high up on the ridge of Bidwell Park. We came across two figures in the distance, growing larger as they moved in our direction. Heat distorted the outlines of their shapes in wavy angles, like a mirage in the desert. As they got closer, I recognized them as Ralph Morrison and his wife, Sue. Ralph was a bigger, more substantial version of his son Paul: dark hair, square jaw, and a highway patrolman's handlebar mustache hidden under a John Deere hat. Sue had a long angular face, and she peered over Ralph's shoulder like I was a mugger in a dark alleyway.

"Welcome home," Ralph said.

"Thanks," I said, even though I'd been back for well over two years.

Ralph pointed at Arthur. "You keeping that feller cool?"

"Yup," I said. I patted Arthur's belly. *Yes, Ralph, my dog is just fine. Thank you.*

We made small talk. "Sure is a hot one." "Yes." "Summer is here for good." "Sure is." I asked about his boys, even though I knew the answers. I didn't mention how I had seen Paul up at Forest Ranch driving around with Lacey. I tugged on Arthur's leash a little to move past them, but I could tell Ralph wasn't done talking.

"I understand you're representing the Watts boy."

"That's right."

"Scotty was always up to no good," he said.

I shrugged. *Fuck you, Ralph.*

"I feel bad for the victim's folks. Their son out there rotting in the dirt and all that," Ralph said.

"I really can't talk about the case, Mr. Morrison."

"Someone should really tell his parents where the body is buried."

"I can't imagine what the family is going through," Sue chimed in from over his shoulder.

I just smiled at them both and nodded. Arthur groaned and licked my leg. *Fucking Chico. Get me out of here.*

"Well, nice to see you both," I said and made another

attempt at moving past them on the trail.

As I passed, Ralph laid his big hand on my shoulder. "I trust you'll do the right thing, son," he said. Ralph was the kind of guy who called you son until you were fifty, so long as he was a few years older than you.

I smiled at him. "Have a nice day," I said.

Arthur and I walked farther along the ridge, and I didn't look back. I seethed inside. "Do the right thing." What the hell did that mean? As if I knew where the body was. As if I'd killed him and dumped the body in some location I was keeping secret. *"Do the right thing." Fuck you, Ralph. You're what's wrong with this place. People like you are why small-town defendants can't get a fair trial. "Innocent until proven guilty" is supposed to mean something, you ignorant asshole. Rumors and accusations aren't facts, and you're an idiot.*

* * *

When I arrived at the office on Monday morning, Shelly greeted me with a new stack of client files.

"Any update on Scotty taking the plea?" she asked.

"Unless someone has a dramatic change of heart, we're going to trial."

"Sorry to hear," she said.

I purposely said "someone" and not "Scotty" since I held out hope that Emma might be able to convince Sullivan to offer a more palatable plea deal. Wishful thinking, I suppose. The "Justice for Josh" campaigns were all over town.

* * *

On Tuesday, Will and I lost our men's-league basketball game. I had to hear him yammer on about some new drone he was going to buy that he planned to fly all over the golf course below his house. He told me about a million-dollar settlement he had just closed. I wanted to punch him.

On Wednesday, I visited my mother. Thin Mustache

explained that she'd been particularly docile that week, and I wondered if they were getting her medications right. "We're giving her the same," he explained. "She's just sleeping more. That's all." I was starting to like Thin Mustache. He seemed like he cared about my mother's care, even if he was just good at faking it.

On Thursday, I had dinner with my dad and sister. Dad made shrimp tacos. I was impressed.

"These are pretty good, Dad," I said.

Without looking up from his meal, he said, "They should be good. They're takeout. I threw away the packaging before you guys got here."

While my sister talked excitedly about summer plans for the congregation, I thought of Eileen and Ray Watts. I wondered what their family dinners looked like. I pictured Eileen guiding spoonfuls of soft food into Ray's mouth, the indignity of the mushy goop falling down his chin and into his lap. I thought about Scotty in jail. I thought about John again. All that thinking made me sad.

* * *

It was late in the day. I was sitting in my office reviewing a new case when I heard the ding-dong chime of our doorbell. Shelly usually locked the door when she left for the day, and it was after 4:00 p.m. I figured she must have forgotten something. I waited for her to call out to me, and when she didn't, I listened for her rustling around for whatever she'd forgotten. Instead, I heard nothing. A rush of air blew past my office, and I got up.

"Shelly?" I called out. No response. "Hello? Did you forget something?" I walked into the hallway. "Shelly? You there?" I rounded the corner to the front, with her desk in full view. The waiting room was empty. Her chair was empty. Her purse was gone. Monitors hummed. Rays of afternoon sunlight caught dust floating up from the floor. My heart started pounding. I checked the front door to see if it had been opened. It was still locked. *Huh. The doorbell must have malfunctioned.* I walked back toward my office, but before I went in, I stopped. The door to John's old office was closed, but I thought I heard a low hum coming from inside. I chuckled to myself. I walked a few steps down the hallway, and the low humming got louder. I jiggled the door handle. It was locked. But standing there, I recognized the hum as a low mechanical whir. Defying logic or reason, I went back to my office, grabbed a set of keys out of my top drawer, walked back to John's door, unlocked it, and pushed it open.

Papers were scattered everywhere, all over the desk. A small fan oscillated back and forth. John sat reclining in his big leather chair. The fan's breeze blew his wavy black hair off his scalp. He combed a hand through it and smiled.

"Butte County!" he said. "Working late?"

I smiled. "Hi, John."

"Are we having fun yet?"

I was not having fun. I was lost. I was tired. And I didn't know if I was doing anything right. As though I had spoken the words, he replied, "Listen, you need to go home. Get some rest. Relax. I like that new dog of yours. Go to the park with him. Get a date, for God's sake. Live your life."

"I suppose I should," I said.

"I just wanted to check in, that's all," he said. "Oh!" He grabbed a green leather-bound book off his desk, stood up, and presented it to me. "I also wanted to show you this."

I read the spine: "*The Conscience of a Lawyer*, by David Mellinkoff."

"Ever read it?" he asked.

"No."

"It's pretty boring. About some ancient case. Deals with ethics—what to do when you know your client is guilty and you're going to trial. All that jazz." He leaned closer and smiled. "Not exactly our case, is it?"

"Is it? I don't know," I said.

"Well, yours is the harder case," he said. "What to do with uncertainty. What to do when you're not sure if your client is actually innocent. All the evidence points to his guilt, but there's a small sliver of doubt about it all. The harder case is when you're not sure if your client is tricking you. If the whole thing is a con. The harder case is *The People of Butte County v. Scotty Watts.*"

He walked back behind his desk and sat again. "Anyway," he said, "I wanted you to have the book because there's a great quote in there. Meant to give it to you and I never got the chance. I highlighted the quote for you. Check it out."

I leafed through the pages. "Thanks," I said, "but I don't exactly have time for recreational reading right now." I flipped back and forth through the pages, looking for the highlighted portion. "John, where's the highlighted portion? I can't find it." With my head in the book, I heard our front doorbell chime again and looked up. I was standing alone in John's empty office. The papers were gone, the books were gone, and the fan was unplugged and resting silently on its shelf. The lights were off in the empty office, and I stood there for a moment, alone.

TWENTY-TWO

Deer Creek Highway is like a long sloping ramp to heaven. From the valley, the road stretches all the way to the horizon line. Once you reach a certain point, trees start popping up out of the brown weeds and rocks.

As I once again made the drive to Scotty's cabin, the snapshot memories of Scotty Watts both young and old flashed in my mind—his big smile after scoring an impossible layup, his backflip off a high cliff into the dark swimming pools of Little Chico Creek, the nightmarish scene of him waking up facedown in a pool of blood in the still of night, overcome by panic. I wound my car around the road until Arthur and I turned left onto the gravel road of Forest Rim Lane. Rick assured me he was going to make a visit to the crime scene soon, but I was too impatient. Or maybe driving up to Scotty's cabin was a comfortable, familiar habit. I don't know, but driving up to Forest Ranch and being among the cabins and pine trees drew me in. I parked on the gravel road, and Arthur and I walked up to Eleanor Jackson's house.

"Wait here," I told Arthur when we reached her driveway. He sat on the edge of the driveway and watched me go. When I was halfway to the house, I looked back at Arthur, who was now lying in the sun on the edge of the road. I loved him in that moment, and I was glad he was with me.

The wooden stairs leading to Eleanor Jackson's front door creaked beneath my feet, and when I got to the front door, I knocked. There was no answer, and I looked through the sheer curtain covering the windows. The interior was bright and airy and had neatly organized but aging furniture, yet there was no sign of Eleanor Jackson. I knocked again. Still no answer. I walked back out to the road.

"I guess we'll try some other time," I told Arthur as we crossed the road and walked up Scotty's driveway toward his decrepit cabin. I dipped under the yellow crime scene tape that was getting dusty and torn in places. One end had even become untethered from where it was wrapped around a tree. Arthur stopped at the crime scene tape, refusing to go any farther.

"Come on," I said. "Let's go." I grabbed him by the collar, but he resisted. "You want to stay here?" He barked. "All right, fine."

Once inside Scotty's cabin, I took another inventory—the counter where the knife was found, the dining room table where the bowl of cereal had been, the faint outline of the bloodstain on the floor. I paced around the kitchen and living room, just as I always did, and went over my theories of the case. I wondered what the update was on the toxicology report. I thought about calling Rick to get an update. Suddenly I heard Arthur barking with wild urgency from outside. I heard his footsteps on the stairs leading to the front door, and he bolted through the door and into the house. He barked and bobbed around the living room like he was trying to alert me of a fire. I went to the front window and looked out, but there was nothing there. Arthur kept barking nonstop.

"Arthur! Calm down! Stop! It's me!"

I put my hands out. He wouldn't stop barking.

"Arthur! It's me."

Only for a moment did he stand straighter and relax his muscles, and just when I thought his panic was over, right before I leaned down to pet his head, he suddenly turned and

ran back out the front door and down the stairs. I raced down
the steps after him.

"Arthur! What are you doing?" I shouted. He bolted off
into the woods. I sprinted across the lot into the pines to
follow him. Branches smacked my forehead. A spiderweb
caked my face, and strands hung from my open mouth. I
wiped the webbing away and spit what had got in my mouth
into the dirt. I followed Arthur's black splotch of color
through the thick pines, weaving through the thicket.

"Arthur! Slow down!"

We ran for what must have been half a mile, until finally I
came to a small clearing. Arthur sat in the middle of it, looking
almost indifferent. I put my hands on my knees and wheezed
for air, struggling to catch my breath. "Geez." Gasp. "Arthur."
Gasp. "What—" Gasp. I spat a mouthful of dry saliva into the
leaves. "What. The. Hell," I said to him. My heart pounded in
my chest. I breathed deep over and over until I could finally
stand. I walked to him. "What the hell was that all about,
buddy?"

He barked. I was getting pretty annoyed at this point, and I
considered leaving him in the forest if he didn't start
cooperating. "What? What is wrong with you?" He barked
again, and I could tell he was trying to signal something, but I
had no idea what. I looked around the small clearing of pine
needles and leaves. Acorns. Fallen sticks. Rocks. Dirt.

"Arthur, what are we doing?" I asked him. He just looked
up at me as if I should know. "Crazy guy," I said. "Let's go."

He barked once more. I looked at the pine forest around
us. "I know, buddy," I said. "I wish you could tell me what
happened here too."

A breeze blew through the pines, cooling the sweat on my
skin and bringing a chill to my spine. Birds went silent. Silence
closed in around us. Arthur's eyes became clear. Then he
looked up at me and said, "Look. Look around."

"I am!" I said, and I did. Again—acorns. Fallen sticks.
Leaves. Rocks. Dirt. Pine needles. Pine trees. Nothing.

"Okay? I looked around. Now let's go," I said. "Stop being

a weirdo. We're going home."

He got up, and I started to walk back out of the clearing toward the cabin. He followed, but just before we were back in the trees, I saw something out of the corner of my eye. From behind the base of a fallen pine, there was a flash of scarlet red. I walked over to it, brushed some pine needles away, and rolled a softball-size rock out of the way. Lying in the dirt underneath a tree branch was a red bandanna. It was dotted with white-and-gold football helmets—the San Francisco 49ers logo. I looked closer and could see splotches of the red fabric were a shade darker—dried blood.

I thought back to Kelly's description of Arthur. "He's a big friendly black lab," she'd said, "with a blue collar and a red San Francisco 49ers bandanna tied around his neck...They're Scotty's team," she'd told me. "Scotty never let Arthur go anywhere without that bandanna."

I looked at Arthur.

"What do we do with this?" I asked him.

"I don't know," he said. "You tell me."

TWENTY-THREE

Arthur and I left the bandanna there and walked back through the trees to Scotty's cabin. I called Will.

"Nothing. Don't do anything," he said. "What benefit is there to *another* piece of evidence with the victim's blood on it?"

"How do you know it's the victim's blood?"

Will paused. "Who else's is it going to be?"

It seemed like even if the blood on the bandanna belonged to Josh, it didn't hurt to have it tested, because if it belonged to someone else, it would be evidence there was another person in the cabin that night.

"Leave it there," Will said. "See if those idiot investigators can find it."

I told Will I disagreed and that I was going to call the sheriff.

"Fine. If you think it helps Scotty's case, go ahead." His tone was almost bitter. I hung up and called the sheriff.

Arthur and I waited for an hour until a white patrol car turned into the driveway. Another cruiser followed, with a large white van trailing behind. A team of forensic investigators quickly flooded onto the scene.

"Sorry to call you on a Saturday," I said, shaking the

sheriff's hand.

Sheriff Merrick Trumble was six foot two, blond with pale skin, and fit. He was a few years older than me, in his late thirties, but unlike me, he had never left Chico. He'd been a resident all his life. He was a junior firefighter, active on the student government in high school, and was almost done with his law school night degree. I walked him and his team to the bandanna.

"Huh," Sheriff Trumble said, looking down at it. "We had three teams come through here. Can't believe we didn't find this."

"No offense, but it was sitting there in plain sight the entire time. If you guys had three teams come through, they're not doing their job."

"I thought this guy led you to it." He pointed at Arthur, who was staring up a tree at a squirrel that was half-mast up it.

"Well, either way, it wasn't hard to find," I said.

Men in hazmat suits circled the scene, snapped pictures, and filled out chain-of-custody logs. "He yours?" Sheriff Trumble asked, nodding to Arthur. Now Arthur was at the other edge of the clearing, batting at an acorn with his big paws like it was a hockey puck.

"Yeah, kind of. I'm not sure exactly."

Two hours later, the red San Francisco 49ers bandanna was admitted into the evidence locker at the Butte County Sheriff's Department to be tested for DNA. By that time, Arthur and I had already gone home.

* * *

Even from the back of Northgate Community Church, where I stood at my usual post, I could tell my sister's preaching was getting better. The pews were full, the congregation seemed more attentive, and the sermon was interesting enough that for once I didn't spend the entire service gawking at the back of Lacey Price's head, daydreaming about making her laugh. It had been almost two months since

I had seen her and Paul riding together in Paul's truck. Each Sunday I watched them avoid each other, feign disinterest, and silently assert aloofness to the rest of the community. They'd stagger in opposite pews and pretend to be very interested in what my sister was saying. I'd look at Lacey. I'd look at Paul, sitting next to his stupid dad, Ralph, and the rest of his entitled sons. I'd look back to Lacey, then back to Paul. *What are they up to?* I'd think.

After church, I hung by the exit for a moment, thinking I might be able to talk with Lacey. Why was she being so secretive? But doing so would probably require talking to Ralph. Or Paul. Or Cole Morrison, or my JV basketball coach, or perhaps some of my parents' geriatric friends. So I decided against it. I slipped out the back, drove home, picked up Arthur, and took him to play fetch in the park.

* * *

Rick called. The toxicology report results were in. Or rather, as Rick explained, the lack thereof. The detective on the case had never ordered one. Scotty's bowl of cereal was never tested. I asked Rick why not.

"Don't know," he said. "He just didn't."

"What about the knockout drugs? What could Scotty have taken that would've caused him to lose consciousness for so long?" He'd been out for almost five hours that evening. Seemed like a long time to me.

"Pick your poison," Rick said. "It could have been a lot of things. Any benzo. GHB (the date-rape drug). Something called diphenhydramine, which is basically just sleeping pills. You've got a lot of choices there. Maybe we could get Bill Cosby as an expert witness." He laughed.

I asked Rick if they did a toxicology report on Scotty himself. They did, but it had come back negative. There wasn't anything in his system.

"But they waited almost a full day, and it was only a urine sample," Rick said.

"Jesus Christ. A full day? Why so long?" I asked.

"It was over the weekend. Maybe no one was working. Don't know. Some people have lives in this town, you know."

"Well, they shouldn't. They should do their jobs."

"Maybe you should run for district attorney," Rick said.

"I think Sullivan has his hands full as it is."

"Yeah. 'Justice for Josh.' Pretty good slogan if you ask me," Rick said.

I thanked him and hung up. I knew from my time in the navy and the defense bar that knockout drugs like GHB were usually used to facilitate sexual assault crimes, but I had never had one of those cases, so when I went home, I did a little research. I found an article called "Date Rape Drugs and Memory – An Empirical Study."

> In many instances, victims can no longer remember the incident after a period of unconsciousness or antegrade amnesia...
>
> ...date rape drugs are commonly administered in the smallest dose possible to sedate the victim...(and) knowledgeable criminals often use substances that are rapidly eliminated in blood or urine, which makes detection more difficult. Administered substances are often odorless, colorless, and tasteless, and thus ingestion most commonly occurs without being noticed.

Antegrade amnesia. I had to look it up.

Amnesia is the partial or total loss of memory, while antegrade amnesia is when the event triggering amnesia also leads to the inability to recall the recent past. Memory is fickle, and knockout drugs make things worse.

Say, for example, you were sitting alone in your cabin in Forest Ranch one night, eating a bowl of cereal that just so happened to be laced with GHB. You took a few bites of the cereal, passed out, hit your head, and woke up in a pool of blood a few hours later. If the article had anything to say about it, when you woke up, you might not be able to remember what had happened immediately before passing out. That would be an example of antegrade amnesia. You know, just as an example.

TWENTY-FOUR

In criminal trials, sometimes evidence comes trickling in. Witness testimony, cell phone data, GPS tracking, a chemist's findings, an expert's analysis, it all blends together to build and shape two narratives: the prosecution's and the defense's. A new piece of evidence can feel like a small victory, or it can feel like a Jenga piece being pulled from the tower you were building. You learn to take each piece of evidence with a grain of salt.

The failure of detectives to do any timely toxicology report was at least some ammunition for trial. It didn't necessarily mean that I was resting Scotty's entire case on it, but it helped. The more doubt I could plant in the jury's minds about what had happened that night, the better chance I had of saving Scotty Watts from spending the rest of his life behind bars.

I'd almost forgotten the 49ers bandanna was being tested, so when Emma emailed me, telling me to stop by her office to discuss the results, I was genuinely surprised. I was down at the courthouse for a preliminary hearing on another case, and I went by her office. The DA's office in Butte County is a sea of cubicles where paralegals and administrative support crank out memos while attorneys crank away in their perimeter offices. I walked to the end of the hall and found Emma hunched over some paperwork. She glanced up at me and immediately knew I was there to talk about the bandanna.

"There's a third blood type" was all she said when I darkened her doorway. She couldn't have been pleased when she got that news, but she delivered it as though she were indifferent, as though it didn't affect anything at all. "There wasn't much of it, but it's there," she said. I felt like dancing, hollering, or doing some kind of celebration. *I was right. Will was wrong. There was a third blood type.* This news poked more holes in the prosecution's case. I thanked Emma and told her I'd let her get back to work. "The victim's blood is on there too," she said before I left. "A lot of it. I'll email you the report right now."

"Okay," I said and told her to send it to Shelly. I guess it couldn't be all good news.

* * *

Back at the office, Shelly and I scanned the full report. I was leaning over her shoulder at the front desk. She read from the report. "Unknown human blood," she said. "Good news. But it didn't hit *any* of the criminal databases?"

"No...but this is good news!"

"None of the criminal databases? No hits? In any of them?"

"No," I said. But I pointed out that there was someone else there. This was great news.

"Arthur was for sure wearing the bandanna?" she asked.

"Not for sure, but probably. It was a little ways from the crime scene."

"In the middle of the woods. Where kids play."

"I guess."

"Seems like there could be other explanations," Shelly said. "You can't prove Arthur was wearing it. Or how it got there. Some kid could have accidently cut themselves and dripped blood on it without knowing."

No way. That was totally implausible. There was too much blood for that to have happened. Or was there? I wasn't sure.

I felt deflated. I needed Shelly to be on my team and share in my optimism. I needed a break in this case, and what was supposed to be good news felt like another setback.

"I'm just trying to be realistic!" Shelly called out as I walked away.

"I know. Thank you," I said without looking back.

* * *

Will's assessment was even harsher. It was starting to feel like he wanted me to fail. We were sitting on his couch that Tuesday, watching SportsCenter and getting ready for our basketball game. In no uncertain terms, he told me I was losing my grip on reality.

"Come on! Help me brainstorm, man," I said. "Why would there be a third person's blood on that bandanna?"

"Because someone dripped blood on it while they were walking through the forest, just like your secretary said."

"Because someone else was in that cabin on that night!"

"Because some kid cut his hand while playing in the woods."

"Because Scotty was framed!"

"No."

"Who has the motive to frame him?"

"No one."

"A rival drug dealer?"

"This isn't Sinaloa versus Juarez. Scotty was growing a couple acres of weed in his backyard in Podunk, California, that he planned to sell at a co-op. Nobody is going to murder—or frame—someone just to get rid of a little dope."

"Mendocino County has murders all the time!"

"That's where the big boys are. We're in Chico. We're in Butte County. We grow walnuts here," Will said.

We gathered our basketball gear and walked out to the garage. Will thought Scotty was hustling me. "We all grew up together," he said as he backed the Tesla out of the garage. "You know how cunning Scotty can be. He's full of shit, and he's playing you."

I went quiet and thought about it. Maybe Scotty was lying. But then I remembered what John had said: whether or not Scotty was lying...did it matter? My job was to prove his innocence, whether I believed him or not. I just had to assemble the facts. I got light-headed thinking about it.

"You should see the look in his eyes when he tells me he's innocent," I told Will. "If he's lying, he's one damn good liar."

"Most criminals are."

For the rest of the drive, I listened to the stupid hum of Will's stupid electronic car and didn't say another word. We arrived at the gym, and the echo of basketballs clanging off metal rims and bouncing on the hardwood floor reverberated in my ears.

"I'm not kidding, man," Will said. "You're starting to worry me. I think you need to get out more."

I changed the subject. "Did you know Lacey Price and Paul Morrison are dating?" I said as we laced up our shoes. He laughed.

"What's so funny?" I asked.

"You still have a crush on her?"

"What? No. Is it that obvious? Maybe."

He laughed again and said, "I didn't know they were dating. Nor am I surprised."

I asked him what he meant.

"Never mind. And yes, it was obvious you had a crush on her in high school, and it's obvious now."

"Whatever."

A basketball bounced toward him, and he scooped it up and dribbled it off at a slow jog, leaving me to finish tying my shoes.

* * *

Inevitably, many attorneys often think of criminal sentences in the same way finance professionals might think of dollars, or athletes might think of points scored. They are the units of currency that define success or failure. Convincing a client to plead guilty and limiting their exposure to jail time feels like a win because it hedges risk. Better the client serve ten years after pleading guilty than lose at trial and serve twenty. Lawyers are risk-averse. Otherwise they wouldn't have gone to law school, and they're not always thinking about the days, hours, minutes, and seconds clients will spend behind bars. They're thinking about risk. Risk of their client spending the rest of their life in prison. Maybe Shelly and Will were right. A third blood type on Arthur's 49ers bandanna was at best a little more leverage in plea negotiations. That's it.

* * *

It was Saturday afternoon. I was downtown tying Arthur's leash to a bike rack in front of Jamba Juice, about to go inside to get us smoothies so we could cool off. The mid-July sun baked the asphalt.

"Cute dog." It was the sweet song of a woman's voice. Familiarity again. It was Lacey Price.

I pictured the football thudding into the trash can years ago, and Lacey guiding Tex by the arm away from the bullies. I blocked everything else from my mind.

She was so beautiful standing there on the street corner that I wasn't sure if the sunshine or her radiant face was more blinding, and I was relieved when I saw a flash of recognition in her eyes.

"Thanks," I said.

"How long have you been home?" she asked.

"Almost two years now."

"I've seen you in church. Why're you always standing in the back?"

I don't know how she'd seen me. I thought I'd been pretty inconspicuous about it, and I squirmed at the question. She smiled. "You've been hiding!" she said, tapping her temple. "Smart move. Keep a low profile. I'd probably do the same if I were you."

I felt faint, and I got lost in her green eyes, watching them sparkle.

She asked where I was living and what I'd been up to. I told her about Scotty's case. She'd heard about it, of course. "So sad," she said. "Scotty was such an interesting guy."

"He's not dead," I said. I meant it seriously, but she laughed.

I looked down at Arthur. "Old Arthur here is actually Scotty's dog."

"Hopefully you don't have to give him back."

"Hopefully I do. Otherwise Scotty will be in jail for life."

I thought about the day I had seen her riding in Paul's blue pickup and all the weekends I had stood in the back of church wondering. I couldn't get it off my mind. "I think I saw you in Forest Ranch a few weeks ago," I said.

She brushed a strand of hair behind her ear and looked over her shoulder. "Oh. Right," she said.

"You were with Paul, right?"

"Yeah…" she said.

"What's with the secrecy?" I asked. "Sorry if it's rude to pry, but—"

"No, it's fine," she said. "Paul is going through a divorce and all. I don't know. I suppose it's the same reason you're hiding in the back every week." She winked at me and smiled. "We just don't want to broadcast it just yet."

"Oh…" I looked at the ground.

"Oh boy. Who'd you tell?"

"Do you remember Will Norris?"

She threw her head back and laughed. "Oh God," she said. "I guess the secret's out now!"

"Sorry."

"That's okay."

Arthur flicked her hand with his nose a few times until she petted him. She laughed. "What a sweet boy. Look at those eyes!" She squatted and ran her nails through Arthur's coat, massaging his hind legs and rubbing his ears. He whipped his tail from side to side.

I tugged on Arthur's leash. "Okay, okay! He's spoiled enough already."

"I'm going to steal him if you're not careful."

"Don't do it. I have the sheriff on speed dial."

She laughed again and stood. "It was nice to see you," she said.

"You too."

"Good luck with your trial," she said. "Poor Scotty."

"Yeah. It's a bummer."

I watched Lacey walk farther down the street, resisting the urge to run after her, grab her arm, and confess my misplaced desires. The well of emotion bubbled up and embarrassed me. I felt too old for silly romantic delusions, but I couldn't help those aching feelings of longing.

I pictured her again with Tex, and the football tumbling impossibly high in the air. I could never compete with dark-haired country hunk Paul Morrison. I had never forgotten about Lacey in the years I was gone, but I doubt she had thought of me at all.

I decided to forget the stupid smoothie. I untied Arthur, and we walked two blocks to my car. I thought of all the things I should have done or said. I should have been funnier, more charismatic, more interesting. I should have been someone else—the better version of me with all these characteristics—long, long ago when I still had the chance. I opened the door and waited for Arthur to get in. Instead, he just looked up at me. "You really screwed that up," he said.

"Yeah, I know, you jerk. I know. Just get in the stupid car."

TWENTY-FIVE

The California legal ethics handbook declares that the decision on how to plead is entirely the client's. It's also a basic tenant of being a lawyer. If Scotty refused to take a deal, I couldn't force him. But I could always convince him it was the best course of action, and most clients would follow my recommendation. Yet Scotty wasn't most clients. He had his history with the law, and he was stubborn. And I wasn't a stranger to him. I had been the younger, dorkier, less cool kid growing up who followed him, not the other way around. Perhaps it was encountering faces and people I had known while growing up in Chico, or the fact that I'd read his case file a million times, but there was something oddly familiar about Scotty's case.

* * *

Emma and I had biweekly phone calls to discuss the possibility of a plea. She was reasonable but also inflexible. She wouldn't offer anything better than second-degree murder with a fifteen-year cap, on the condition that Scotty disclosed where the body was buried. I realized that the larger forces of Mike Sullivan's campaign for district attorney were driving our negotiations. Emma was conciliatory even when she wouldn't budge, and there was always a hint of reservation in her voice when she refused to offer a better deal.

I would point out the chance of acquittal, highlighting the lack of an actual victim and stacking up other good defense facts like the third blood type on the 49ers bandanna. The case of Josh Anderson's disappearance seemed more complicated than greed between business partners, and at a minimum, the jury might find that it was an argument gone wrong. They'd convict him on manslaughter. "I know," Emma would say. "I understand." She'd sigh into the phone, and I could hear in her voice she was starting to understand the problems with her case. Early assessments may have been damning for Scotty because there was a near certainty that Josh's body would be found. It was still missing, and Emma sounded tired of representing a position she was forced to embrace. This was Mike Sullivan's doing. He wanted the conviction. He wanted nothing less than second-degree murder.

* * *

On my drive to the courthouse to visit Scotty, I once again saw the big metal combine lumbering along the road. Dust clouds billowed out behind it. The same darkened face under a baseball cap, wearing a flannel shirt and blue jeans, sat atop the massive machinery. My Honda's air-conditioning groaned. I felt a bead of sweat run down my back. Hot air spit out of the vents, and I shut it off. I couldn't imagine how hot it was in that field. I looked closer at the dark face hidden beneath the camouflage hat and wondered if I knew him. I wondered if maybe we'd also gone to school together.

Scotty was waiting for me in the interview room, wearing his orange jumpsuit. He wrung his hands together.

"How's everything going?" I asked.

"Fine, considering I'm locked in a cage."

Two weeks ago, when I'd told Scotty we found Arthur's bandanna, he was a little more hopeful. Confinement can crush a man's spirit, and Scotty looked to be wearing down. I told him the results of the blood test on the bandanna, hoping that would lift his spirits. "This means there could have been a third person in the cabin," I said. It didn't. He was as skeptical as everyone else.

"Could be," he said.

"The prosecution will probably contend it came from a hunter or a kid with a cut hand walking through the woods."

"Nobody hunts up there. That's too close to the cabins," he said.

"I know. That's what I said."

"But seems like a jury will probably believe something like that."

"Maybe," I said.

"I wonder how the bandanna fell off his neck in the first place. I always tied it in a pretty good knot."

I agreed. It hadn't been cut, and it was strange how it had somehow fallen off Arthur's neck and got trapped under a rock beneath a fallen pine tree. "It is weird, but we'll probably never know how that happened," I told him. "Right now we just need theories of the case that can prove your innocence."

We sat in silence for a moment, regarding each other. The memory of young Scotty holding a baseball mitt above his head was starting to fade, and it was getting replaced by the image of a bleary-eyed Scotty sitting under fluorescent lights wearing an orange jumpsuit, chained to a table. The vacant stare. The dead eyes.

I could tell talking about the bandanna had stirred something in him. He shifted in his seat and looked off to nowhere in particular. He didn't want to talk about the case anymore, or his chances at trial.

"You know why I'm a Niners fan?" he asked.

I shrugged.

"My dad took me to a game when I was twelve. We sat way up high in the nosebleed seats because it was all he could afford. His favorite player was Joe Montana, and he was shouting, 'Go, Joe! Go!' the whole game. I started doing it too.

'Go, Joe! Go!' I was yelling. I was just a kid, you know?"

He smiled at the memory. It had been a while since I'd thought about Ray Watts, helplessly trapped in that lifeless body with his permanently fishhooked lip. Ray Watts was a Butte County man. He took seriously the dutiful obligation of caring for his family, and he couldn't any longer. The only dignity a man like Ray has left in the latter years of his life is his physicality, and it had been taken from him.

"Montana to Rice over and over again," Scotty said. "Montana was scrambling. Throwing bullets all over the field. Everyone around us was going crazy." He paused and looked off in the distance, getting a little excited. "One play in the third quarter. Niners were deep in their own territory. Montana rolled out. Big defensive lineman chasing after him. He's on the run, just about to reach the sideline, and he hits Rice with a twenty-yard strike. Rice catches it and jukes the safety. He glides all the way to the end zone like his feet aren't even touching the ground. The crowd going crazy. You could feel the energy in the building." He swallowed hard, and his voice cracked a little. "My dad looked down at me with his big toothy smile. His crooked teeth." His lip quivered. "You know how he has those crooked teeth."

I nodded my head; I did know. A tear rolled slowly down Scotty's cheek and fell onto his orange jumpsuit, soaking a dark stain in the material. "When the game was over, a guy outside was selling these cheap knockoff hats." Scotty fought back tears, refusing to allow himself to break down. "Those dumb hats. Goofy gold-and-red colors. Really, really ugly hats." He laughed. "My dad was so excited, he bought me one. The next six months. Never took it off. I loved that hat."

Scotty wiped his eyes with his sleeve and hid his face.

"Sorry," he said, sniffling.

"It's all right," I said.

He looked up at me. "Anyway, I didn't really care about the game, but that hat meant everything to me. That day meant everything to me. I think I'm still a Niners fan because that was the last time I felt like the world was an okay place."

TWENTY-SIX

Nothing ever seems to get done at the Butte County Courthouse during the hottest month of the year. August is for end-of-summer vacations. Attorneys, judges, expert witnesses, court staff, bailiffs, they all head off in different directions in August. A witness interview is rescheduled, a court deadline is moved back, a motions hearing is pushed, and the trial time line gets pushed back further and further. Like dominoes. Sheriff Trumble was visiting family in Idaho. Deputy Haskins had taken his family camping in Lassen National Forest. Judge Waitskin had left on a sailing trip around the Greek islands with his wife. Emma had flown to Hawaii for a weeklong vacation with her husband and two kids. Even Rick had gone fishing in Mexico. Relevant personnel scattered vacations throughout the month as though each had implicitly agreed that August could be torn from the calendar. Progress on Scotty's case stood still, and the long summer days dragged on. My mother's condition didn't change much. She slept, she drooled, and she rambled. Thin Mustache would check on us, and I'd get embarrassed when he'd walk in and I'd be wiping tears from my face. I don't know why, but I did. My father golfed. He burned steak, overcooked potatoes, and gruffly mumbled advice to me about Scotty's case. My sister led a women's church retreat to the coast. She preached. Her belly got bigger from the fetus growing inside her. I told Shelly to take a vacation.

Once again Chico felt like a place frozen in amber. There was nothing to do but think.

I visited Scotty twice that month, checking in on him and explaining why his case wasn't moving along quicker. We'd waived his right to a speedy trial at the arraignment. Every defense attorney "waived time" since doing otherwise would make it virtually impossible to adequately prepare a defense, but now we were at the mercy of coordinating schedules. Until everyone got back from their vacations, I couldn't interview witnesses and experts, write an opening statement, map out my direct examinations, or prepare for trial.

I watched the presidential election coverage, but even that seemed to grind to a halt. Other than a Trump tweet or evasive Clinton press release, the candidates prepared for the post–Labor Day stretch.

The "Justice for Josh" campaign took a short break. The "Dubois for DA" signs around town became sparse. Will took vacations to Cabo San Lucas, Hawaii, and San Diego, so he wasn't around all that much. Each time he came back, he would report his sexual conquests to me like a soldier proudly reporting kills from the battlefield.

"Dude, this one chick was *un-be-leev-able*. In Cabo. Tons of blow. This one USC student. Blonde. Big fake tits. Loaded. Pro in the sack. Best night of my life."

"Great," I said.

"I told you you could come with, but you wanted to sit here and mope about your stupid case."

"I'm not moping."

"Jesus, you're no fun," he said.

* * *

High school kids finished the last of their summer camps and adventurous world traveling. Day after day the temperatures soared into the high nineties. When my air-conditioning went out on the third Thursday, I took Arthur in the backyard and sprayed us both with the garden hose. He jumped high into the air and tried to chomp his jaws down on the streams of water. He wagged his tail and perked his ears up. Later that night I caught him sniffing a metal drum barrel I hadn't seen before. It was leaned up against the back of my house, and I didn't want him getting into anything that could hurt him. I couldn't pry the lid open, and when I tried to roll it away, I could barely move it half an inch. The rain must have seeped in and filled it to the brim, and it became an endearing fixture of my backyard landscape. It was the kind of thing you'd find in a backyard in Chico anyway.

With August came John. He was back as a constant presence in my life, and while I sprayed Arthur with the hose, he stood off to the side, watching us, smiling. He started coming around more, but he also started acting weird. I told him I was reading the book he had given me, David Mellinkoff's *The Conscience of a Lawyer*, but that I couldn't find the highlighted portion. He would ignore me as though I hadn't said anything. I read through the passages looking for clues, but no matter how hard I looked, I couldn't find the section he was talking about.

It was late one night when he sat across from me at the dining room table, watching me eat. The sun had gone down, but the earth was still radiating heat. John sat there wearing his three-piece suit. I'd got accustomed to him ignoring my questions, but it was also getting on my nerves. He hadn't been doing this before, so why now?

"Do you want some food?" I asked him.

He rose out of his seat, walked to where Arthur was munching down a bowl of dog food, and patted him on the head.

"John," I said louder. "*Do, you, want, food?*"

He looked over at me and smiled like he was reflecting on a pleasant memory, but instead of answering, he walked over and sat on the couch, slumped down in the cushions, and wiggled his way into comfort. He looked to the blank TV as though thinking of something far off. Like he was the only person in the house.

"Fine. Whatever," I said.

I finished my last few bites and went into the kitchen to clean my plate. When I turned back to the living room, he'd left.

A few days later he joined Arthur and me on a hike in Forest Ranch. We'd been hiking for about a half hour, and the sun was starting to rise higher in the sky. Arthur walked behind me, John behind him. We trudged along the dry, rocky hillside. "Am I working too hard on this case?" I asked. Hearing no response, I turned back. "John?" He focused his eyes on the path in front of him, stumbling over rocks in his brown leather dress shoes. "What do you think about Scotty's case? You got any advice?" I asked. I kept hiking, waiting for a response. "John?" I shouted, looking back at him. He just kept walking and stumbling over the uneven ground. "What kind of idiot hikes in a suit?" I asked.

The next weekend, I took Arthur to the park. John stood ten or fifteen feet away with a stupid grin on his face. "I'm almost done with that book you gave me," I said. I threw Arthur's stick high into the air for him to fetch. John ignored me and watched Arthur run after it. "You said there was something highlighted," I said. "Nothing was highlighted."

John put his hands in his pockets and looked over my shoulder to some teenagers splashing around in the creek.

"John! Goddamn it! You never highlighted anything in the book. Remember?" I took a couple of steps over to where he stood smirking. "Do you remember? Hello?" I pushed his shoulder. He stumbled back but kept the same stupid smile on his face. He looked up into the trees, then back at me. Then he turned and walked slowly away.

"Leave me alone!" I yelled as he walked off toward a grove of trees lining the park. I grabbed Arthur's stick and chucked it again. Arthur ran after it. John didn't look back, and I watched the outline of that stupid three-piece suit disappear into the tree line. I've always hated August, and I was glad when it was over.

TWENTY-SEVEN

On Labor Day, I drove up the highway to Forest Ranch, this time for a meeting with Eleanor Jackson. Apparently the only people with no Labor Day plans were me, Arthur, and an eighty-five-year-old woman who lived in the forest alone.

Walking up her driveway, I couldn't help but admire the immaculate two-story white cabin she lived in. As I climbed the stairs leading to her front door, I heard the groan of the wooden stairs under my feet. I knocked and waited. I noticed the top hinge of Ms. Jackson's front screen door had come off. I knocked again. Nothing.

"Ms. Jackson!" I called out. "Hello?"

She'd probably forgotten about our appointment and was napping. I knocked again, louder this time. I heard a scratchy voice muffled through the door.

"Just a second. Just a second, honey," she said a couple of times. The door swung open.

Eleanor Jackson had curly white hair and wore a flower print dress. She was wiry, about five foot five, and the healthiest-looking eighty-five-year-old I'd seen in my entire life. A beaming smile revealed a full set of teeth.

"Hello, ma'am," I said. "I'm the criminal-defense attorney that called. I'm representing your next-door neighbor, Scotty

Watts." I pointed at the house behind me and down the hill across the street. "We spoke on the phone."

"Oh, yes, yes. Do come in."

She led me inside and offered a seat on her couch. Her house was meticulously clean. She lived alone. Her husband had died many years ago. She told me she loved living up in the trees where she could hear the birds chirping and see deer and foxes roaming in her backyard. She offered me a glass of water, and while she shuffled off into the kitchen I scanned the room, taking in her decor. There were framed family photos, an old cuckoo clock on the wall, and a map of Georgia with a big peach superimposed over an outline of the state. She came back from the kitchen and set the water glass on the coffee table in front of me. "There you go, sweetie," she said. Her bright-brown eyes sparkled. A fan buzzed in the corner of her living room. She seemed unfazed by the muggy afternoon.

"I grew up in the South," she told me. "I can handle anything."

I pointed to the peach map and confirmed the obvious. "Georgia?"

"Yes. That's right. My husband and I. We were high school sweethearts. But I lived there in a different time. I think things are better now, but I still don't think I could go back. This is my home now." I asked her how well she knew Scotty. "I don't do much with my days. I go on long walks through the woods, I read until my eyes get tired, and I listen to the radio. I'm home so much. I see people come and go. It's like I told the officers, I saw that boy who used to visit Scotty pull up in that fancy white truck of his, and he got out and went inside. That's all I really know." She paused for a moment, then continued, "I generally mind my own business and try to stay out of the way, but sometimes I can't help but see things."

I nodded. Then I stood and looked out the front window facing Scotty's cabin. "You're sure you saw a white truck pull up that day? Because it seems like the view is pretty well obscured by those pines."

"I know, I know. The police said that too. But I'm sure.

Like I said, I don't do much with my days, but I like to sit on my front porch and listen to the birds. That's what I was doing that evening." She gestured outside the window to her front porch, where a couple of old rocking chairs sat with a small table between them. "I'd seen that truck pull up many times before, so I knew what it looked like. I know the boy that got out."

"Do you wear glasses?" I asked.

"Oh, honey. You'd think I'd be blind as a bat by now, but I've been blessed. My vision is just fine."

"What about Paul Morrison?" I asked. "Does that name ring a bell?"

"Oh yes," she said. "Young man with short black hair? Lives up the road?"

"Yes, that's him."

"I'd see him from time to time."

"Here? On your street?"

"Oh yes. Him and Scotty would be hollering at each other about Lord knows what. Looked like some neighborly disagreements."

"How long ago was this?"

"A couple of years."

"They ever get physical?"

"You mean like swingin' punches at each other?" she asked. I nodded.

"No. Just a bunch of hollering. They'd both always calm down after a while," she said.

"That day that you saw the white pickup...did you ever hear a gunshot?"

"No."

"And you were here all evening?"

"Yes."

"Do you have any trouble with your hearing?"

"I can hear you just fine." She reached up at her ear and pulled out a small hearing aid no bigger than her fingernail. "But only thanks to these. These little darlings work great!" She examined the hearing aid between her fingertips.

I smiled at her. She smiled back.

"The hinge is loose on your front screen," I told her. "Would you like me to fix it?" She beamed. She nodded and disappeared downstairs. She came back holding a small tool bag, and we walked outside to the front porch. I rustled through the tool bag for a screwdriver. When I found one that fit the screw, I reached up and started to turn it back in place.

"The men from the sheriff's office said I would need to go to court and testify," she said.

"That's right."

"I don't like the idea of going to court much."

"Me neither, Ms. Jackson. Me neither."

The hinge secured tightly now, I tossed the screwdriver back in the tool bag. I walked with her back downstairs to the garage to put the tools away, and then we stood in the driveway together.

"Ms. Jackson, you must take those hearing aids out at some point, right?"

"Only at night."

"Are you a pretty heavy sleeper?"

"Not really. Ever since my husband passed away, I wake every couple of hours and reach across the bed to feel if he's there."

Her face darkened in a droopy sadness, but she let the moment pass and then gave a good-natured laugh. "I don't even think about it. I just do it. I just can't sleep without him there."

"That must be nice," I said.

She looked at me crossly. "Oh no, it's terrible not having him around."

"I'm sorry. I meant it must have been nice to have someone you love that much. To have someone you can miss in that way."

She smiled. "Yes. It was. We were married forty-two years, and it was quite nice." Ms. Jackson insisted that she walk me to my car, so we made our way down the creaky steps and down the driveway toward the road.

"Ms. Jackson?" I asked. "If someone fired a gun in the middle of the night, over near Mr. Watts's place, do you think it'd wake you up?"

"Oh yes. I think so." She nodded. "Like I said, I'm a very light sleeper these days. Yes. I would've heard it."

"Even without the hearing aids?" I asked. "You're pretty sure about that?"

She smiled. "A fallen tree branch wakes me up. I once woke up when a cool breeze blew through the house. I'm pretty sure a gunshot would do it."

I thanked her, got in my car, and drove away.

TWENTY-EIGHT

I was on the phone with Shelly.

"It turns out Eleanor Jackson is a sweet little eighty-five-year-old woman with perfect vision who spends her days spying on her neighbor," I said. "What the hell am I going to do with that? I have to attack the credibility of a sweet old lady—"

She cut me off, "It's Labor Day! Go home!"

"Sorry…"

"That's all right, but you need to take a break. You're running in circles."

I apologized again and told her I would go home right away. "Good," she said, and we hung up.

But I didn't go home right away. Right before turning onto Highway 32, I remembered standing there a few weeks earlier, seeing Paul Morrison driving that old blue pickup with Lacey in the passenger's seat. I remembered Lacey's hair blowing in the wind. I remembered her looking over to me and smiling. The memory compelled me to switch my blinker on and turn left to head farther up the mountain.

Paul's house wasn't hard to find. There are only two left turns past the Forest Ranch Lane: the first is Conestoga Way, and the second is Garland Road. I turned onto Conestoga Way and saw the blue pickup in front of a three-story cabin with a gleaming slate roof. It looked brand-new. The truck, the new house—it had to be Paul's. Plus, there was only one other structure that could even be considered a residence on Paul's street, and that was a tiny abandoned shack made of sheet-metal siding.

I parked, walked up the steps, and knocked on the front door. I heard rustling from inside and waited for a minute or two until Paul eventually appeared in the doorway. He wore blue jeans and a T-shirt. I was a bit startled when the door swung open and I saw him standing there. It was Labor Day, after all.

"I didn't think you'd be home," I said.

"Then why'd you come?"

We hadn't spoken in more than a decade, and this was how our conversation started. I didn't have an answer for him.

"Been some time," he said.

"Yeah, it has."

"How can I help you?"

"Can I talk to you about Scotty?"

He scoffed. "Heard you were defending that deadbeat. What do you want to know?"

"Did he ever cause any trouble for you?" I asked.

"Scotty's nothing but trouble."

"But for you specifically. Has he ever caused *you* trouble?"

"No."

"He never messed with your crops?"

"Crops? What crops? The only thing I grow up here is a few vegetables in my garden out back. The family farm is down in the valley. They ain't up here. He's downstream from me anyway."

"Fair enough," I said.

"Is that it?" He was anxious to close the door. I could tell. But I had more questions.

"His neighbor...Do you know Ms. Jackson?"

"Yeah, I know her."

"She mentioned you and Scotty have had some

disagreements. She says you guys got into it a couple times."

Paul pursed his lips. "Scotty used to throw a lot of real loud parties. The whole forest could hear 'em. So yeah, I went down there and gave him a piece of my mind."

"Anything ever get physical?"

"What are you implying?"

"Can you tell me what you were doing the night the cops came to arrest Scotty?"

Paul laughed. "This is what you came here for? Cuz you think I'm a suspect?"

"I'm just doing my job, Paul."

"How about you turn around and get the hell off my porch before I go grab my shotgun?"

"Did you guys ever come to blows?"

"It was nice of you to drop by. I'll bet your dad is real proud."

Paul started to turn back into the house. I heard a woman's voice from inside. "Who's there?" she said. It was Lacey. Of course.

Paul smiled at me. "Take care now," he said, and he started to shut the door. Just before it shut in my face, I heard him call upstairs, "It's no one." Then the door clicked closed.

TWENTY-NINE

When I first moved back home, California was still in the throes of a horrific drought. Governor Brown implemented policies encouraging water conservation and even mandated a few regulations requiring it, from reimbursements for drought-friendly gardens, to deductions on utility bills for limiting water use, to the number of days per week you were allowed to wash your car. The concern of the average California resident centered around not being able to run a hot bath, take a long shower, or water their garden or lawn. These days, those fears have momentarily abated. The year 2017 was not a drought year. But the outsize effect Northern California has on the state's water supply means the issue is never too far from the minds of Butte County residents. The Oroville Dam alone supplies drinking water to twenty-five million people in Southern California and irrigates millions of acres of Central Valley farmland. The dam is located just east of the Butte County Courthouse, and its outsize influence on the entire state is why, when it almost busted earlier this year, it made national news. It would have been bad.

California is no longer in drought conditions, but decision makers and major stakeholders constantly monitor the water supply since they know drought conditions could lead to catastrophe. Among those decision makers is Ralph Morrison, the patriarch of Butte County's most prolific farming company, Morrison Family Farms. Agriculture is a billion-dollar industry in Butte County, and farmers grow a variety of crops— primarily walnuts, almonds, and rice. Each of those is a water hog, and when news came out that almonds use a lot of water, Morrison Family Farms came under attack. Ralph Morrison took notice. Formerly apolitical, he joined the Almond Board of California. He campaigned. He lobbied state representatives. He started attending city council meetings and sessions of the Board of Supervisors.

The Morrisons were a powerful-enough influence that they were a favorite topic of gossip around town, and my family probably knew the gossip better than most. First, Paul Morrison was the same age as Scotty. Second, after Ralph Morrison suddenly became politically active, he and my father became close friends. Or maybe they just worked together. It was always hard to tell with fathers in Chico. The strongest sign of affection for fathers in Butte County is engaging in anything more than polite conversation. Men like Ralph and my father subscribed to the old-school country-boy ethic of protecting your land, your family, and your beliefs. They were cut from this same cloth, belonging to a salt-of-the-earth, blue jean–wearing club that fought fiercely to protect those beliefs.

Of all the theories of Scotty's case that I could have chosen to try to exonerate him, I couldn't tell you how I chose what I did. I could say I followed a trail of evidence that inevitably led me to it, or I could tell you I concocted the most damning narrative of conspiracy and corruption to rebuke my hometown and rebel against people I felt had slighted me. I suppose it's somewhere in between, and looking back, I probably should have listened more to people like Shelly and Rick.

I could see right away that Rick and Shelly did not like where I was going. We met in my office to brainstorm theories of the case. I told them about my meeting with Paul. I reminded them of what I just told you: California is perpetually frightened of a drought; many crops grown in Butte County use a lot of water; and Ralph Morrison had outsize influence on the California Department of Water Resources review board, the Board of Supervisors, and other agriculturally based political interests.

"What other crops in Butte County are water hogs?" I asked.

Their eyes flitted back and forth. They could tell I'd been doing some research on my own.

"That don't go on your kitchen table."

They looked at each other and shifted in their seats.

"It's green."

Nothing.

"Weed," I said. "We grow weed."

They were well aware, they reminded me. Any Chico resident who's been in town for a few years knows there's a segment of the population in Butte County that takes a special pride in producing top-quality cannabis. Butte County is a neighbor to the nation's pot-cultivation mecca—an area covering thousands of acres spanning Mendocino, Humboldt, and Trinity Counties, lush and fertile land affectionately known as the Emerald Triangle that enjoys moist Pacific Ocean air, soil both firm and soft, and a cool breeze blowing inland, thus making it perfect for crops. The Emerald Triangle is well known among marijuana connoisseurs. Most of the Emerald Triangle growers are contract employees cultivating large quantities for dispensaries and Mexican drug cartels. Growers in Butte County are usually much smaller. Growers in Butte County are more like Scotty Watts.

I had printed out dozens of news articles documenting the struggle between law enforcement personnel in Butte County, farmers like Ralph Morrison, and pot growers like Scotty Watts. With Shelly and Rick looking at me dumbfounded, I stood and started passing the hard copies across my desk, calling out the headlines as I did.

"'Nearly 14,000 Pot Plants Seized in Oroville Grow Operation.'

"'Butte County DA Using Environment against Large-Scale Pot Growers.'

"'Proliferation of Pot—Sheriff's Deputies Bust Several High-Volume Marijuana Farms.'

"'Medical Marijuana Plants in Violation of County Ordinance Seized.'"

Shelly furrowed her brow and shook her head. "I don't know."

"This is not a good idea." Rick said.

"Just hear me out," I said.

I remember my father mentioning offhandedly a longstanding and undeclared war between farmers like Ralph Morrison and people like Scotty Watts. The "legitimate" farmers despised the marijuana growers because they did anything and everything to get their crops to grow, often disregarding county ordinances or state environmental laws. Marijuana growers would divert streams, use household weed-killing products, or grade the land to flatten soil for a grow site where there was none. Diverting a stream or grading the land illegally could drastically affect the water supply, and using household products could contaminate the water and produce a chemical-ridden, unsellable crop.

Whenever the topic of marijuana production came up, my father would say, "If you put any farmer on a jury against a pot grower, I guarantee you they will vote to convict."

I looked at Rick and Shelly, gauging their reactions.

"Then we shouldn't have farmers on this jury," Shelly said. "But a conspiracy theory? That's a bridge too far."

"The jury isn't going to like it," Rick agreed.

I sighed.

"You're going to make a lot of enemies," Shelly said.

"It doesn't have to be true," I pointed out. "It just has to be plausible. And I don't care about creating enemies."

"It's not plausible," Shelly said.

"I at least want to see where the research leads. Let's look into it," I told them.

I could see that I wasn't going to convince them, but they

didn't have a choice. We were going to investigate it and see where it led.

I know I should have listened to them, but sometimes a theory of a case gets so ingrained in your thoughts that you can't stop thinking about the ways it could be true, and you become more certain that it's the only answer. It morphs from a plausible defense to something you really start to believe.

THIRTY

Fall arrived. Leaves turned a lighter shade of green, and a charred color appeared at the edges like they were burning from the outside in. The school year started, and Chico State students swarmed downtown. Football season began, and my social media accounts became cluttered with Green Bay Packers posts. The first regular-season game of the 2016 NFL football season had arrived. Aaron Rodgers was facing the Jacksonville Jaguars, and while Will didn't need an excuse to throw a party, he decided to celebrate the occasion. He was throwing a barbecue, he said, and I should come. It would take my mind off Scotty's case. I remember that day clearly for two reasons: first, it was 9/11, and second, Lacey Price was there.

I was sitting in my car in Will's driveway. I looked to the back seat where Arthur was lying down. "You ready, buddy?" I asked. He yawned. We got out of the car and walked up to the massive wood front door of Will's McMansion. I knocked. Moments later, Will appeared wearing a tank top with drink in hand.

"Hey! There he is!" he shouted. He gave me a high five. Arthur barked, and it startled Will. He jumped back. "Oh! Shit! I didn't know you were bringing a dog!" Arthur barked again.

"He's harmless," I said.

"Just keep that stupid mutt away from me," he said.

"I didn't know you didn't like dogs," I said.

"Yeah. Mangy, dirty animals. They should be in the wild," he said.

Who doesn't like dogs?

Loud, thumping bass music shook the walls. Will and I must have been a decade older than anyone in there. College-aged frat boys paraded shirtless around the party. Bikini-wearing twenty-something women overflowed from the living room into the backyard. At the back of the house, giant glass doors had been flung open to expose the entire back wall. The ceilings of the living room seemed impossibly high. Light flooded in. Wafts of meat blew off the grill from the back deck. Arthur sniffed the air. Everything looked much different from when I had visited Will on Tuesday nights. The mansion always felt dark and sad. Now it was bright and full of life. I felt like I was on the set of *Entourage*.

Arthur plodded over to a group of women sitting poolside, dangling their feet in the water. When they saw Arthur approaching, they swooned. They petted his head, scratched his belly, and kissed his snout, remarking at how sweet he was. I followed him, hoping this might be a chance to talk to them. But just before I opened my mouth to say hello, a kid with high cheekbones swam up to them, grabbed on to one of their ankles, and pulled her in. They squealed. A moment later they were all in the pool, laughing and splashing one another. I stood on the edge with Arthur, watching them. We stood there for a moment, looking around at all the beautiful people talking in groups, and I looked down into my drink. When I looked up, I saw a man standing at the edge of Will's backyard behind some bushes. The trees and hedges almost totally obscured my view of him, but I could see that he was waving at me. He stepped aside into a small clearing, and I could see that it was John, wearing his three-piece suit. I didn't want to see him, but there he was. Fortunately Will walked up and pulled me away, directing my attention to a group nearby.

"Ladies!" he announced to the group next to us. "This is

my big-dicked friend I've been telling you all about." The girls laughed and told Will he was gross. I agreed and blushed. Will made a grotesque distance measurement with his palms and then introduced me to a woman he called his "girlfriend," but they both laughed and rolled their eyes when he said it. Someone handed me a beer, and I chugged it.

Arthur and I milled about by the side of the pool for most of the party. Arthur drank pool water. I admired the tanned, toned body of a short little blonde, but I must have admired too long since she looked disgusted when she caught my eye.

Later, Will called me over to the grill. "Hold this," he said, and Will piled meat onto the serving tray he had handed me. I set the tray on a table well apportioned with condiments and fixings for the burgers and hot dogs. Attendees swarmed and worked down the line, piling their plates high.

Later, Arthur and I watched the football game. Aaron Rodgers threw a screen pass to his running back, Eddie Lacey, who ran deep into Jacksonville territory. A few plays later, he threw a twenty-nine-yard touchdown pass.

"Incredible, isn't it?" Will said. "Can't believe we grew up with that guy. Now he's worth hundreds of millions of dollars." Will took a big swig of his beer.

"Yeah, it's pretty amazing," I said.

"You need another beer." Will left. He returned moments later and handed me a drink.

The game went to halftime. A tall slender man walked out of the room and down the hall with a girl wearing an American-flag bikini. He led her by the hand toward one of Will's extra bedrooms. A woman next to me slept with her head in her friend's lap. The friend saw me watching her and scooted farther away. I realized I'd lost track of Arthur. I stood and located him in the backyard playing tug-of-war with a group of girls. I walked into the kitchen. Will was texting on his phone and smiling.

"You know," I said, interrupting the text messaging, "I tried to get him to take a deal."

He dropped his phone to his side, tilted his head back in

exasperation, and rolled his eyes.

"Stop," he said. "We're not talking about Scotty's trial."

I felt guilty about what was going on with Scotty's case, and I felt guilty for being at Will's party when I should have been working. I explained to Will that Scotty had refused to take a deal even though I thought it was in his best interest.

"We should do shots," Will said. He was ignoring me, and I was already drunk.

"Imagine you were in your house, and in the middle of the night, while you were sleeping, someone broke in and drugged you. You wake up, hours later, in a giant puddle of blood, with no recollection of what happened," I said.

"Who said someone broke into his house?" Will asked.

"I don't know. But imagine that scenario. The same situation as Scotty. Except it's you. Would you take a deal?"

For a brief moment, Will had a far-off look in his eyes, and I thought he was pondering the question. I waited for his answer, but then he went back to texting on his phone. He hadn't been contemplating Scotty's fate; he'd been contemplating his next text. When he was done, he looked up, punched me in the shoulder, and said, "I'm gonna get you another beer."

With 9:14 to go in the game, the Packers made a twenty-three-yard field goal. I got up to use the bathroom. Will and a group of college kids were in the living room surrounding Arthur. They were taking turns giving him commands. After each trick, they'd feed him a piece of steak.

"Dude, this dog's a pussy magnet!" Will shouted at me.

"Don't feed him too much," I said, and just at that moment, Lacey appeared over my shoulder.

"He's not wrong," she said, patting Arthur on the head. "Chicks love a cute dog."

"Oh," I said.

"How's it going?"

"Fine." My mind raced. I wondered where Paul was.

She gestured toward the bathroom. "Don't let me keep you," she said. I was caught off guard and didn't know what to say to her.

Alone in the bathroom, I cursed my own awkwardness. When I walked back out into the living room, I saw Lacey standing by the back doors and approached.

"Looks like the Packers are gonna pull it out," she said.

"Yeah," I said. "Where's…uh…"

"Paul?"

"Yeah."

"Things aren't really going that well."

"Sorry to hear," I said, even though, of course, I wasn't.

We stood watching the football game together. A while later, I caught Will looking at us from across the room. The corner of his mouth curved up slightly in a wry smile. Something about the way he looked at us made me hate him. I wanted to walk over and punch him in the face. But whatever the intense emotion bubbling inside me was, I somehow channeled it into courage. I turned to Lacey.

"Do you want to get lunch sometime?" I asked.

She smiled and paused like she really had to think about it. This is never a good sign, but then she said sure, and we exchanged numbers.

* * *

I don't know what happened the rest of the day because all I could think about was Lacey Price. I pictured her shouting at those bullies and launching that football across the entire courtyard. I pictured her looking at me from Paul's blue pickup with the wind blowing gently across her face.

I left the party once the game was over, and when Arthur and I walked outside, the late-afternoon calm of small-town Chico washed over me. The reverberating bass still shook the walls, but it was muffled and distant now. For the first time in as long as I could remember, I wasn't thinking about Scotty's case, about who had killed Josh Anderson, or about Paul Morrison or his father, Ralph. My brain went totally empty, and the euphoric high of romantic possibility consumed me.

"Lacey Price," I said to myself. Just saying her name made me smile.

I opened the car door for Arthur to jump in, but he sat and looked up at me.

"Lacey Price...It sure would be nice, wouldn't it?" I said to him.

He gave me a blank stare and remained seated.

"Come on. Get in," I said.

He hesitated. "She's very nice," he said.

"Yes, she is," I told him. "Now get in the car."

He jumped in.

THIRTY-ONE

Four days later my mother died. I was in my office reviewing a criminal complaint against a new client when my sister called. It was Thursday, September 15, at 3:52 p.m. Right when I heard my sister's voice, I looked at the clock on my computer screen like I knew it would be a moment I'd need to remember. That date and time are seared into my memory.

"Mom's dead" was all she said. Those were the first two words out of her mouth. She just said it, without fanfare or preamble. I could hear that she'd been crying. I couldn't speak, and I stared at the little numbers in the bottom right-hand corner of my computer monitor. The last digit changed—3:53 p.m. now.

That's how these things happen, isn't it? You get a phone call, someone pays you a visit, or there's always some intermediary who delivers the news. Not that you'd want to actually watch the death of a loved one, but the separation from the actual event makes the whole thing distant, impersonal even. When my sister said those two words, all I could manage was to say her name, as though we had a bad connection and I hadn't heard her.

"Did you hear me?" she said, her voice quivering now. "Lakeside called. They couldn't get ahold of Dad. She passed twenty minutes ago. Can you go down there please? I can't go right now."

"Sure," I told her.

After months of watching my mother in an almost vegetative state, wishing for death's mercy, the irreversible finality of it had arrived. I told Shelly I would be out the rest of the day and left the office in a daze.

I couldn't muster any emotion. I don't know if it was shock or emptiness or confusion, but I felt nothing but a vacancy as I drove to Lakeside. I was envious of my sister. She'd had herself a good cry over the news. I wanted to feel closer to the moment, and I wondered if something was wrong with me.

"It was her time," John said from the passenger's seat.

"You're back to talking now, are you?" I said. "Done with the silent treatment? Done acting like a weirdo?" I hadn't forgotten about August, and seeing him at Will's party had been the first time in a while. He acted like nothing was wrong.

"You needed a break," he said.

"And that's the advice you're giving me?"

"What?"

"*It was her time?* Really, John? An empty platitude? Not now," I said.

He shrugged. "Well, it *was* her time."

We drove the rest of the way in silence.

* * *

Thin Mustache and the other staff were huddled in the hallway outside my mother's room. Some I recognized, like Hispanic Nurse, who smelled of creamy lotion and fresh-cut flowers. Some I didn't, like the young man with a dragon tattoo on his left forearm, who must've been barely eighteen. The Lakeside director, an unremarkable man in a cheap suit, greeted me with a handshake. We'd previously seen very little of him, yet here he was offering his condolences. Everything's a business, I suppose. He led me inside.

I was confused looking down at my mother's bed. I didn't

see her there. I almost asked where the body was, but before I did, the manager pulled back the thin top sheet to reveal her frozen face. Her mouth gaped open as though she were midsentence, and her head looked too large for her body. The rest of her was nothing more than a shriveling, withered jumble of limbs. We stood over the bed like scientists considering a lab experiment. The room smelled of musty, damp cloth. I had a sudden flash of anger. I wanted to ask Thin Mustache, "What's that smell? Do you guys wash the sheets around here or what?" He had been my only point of contact, my comrade during all those visits watching my mother slowly wither away. I shouldn't take it out on him. After all, *we* put her here. But I felt guilty and enraged all at once, and I wanted to take it out on someone.

John walked in and stood at the foot of her bed. I didn't want him there. He shrugged casually, as if to say, "What can you do?" And when he did that, I wanted to punch him.

Moments later I heard sobbing from down the hall, and my sister appeared in the doorway, and Hispanic Nurse helped her into the room like an athletic trainer ushering her off the field after a sprained ankle. She hugged me tightly, burying her head into my chest, and I felt the cool moisture of her tears soaking through my dress shirt. It was the closest I'd felt to my sister since we were kids, and I realized it had been a long time since I'd enjoyed the comfort of a human embrace. The Horton-Norris Funeral Home van arrived, and three employees waited patiently in the hallway until I nodded for them to take the body away. Two strong men wheeled my mother down the hallway and out of the home. My sister and I followed. We walked through the automatic doors, watching them load the gurney carrying my mother's body into the waiting van. We stood under the low gray sky and watched the van grow smaller as it motored away. The Lakeside manager said goodbye. Thin Mustache said goodbye. I nodded at him, I hope in a way that expressed my appreciation. He'd looked after her for two years, and even though I knew he was just doing his job, I suppose I had an affinity for him. Hispanic

Nurse said goodbye. They all walked back inside through the automatic doors, leaving my sister and me standing in the parking lot alone, disappearing from our lives forever.

My sister and I stood for a long moment in silence. We watched cars pass up and down the street until she looked up at me. "Where the hell is Dad?" she asked.

"I don't know," I told her.

* * *

The funeral was on Saturday at my sister's church. My sister gave the eulogy, of course. I sat in the first row next to the aisle. I don't think I'd been that close to the lectern since I was a kid. I hate funerals, which is always a funny thing to say since no one likes funerals. *I hate funerals*—it's just one of those things you say. But I had particular gripes. I resented the forced social pressure to be present. Strangers offering condolences made me uncomfortable.

After the service, I stayed seated in the front and talked with John, who sat next to me.

"What is the purpose of funerals anyway?" he asked. It seemed like people gave John no attention, so I suppose he was determined to dominate mine. But I was sort of glad for his company in that moment. I didn't answer John, and an old woman in a big hat with lots of lace walked up and shook my hand. She told me she was sorry for my loss.

"You sound sorrier," I said.

"Excuse me?" the woman asked.

"Thank you," I said, and she shuffled away with a concerned look on her face. I turned to John. "I don't know what the point is either."

"Is it for the living or the dead?" he asked.

"I suppose everyone is different."

"I wonder if it's a dated tradition that we should get rid of," he said.

"John?"

"Yeah?"

"Shut up."

* * *

The reception was held at my father's house—the same house he shared with my mother for so many years. Strangers with grave faces shuffled solemnly around our house eating potato and macaroni salad, vegetable platters, carrot and celery sticks dipped in ranch, and store-bought chocolate-chip cookies. They shuffled with eyes downcast, using quiet voices. John and I stood in a corner of the room.

"All these people are just waiting until the socially appropriate time to leave," John said.

"You mean like us?"

He laughed. "Maybe."

I missed my mom, but I'd been missing her for quite some time at that point.

My sister commiserated with everyone. She was always a great host. When she walked up to John and me, I thanked her for taking care of everything. I told her she did a great job with the eulogy. Tears welled in her eyes. We hugged. "Sorry," I said, "but I have to go. I have to get home and feed Arthur, okay?"

She nodded. "It's okay." She was so understanding, so sweet.

John and I drove back to my house off Honey Run Road. We walked to the back of the house and found Arthur in the backyard. He looked up at us happily, totally unaware of the solemn day. He was busy digging a hole by the fence line.

* * *

A week later, Rick and Shelly marched into my office side by side like soldiers to battle. We had planned to meet that day, but our meetings were casual roundtables where we batted around ideas. They looked like nervous sales associates. Rick clutched a folder to his chest like it was a treasure he didn't want to share. I could tell they had something to tell me.

"Don't get too excited," Shelly said. They sat. I asked them why they were acting so weird. Rick opened the file folder and rifled through some papers. Shelly and I watched him.

"Complaints were made," he said, sliding a sheet of paper across my desk.

"Why didn't you just email this to me?"

"We wanted to talk to you about this without you seeing it first," Shelly said.

Rick handed me another sheet. He explained what it was that they had found.

Two years ago, Paul Morrison had complained to the sheriff that Scotty was violating a county ordinance. The ordinance limited the number of marijuana plants you could grow on your property. Then Paul filed another complaint alleging that Scotty had diverted a stream to use for his marijuana grow.

"Okay," I said. "But I talked to Paul—"

"He went to the DA too," Rick said.

"For both complaints," Shelly said.

"What happened?"

"They issued Scotty a warning," Shelly said. "They told Paul they couldn't prove the water violation and explained that they didn't have the resources to drive out to every property and count every marijuana grower's plants."

I looked at the pieces of paper in front of me. Three of them were just blank sheets with handwritten notes. One was a sheet that looked like meeting minutes from a Board of Supervisors meeting, but there was a big redacted portion in the middle.

"There's another thing," Rick said. "Scotty and Josh went before the Board of Supervisors five separate times over the last three years. Applying for a zoning permit to open a dispensary."

Shelly spoke up. "They were denied each time."

"Okay," I said. "So what?"

Shelly and Rick gave each other that look again. Rick spoke

first. "Ralph Morrison was at the meetings."

"Your dad was presiding at two of them," Shelly said.

Rick cleared his throat. "And there's a problem with the meeting minutes."

THIRTY-TWO

I was starting to feel more and more convinced of Scotty's innocence and more and more guilty about the fact that he was behind bars. Maybe that's why I started drinking again.

* * *

Mary Buyske was a forty-five-year-old single woman who lived alone with at least one cat. She had got the job as secretary for the Butte County Board of Supervisors two months after graduating from Chico State, and that summer would mark her twenty-year anniversary at the position. She prepared the meeting minutes for the Board of Supervisors. But as Rick explained, Ms. Buyske's meeting minutes included only what the board wanted. Institutional selective memory, as it were. There were gaps in the schedule, blank portions of testimony, witnesses who appeared before the board but went unlisted in the notes. Rick hadn't learned all this on his own, of course, since another interesting characteristic of Ms. Buyske, other than her love of cats, was her near photographic memory. Everything Rick knew about the board, including Ralph Morrison's strangely vocal presence at the hearings involving Scotty, who testified and who didn't, and what got recorded and what didn't, Ms. Buyske had told him. There were records of Scotty and Josh appearing twice before the board, but Ms. Buyske remembered in vivid detail three other times. Scotty had mentioned to me offhandedly that he'd gone before the board to get a business license, but never in this detail. Ms. Buyske's memory was either better than Scotty's, or I hadn't been asking the right questions. Ralph Morrison's attendance was in the minutes twice, but his testimony wasn't. Yet Ms. Buyske remembered him there, and she specifically remembered my father telling her to exclude Ralph's appearance.

Why? Why would my father do that, for any reason other than he had something to hide?

She remembered Ralph's vocal opposition to Scotty and Josh opening a marijuana co-op as well as a very candid conversation with my father regarding Scotty's alleged water and agricultural violations. The discussion at these meetings was wide-ranging, including Scotty's cultivation practices and whether the marijuana grow in his backyard was in compliance with the law.

"Is she willing to testify?" I asked Rick.

"I'm not sure it's such a good idea," Rick said.

"Now what sense does that make?" I asked Rick. "With all due respect, Rick, that's not what I asked. I asked if she was willing to testify."

"She didn't even know what she was saying. This theory of yours…"

I saw Shelly nodding her assent out of the corner of my eye.

"Would you like to add something?" I asked Shelly.

"Think about it," she said. "Even if the Board of Supervisors and Ralph Morrison hated Scotty and Josh and hated what they were doing, don't you think it's a little extreme to kill someone over it?"

"Yes! That's the point," I said. "It is extreme. And a jury will think it's extreme, and they'll exonerate Scotty because of it." I could see from the expressions on their faces that they weren't going to budge. We were never going to agree. "Fine," I said. "If she won't testify voluntarily, one of you contact her and let her know a subpoena is on the way."

Rick stared bleary-eyed at a spot on my desk. Shelly slumped in her chair and looked up at the air-conditioning vent, as if hoping a different course of action would drop from the sky.

"I'm trying to come up with a theory of the case that will give my client a chance, and I don't have a lot else to go on right now," I said. "So unless one or both of you has a better suggestion, this is what we're going to do."

They pursed their lips and shifted in their seats.

"One more thing," I said. "I want alibis for everyone. Ralph, Paul, every single one of the Morrison boys. Hell, I want an alibi for Lacey Price. I want to know what everyone in this goddamn town was doing the night of March 12. I want them all accounted for. The police didn't do their job, so we're going to do it for them."

* * *

Apart from whether your client should accept a plea deal, the biggest consideration a criminal defense attorney has is whether their client should testify. The default answer is to not call them to the stand. Lawyers are trained at manipulating language in a way that makes it appear witnesses are lying, even if they aren't or they've made an honest mistake. A good prosecutor can make small and irrelevant inconsistencies in a person's testimony seem like evasive concealments of fact. Concealment of facts equals lying; lying equals guilt. That's how your typical juror would see it, and exposing Scotty to Emma's cross-examination scared me. A lesser attorney would not have frightened me so much, but Emma did. I'd seen her eviscerate people on the stand. On the other hand, while Scotty's testimony wasn't that helpful, it also wasn't really inconsistent. The antegrade-amnesia science and Scotty's inability to remember would dovetail nicely with the only theory I could go on: Morrison Family Farms was fed up with Scotty diverting water and using toxic chemicals to grow weed. They had learned Scotty's habits at home. They knew about Scotty and Josh's meeting. They snuck in the cabin while no one was there. They laced Scotty's milk or cereal or both with GHB or some other knockout drug. Scotty ingested it and passed out. Josh arrived. The killer murdered Josh, disposed of the body, and framed Scotty for the murder. Scotty didn't remember what had happened because of the knockout drug, thanks to antegrade amnesia. Scotty would take the stand and repeat that he didn't remember. There was no body to implicate Scotty, only circumstantial evidence, and Scotty would go free.

Was this theory far-fetched? Yes. That's a remarkable amount of effort by the Morrisons, first of all. Second of all, if they were going to frame Scotty, why would the Morrisons dispose of Josh's body so it couldn't be found? Those questions were not going to be answered, but I also had nothing else to go on. It was my best option. It was Scotty's best option.

As counterpoint, if the jury didn't buy that theory or didn't like those lingering unanswered questions, putting Scotty on the stand and having him repeat "I don't remember" would appear evasive. "I don't remember" is a convenient excuse for someone charged with murder, especially when there are no other witnesses, there's no good explanation why your DNA is all over the crime scene, and you're found covered in the victim's blood.

I went over all this with John while we drove to the courthouse. He ran a hand through his wavy black hair. "I don't put my client on the stand unless he's going to get up there and explain to the jury why he's innocent," he said. "Without contradicting himself with any prior statements."

"So you wouldn't put him on?"

"I didn't say that."

"Are you trying to be unhelpful?"

John shrugged. "Ask him what he wants to do."

Yes, John. That's what we're doing. We're driving to the courthouse to ask him. You moron.

* * *

"We need to talk about whether or not you're going to testify," I told Scotty.

We were back in the bare-walled interview room. He shrugged and mumbled something about "doesn't matter."

"You're going to need to have answers if the prosecutor asks about the fingerprints on the knife, the truck out front, the DNA match, the pool of blood, and the motive."

He shrugged. "I don't. I don't have answers to that. I don't remember anything. I told you."

"We have to talk about whether you're willing to testify."

"Okay."

"Are you?"

"I don't know."

"It's your one chance to get up in front of the jury and tell them your side of the story," I told him.

"But my story doesn't add anything."

"I know."

"Will it make a difference?" he asked.

"I don't know. Usually I can tell, but in this case, I don't know."

"I'll do whatever you think is best," he said.

That settled it—nothing was solved, and we'd have to answer that question closer to trial.

I asked Scotty if the marijuana field was graded for crop cultivation or if they did it themselves.

"I don't know. Josh did the grow, not me."

I asked if they diverted streams or other water resources.

Scotty shrugged. "No idea. Maybe."

What products did they use to fertilize the plants? Again, he didn't know. What about Ralph's complaints? Did Scotty know about them?

He laughed. "Everyone in this county hates my guts. Go

back up to the cabin. You can ask any farmer in Forest Ranch. Hell, any farmer in the valley even. They didn't want nothing to do with me. So did I know about them? No, not really. But am I surprised? No. I'm not. People thought I left my parents stranded. You know how this town is."

It was true. A false rumor could spread faster than a summer brush fire, and the town did have a way of ganging up on you.

"So if you're asking me if I think I was framed or who I think might've done it, my answer is the same it's always been: I don't know. The Morrisons? Sure. Just as easily as anyone else, I guess."

I looked over at John. He was standing in the corner. "I don't know. You're on your own," he said. "You didn't want my help."

"What're you looking at?" Scotty asked.

"Nothing," I said. "Do your parents still live over off West Fourth?"

"I think so," he said. "I'm actually not sure."

I opened his file, hoping a flash of inspiration would hit, but my eyes glazed over. Suddenly the ghastly fluorescent light made the pages appear so bright and reflective, it felt like I was looking straight into the sun. My eyes started to burn. I shut them. The room started to shake. I rubbed my eyes like a weary traveler.

"Are you all right?" I heard Scotty say, but it sounded like I was in a vacuum. When I opened my eyes, Scotty looked concerned. John was gone.

"Yeah," I told him. "I'm fine."

"You look worse than I do," he said.

"Thanks," I said. "Tell me how you really feel."

THIRTY-THREE

My father never seemed to enjoy the domestic life he'd created for himself. I wouldn't go so far as to say he hated it, but I think he endured it more so than lived it. He had a Protestant work ethic, a flat affect, and old-school Chico values. He woke up early each day, put in nine hours of hard work, came home, ate dinner, read the newspaper, and retired early. We didn't speak much. I watched him stoically plod through his days like a soldier marching through a vast and endless field. While I'm sure my opinion is colored by the misperceptions of a sensitive child, his attitude toward me appeared to be somewhere between indifference and obligation. I imagine the most enjoyable parts of his life were spent apart from his family.

As I got older, his emotional exterior only hardened. When we did speak, our conversations were never profound or detailed. The closest thing to bonding involved discussing current events. We avoided any meaningful or deep conversation, and after Mom died, I figured we'd live out the remainder of his days like reluctant coworkers forced to work closely together. We'd continue to keep our distance since there was no reason to change things now. But with Scotty's case, suddenly our lives were forced together, and we were involuntarily intertwined.

He'd asked Ms. Buyske to selectively record the Board of Supervisors' meeting minutes, but why? How close was he with Ralph Morrison? What were his motivations in Scotty's case? He knew I was representing him. Did he not remember Scotty's applications to the board? Or Ralph's appearances? Was the omission evidence of deception or lapse in memory? Whatever the case, I knew that broaching the subject would not be easy.

Driving to the Thursday-night dinner that my sister, father, and I felt obligated to continue in my mother's absence, I considered not even bringing it up—Mary Buyske to testify. We had the records of the board meetings. It would all come out at trial, and that might be enough. And if there was an innocuous reason or some explanation, I should force the prosecution to explain it. I could catch Emma on her heels. Tipping my father off might tip my hand to Emma.

Curiosity got the best of me. Dinner was served. We filled the spaces between silences how we always had, with the usual banal small talk you might engage in with an old acquaintance you hadn't seen in a long time—sports, the Green Bay Packers, Aaron Rodgers, current events. The Packers were struggling. Cell phone batteries were exploding and getting banned on airplanes. The Sacramento mayor had beaten someone up. Another black teen had been shot by a white police officer. Donald Trump was debating Hillary Clinton the following week. "Such a shame," my father said about the campaign. "Embarrassing" was how he described the election. It was a nonpartisan rebuke.

We talked local elections. The mayor faced only a weak challenger. He would win. My father would run unopposed and retain his seat on the Board of Supervisors, as would each of the municipal judges in the county. The district attorney race appeared to be the only interesting one on the ballot. Bill Dubois was turning out to be a real challenger for Mike Sullivan. The "Justice for Josh" campaign was the closest thing to attack ads you'll find in a Butte County election. I used to think the effect on Scotty's case was forcing Emma into an unreasonably harsh offer, but given Scotty's past, I'm not sure he would've pled guilty to anything. We spoke in fits and starts until finally I had to ask him.

"Dad," I said. He looked up from his meal at me. "A couple of years ago, Scotty applied for a zoning permit. He went before the board. Do you remember that?"

"Yes. Vaguely."

"Why didn't you mention it to me?"

"I didn't remember until just now." *That sounds like bullshit.* "How is this relevant?"

"You denied his permit."

"We did?"

"Yes. Why?"

"I'm pretty sure it ran contrary to the zoning policy," he said. "Not a hard decision as I recall." *You just said you didn't remember,* I thought.

I kept at him. "But he applied five different times. Kept modifying it. He worked closely with the board." Surely he remembered that sustained effort, right?

"I do remember him coming before us more than once. But he never did the application correctly. The denial was routine. It was an afterthought."

"Ralph Morrison was there," I told him.

He set his fork on his plate and looked up at me. "Where are you going with this? What is the question you want to ask me?"

"Ralph Morrison was there. Every single time."

"So what?"

"Are you guys friends?"

"This is ridiculous."

"Why does the board take meeting minutes selectively?"

He took a sip of wine. The faint sound of a jazz riff ended, and until the next song began, the house was totally silent. I could see that my father wasn't going to answer any more questions. He went back to eating his dinner. His head was buried in his plate.

"Let's talk about something else," my sister said.

A moment passed before my father spoke again. I knew he had to have the last word. "I can appreciate that you want to do a good job for your client. It's admirable. But I am not alone in thinking your handling of this Scotty Watts case is going poorly." He took another sip of wine, bringing it slowly to his lips then setting it gently on the glass table. "Frankly it's becoming increasingly embarrassing to explain your conduct to people in this community."

I felt like a teenager once again. I let it go. I knew he wouldn't discuss it any further.

My sister broke the prolonged silence that followed. "I'm visiting Mom next weekend," she said. "I think we should go as a family." No one looked up. "Please?"

"Sure," I said.

My father gruffly agreed. After dinner, I drove home and took Arthur for a walk.

THIRTY-FOUR

My sister had finished her sermon, but I was already outside waiting. The congregation funneled out, and I hung on the periphery by the front steps, trying to muster the courage to finally talk to Lacey. I still hadn't texted or called since I wasn't sure what I'd say. She walked out with a group of friends, and when they peeled away from her, I started to make a move. Paul appeared. He said hello and touched her arm, and watching their conversation left me with a sinking feeling, like my heart had fallen into my stomach. He said something that made her throw her head back and laugh. She touched his arm playfully. I could watch only for a few moments longer before I spun on my heels and stomped toward the parking lot to my car.

It was probably a stupid idea anyway.

But a few days later, Arthur and I were in the park playing fetch. Three girls about my age were riding on the bike path toward me, illuminated by rays of sunlight cutting through the fire-colored leaves. When they got closer, I recognized it was Lacey with two friends I didn't know. Lacey saw me and got off her bike. Her friends continued up the road toward the parking lot.

"What happened to lunch?" she asked.

"Do you really want to go?"

"Yeah. Of course."

"What about you and Paul?"

"It's complicated," she said.

I told her that Scotty's trial was starting soon, and we agreed on going out the following Tuesday before I got too busy with the trial. We talked for what was probably only a few minutes, but it seemed like an entire afternoon. She leaned on her bike, and every so often I'd toss the stick for Arthur to fetch. We talked about Scotty, referring to him in platitudes like what a shame it was and how it was wasted potential and charisma. I told her about the tough hand Scotty had been dealt, considering the circumstances of his first run-in with the law and his dad's illness. Then I asked what had brought her to Will's barbecue.

"I don't remember you guys hanging out too much in high school," I said.

"We hung out a little after you left," she said. It seemed like something about the question bothered her.

"He's a wild man," she said. I felt like she wanted to tell me more, but I left it at that. She bent and patted Arthur on the head. She picked up his stick and gave it a toss. "You were always so quiet in high school. Always off by yourself." She tilted her head and smiled at me when she said this, like she appreciated the oddity. "I'm glad things turned out okay for you."

I didn't respond. I thought about this for a moment, thinking back to college, to law school, to the navy, and to coming home. Did things turn out okay for me? I wasn't sure.

* * *

I agreed to meet Will for one drink that Friday since Scotty's trial would be starting soon and I'd soon be too busy for socializing. When I emphasized I'd be meeting him only for one drink, he said, "Sure thing, buddy."

When I arrived, he was chatting at the bar with a good-looking young couple. "There's my weirdo protégé right there!" Will shouted.

"We're the same age," I said. I turned to the good-looking couple. "I'm sorry you've had to deal with him."

"We don't mind," the man said.

"He's fun!" the woman said.

Will announced he wanted to buy a round of drinks. He said "drinks," but we took shots. I told him that was enough, but he goaded me into getting another drink. I milled about and listened to Will's perverted comments, and when my drink was finished, I told him I was going home. I wanted to prepare a little more for Scotty's trial. Will's mouth turned into a crooked mischievous smile. "You seen those fat titties yet?" he said with a glint in his eye.

"Why do you have to talk like that? And I don't know what you're talking about."

"Lacey Price. Have you seen them?"

"No."

"Wait till you do." He reared his head back. "Good God, are they perfect! Heavenly," he said.

My jaw clenched. I gritted my teeth together. "How would you know?" I asked.

"She didn't tell you?" The bartender set cocktails in front of us.

"Tell me what?"

He chuckled. "Lacey is…adventurous. We used to bone like twice a day for about six months."

"What?"

"Yeah. Total nympho. Goes wild in bed. It's really great, actually."

Blood rushed from my brain to my feet. He kept going.

"Crazy horny. She used to—"

"Okay. I got it," I said. "I don't need details."

"Hey, don't get all butthurt. It's not like I'm the only guy she's ever had sex with. Shit, man, Lacey was railed by like every single dude in high school."

"No, she wasn't."

"Yeah, she was."

"Whatever. Let's talk about something else."

"Do you want another drink?" Will asked.

"Sure," I said. Going home and stewing on my couch thinking about Lacey and Will rapturously engaged with each other seemed like a bad idea.

Two drinks later, the room started spinning. We were at a new bar across the street. Things started moving in slow motion. My mind drifted off, and I pictured her in Paul's blue pickup, driving up Highway 32 with the wind blowing through her hair. I pictured her looking over at me and smiling. I pictured her back in junior high leading Tex away by the arm.

Will shouted over the blaring music that we were going somewhere else. We walked across the street to a dingy narrow bar crowded with locals. The men wore ten-gallon hats and blue jeans. Among them was Paul Morrison himself, sitting at the bar and sipping on a Sierra Nevada beer. His brother Cole next to him.

There was nowhere to go. Will and I edged up closer to Paul and Cole. They nodded at us and said hello, and Will leaned in to chat with them. I stood over Will's shoulder out of view, and over the loud music and barroom chatter, I couldn't hear what they were talking about. Seeing my reflection in the mirrored glass behind the bar was like looking through a window at a stranger I knew very well. I imagined Lacey and Will sport-fucking on his couch, in his kitchen, in his pool, on the patio in the backyard—screwing like it was the end of the world. I imagined them in pornographic scenes, gyrating like stuck pigs. I heard Lacey's voice in my head squealing with delight.

"You want another one?" Will asked.

I nodded. He ordered four shots, and the Morrison brothers clinked glasses with Will and me. Paul eyed me with suspicion. We downed the shots. I couldn't quite hear, but Paul said something to me like "Nice to see you again," a threatening grimace on his face.

A group walked by, and each one bumped into me on their

way to the exit. Beer spilled on my clothes and shoes. "I'm gonna go to the bathroom!" I shouted at Will and stumbled off.

I shut the door and looked at my phone. It was 10:30 p.m.

When I came back, the stranger in the mirrored window was looking at me again. His face was deadly serious. But John was standing next to him in the reflection. I looked to my side where he should have been, but he was only behind the bar, in the window. John and the stranger stood perfectly still. John's smile grew in slow motion until his lips were stretched grotesquely from ear to ear, a cartoonish row of crammed jagged teeth in his mouth. I couldn't look at the reflection any longer.

"Let's get out of here!" I said to Will.

"What?" He couldn't hear me.

"Where's Lacey?" I asked Paul.

"You're pretty wasted, bro," he said.

When I turned back, Will was gone. I looked around to find him. Suddenly Paul grabbed my arm, and I saw rage in his eyes.

"You know," he said, "when we were growing up, I never thought much of you. No one did." The alcohol churned in my stomach. I almost fell over. "You weren't going to be anyone. Just another nobody. But you're worse than that." He scoffed. "Defending Scotty Watts. What an honor that must be for you. You two are perfect for each other."

"Take a swing!" John shouted in my ear. Suddenly he was there in the bar. "How dare you let him talk to you like that!" John screamed. Paul had a smirk on his face. "Do it!" John yelled. Jesus. Can anyone else hear this? I thought.

Paul spoke. "You gonna do something or just stand there with that stupid look on your face?" The moment passed. I didn't do anything. I turned for the exit, leaving Cole, Paul, and John to watch me go.

"Pathetic!" John shouted at me.

I rushed outside into the cold night air. It brought clarity to my eyes, for only a moment, but I seethed. I should have broken a bottle of beer over the bar and cut Paul's throat.

* * *

"Blackout" isn't always the best word, is it? After a night of heavy drinking, bits and pieces of the night come back to you. It's more like gaps in your memory, like trying to recount a story you've been told. I woke up the next morning on Will's plush cream couch, shivering cold, with only a thin sheet covering me. My eyes were only partially open when a blurry shapeless red figure glided across the room.

"Looking a little rough this morning," a woman's voice I didn't recognize said. I heard the front door open and close, pulled the sheet over my head, and shut my eyes tight. I ran my sandpaper tongue over my lips. They were so dry, they felt like brittle chalk. I recounted the previous night's events like snapshots of my memory:

—Talking with Paul at the narrow bar, wanting to punch him. John yelling in my face.

—Flailing around on the dance floor of a club, looking longingly into the eyes of a moonfaced girl I'd never seen before.

—Searching through my phone for something.

—Seeing the sign for O'Haras, sobering myself for the entrance.

—Walking into O'Haras, seeing Kelly behind the bar.

—Will leaning over the bar toward Kelly, waving a credit card in his hand.

—Kelly shaking her head at him.

—Will leaning aggressively in.

—Kelly motioning to security.

—Riding alone in the back seat of a car under a full moon.

What was a dream, and what was a memory?

I wasn't sure. I lay on Will's couch for a while longer. I got up, forced down a glass of water, and found my way home.

THIRTY-FIVE

Sunday.

Scotty's trial was in one week, and I couldn't fathom that there was more evidence to uncover, imagine that there were more theories to consider, or think of more witnesses to speak to. But it'd been a while since I'd driven up to Forest Ranch, and I'd missed it. There was something about the routine of driving up Deer Creek Highway to Scotty's cabin that was comforting, like it was part of an old routine I'd taken up again. I missed breathing in the pine-scented air and listening to the quiet sound of the wind rustling through the trees. Maybe the peacefulness of the place helped me think. I don't know. I also went up there because I could tell Arthur was restless. I was sitting on my couch watching football, and he started throwing shoes at me. He'd walk from the couch to the front door, grab one of my sneakers in his mouth, walk back to me, and fling the shoe in my lap.

"Yes? Can I help you?" I'd ask, even though I knew what he wanted. I'd put the shoe back in its place, but he'd plod back over, grab it in his jaws, walk back to me, and fling it again. I'd seen this routine before. He did this with tennis balls when it was time for fetch, or boxer shorts when he was ready for bed. Smart dog. After a few trips back and forth, he sat up on his hind legs and reached his paw onto my lap like a man waiting for service at a counter.

"Let's go," he said.

"Okay, fine," I said. "Let's go."

When I turned onto Forest Rim Lane, I rolled slowly past the vacant lot Kelly had told me about and looked at the remains of the home burned down years ago. As I rolled past the driveway, I saw John standing in the clearing. He gestured to me to come over as though he'd been waiting there all morning. I stopped the car.

What the hell is he doing here?

Arthur and I walked to the driveway to meet him. He spread his arms and smiled. "Been waiting awhile," he said. "Ready for trial?"

"As ready as we're gonna be," I said. Then I admitted, "It's probably going to be a bloodbath."

"There's only so much you can do," he said. "Don't be discouraged."

He gestured for me to follow him to the back of the lot. "I wonder if this will help," he said and led me to where the pine-needle floor turned to dirt, just before the pine-tree forest got thick. He stopped and pointed to a spot at our feet. The earth was broken up a little, but there didn't seem to be anything special about that spot. Rocks. Dirt. Pine cones.

"What?" I asked.

"Look closer."

I did, and I saw a slight indentation running for a few feet, like a track pushed into the mud. Another indented track ran parallel about six feet apart.

"*Tire tracks?*" I said. John just shrugged.

They looked like they had been created months ago. Or was I imagining it? It was hard to tell. You could barely make out anything in the dirt, and part of me felt like I was imagining something that wasn't there. The marks in the dirt had a familiarity to them.

"You tell me," John said, as though I were supposed to know.

I thought and thought about what they could mean and how I could know. I considered whose car might have made them and who might be parking in the lot next to Scotty's, and for what reason. A realtor maybe? Hunters? Hikers? Then I realized how silly all that thinking was.

"This is stupid," I told John. "March was seven months ago. Why are you showing me this now?"

John shrugged and put his hands in his pockets. "Just trying to help," he said.

"The tracks could have been created anytime between the night of March 12 and now by a million different cars. Plus, even if we assume these tracks are from some car that parked in this spot the night of March 12, the forensics are useless." I was getting angry, and John was becoming a distraction again. "John," I said, "this might be the most useless thing you've ever shown me."

"Like I said, I'm just trying to help. Take it for what you will," John said.

He picked up a pine cone and chucked it into the forest.

What a waste of time, I thought.

Just when I thought John would cease to get on my nerves, he showed up and pointed out some useless patch of dirt that *might* have been relevant seven months ago, stirring up doubt and confusion in my mind. Birds chirped. John lifted his head to the canopy of trees above as if he were searching for something in them, and he put his hands in his pockets and wandered off like a man taking a Sunday stroll in the park.

I looked down at Arthur. His back was straight and ears perked up, like a hunting dog tracking the location of a downed bird. I followed his gaze. He was looking through the forest in the direction of Scotty's cabin next door. I could make out an untrodden path through the sparse pine forest to the wooden stairs leading up to Scotty's deck. From where we stood—at the back of the lot where the tracks were—someone could walk through the forest and be at Scotty's back door in two minutes. I could see the back stairs of Scotty's cabin from where we stood. If one were to have parked his car right there, walked through those pines, and ascended those stairs, he could have quietly opened Scotty's sliding-glass door and been positioned directly behind him. And if he would have done so on the night of March 12 between the hours of 7:30 and 8:00 p.m., he would have found Scotty eating his cereal alone in his cabin, with his back to the window. I looked over toward Eleanor Jackson's house. You couldn't even make out a faint outline of it; the forest was so thick.

No. This is ridiculous. I couldn't present any of this in front of a jury. I'm wasting my time. John's wasting my time.

I shook it off and looked over to the other side of the lot, where John was examining a leaf like a park ranger considering its health.

"Come on, Arthur," I said, and we trudged through the bushes toward Scotty's cabin. When we broke through the clearing to the back of Scotty's lot, Arthur and I stood there for a moment and considered the path from the tire tracks to where we stood. We looked up at Scotty's cabin. I could see the reflection of the sliding-glass door on the second story. I looked at Arthur.

"What are we doing?" he asked.

"I don't know," I said. "This is pointless, isn't it?"

"I don't know," he said, and I decided that it was.

"Let's go home," I told him, and we did.

* * *

Later that night, Arthur and I watched Aaron Rodgers and the Green Bay Packers race out to an early lead against the New York Giants, but stupid John had planted that idea in my head, and I couldn't stop thinking about those tire tracks. Perhaps they were Scotty's last hope. Perhaps they were something else. I grabbed Scotty's file and opened the investigative report. I looked at the weather details the detective had notated. For the late hours of March 12 and early-morning hours of March 13, the detective had written, "Clear sky. No rain. High winds."

High winds.

I opened my computer and searched for "weather for March 12, 2016." I found comprehensive recorded weather statistics dating back years. March 12. It turned out that the detective's notation of "high winds" had been a gross understatement. On the night of March 12, 2016, Forest Ranch had experienced winds of almost fifty miles per hour—more like gale-force winds. Gusts like that would howl so loudly, you wouldn't be able to hear yourself think. You also wouldn't hear someone walking up the back stairs of creaky wood steps leading to the sliding-glass door of your cabin.

Had it rained earlier that day? I looked at the precipitation information.

It *had* rained. Almost a half inch.

A half inch of rain.

Just enough to moisten the untrodden forest ground. Just enough to leave tire tracks in the mud.

THIRTY-SIX

There was a knock at the front door, and Arthur snapped his head in the direction of the sound. He slid off the couch and jogged over. I opened it. Eileen Watts raised her doleful eyes to meet mine. Her arms rested on the back of Ray's wheelchair. The night was dark and still. Ray drooled helplessly onto his shirt, a blanket draped over his legs. A strand of gray hair fell in Eileen's face, and she pushed it behind her ear. It'd been months since I'd seen Ray and Eileen outside the grocery store.

"I'm sorry for bothering you on a Sunday," she said. "Do you have a moment to talk?"

It was quite all right, I said, and yes, I could talk. I helped her wheel Ray inside and positioned him next to the couch. I poured her a glass of water and sat across from her. Arthur sniffed at Ray's arm, and Ray groaned in disapproval. I grabbed Arthur's collar and pulled him away.

"I'm sorry I didn't recognize you at the grocery store," Eileen said. "It's been so many years. You're all grown now."

"It's okay," I told her. It had been a long time. "No problem at all."

"I've been meaning to come…" she said. "But it's hard to get away with Ray, and work, and…"

"It's fine. I understand," I said. "What can I do for you?"

"I wanted to thank you," she said. She held her water glass between her knees and drew a clear line through the condensation with her finger.

"Oh. No problem," I said. "I'd do it for free, seeing how Scotty and I were close friends." This wasn't exactly the truth, of course. Scotty and I were not close friends, and we never had been. It was like claiming Aaron Rodgers and I were close friends.

"I know it must be hard to defend someone you know is guilty," she said.

"Sorry?" I asked. I was confused.

"I just mean…I just hope…" She struggled for the words. "I just hope Scotty takes responsibility for what he did."

"Mrs. Watts—"

"Please, call me Eileen."

"Eileen," I said, "I'm not sure Scotty is guilty. I don't know."

She smiled at me. "I understand. You have to say that."

"No, I don't," I said. "I really mean that. I can't talk specifics about the case, but there's a lot of questions about what happened that night, and not all of them point to Scotty's guilt."

Eileen pursed her lips. "You were always a very good boy," she said. "A very good boy." She sighed, thinking about the years that had passed. "Moving away. Law school. The navy…I'll bet your parents are proud."

I thought about my fragmented family and disgraceful career. My mother was dead. My father and I spoke intermittently. His questionable practices on the Board of Supervisors might drive my entire defense case at Scotty's trial. I had been kicked out of the navy. I'd lost my mentor. I had few friends. I had a desperate longing for a high school crush. I had resentment and nostalgia for the place I lived. I was confused, lonely, and lost. *Were my parents proud?* I don't know. I doubted it. But Eileen didn't need to know any of this, so I just smiled and said, "I hope so."

Ray groaned. Eileen nodded, as if assenting to whatever he

was trying to communicate, and turned to me. "I suppose I really came here because I feel so bad for that poor boy's family. That Anderson boy. I know what it's like to lose a son, and if you can convince Scotty to tell the police where his body is, it would make Ray and I feel much better."

"I can appreciate your concern, but I honestly don't know if Scotty can tell the police where the body is. He really might be telling the truth," I said. "And I know he wants your support during his trial. I know he'd like to reconcile with you both."

"He wants our help?" she asked.

"Yes."

"Did Scotty tell you exactly why we don't speak anymore?" she asked.

I told her what I knew, that she and Ray were disappointed in Scotty for selling weed. I recounted everything Scotty had told me—about what had happened after high school, about helping Ray with the plumbing business after he was released from jail, about Ray getting sick, and about trying to help support the family however he could. "All he said was that at some point you stopped accepting his help."

Eileen laughed sardonically. "*We* stopped accepting *his* help? Ha! That doesn't surprise me. He's not telling you the truth. We tried. We really did. But I refused to have a drug addict living in our house." She gave me that look of pity again. "Scotty did work hard, for a time. I think he was trying. He was living at home. But I started finding needles in the bathroom. I'd confront him. He wouldn't tell me what was going on. Ray and I aren't stupid, you know. He'd be awake for days and then totally worthless for days. He was erratic. Unreliable. Ray missed appointments. Scotty missed shifts at work. Finally one day I'd just taken Ray to his physical therapy appointment. When I came back, I found Scotty passed out in the bathroom with a needle in his arm. He was lying there with his head against the bathtub as limp as a sack of potatoes. I thought he was dead."

I shifted in my seat.

"I couldn't take care of two people anymore," she said. Her eyes glistened. "So I kicked him out. He moved up to the cabin. He sent us a little money at first. And it's true: I cashed the checks for a while. I did need the help. But he'd become a different person. It felt wrong, and I knew where the money was coming from. I exhausted myself trying to help him. It became too much."

I felt like I'd just had a shot of iron injected into my spine. I didn't know what to say. I looked at my hands.

"It's funny how only one part of the story can come across, isn't it?" she said. "I'm sorry he lied to you."

She shook her head and looked into her drink. "You were always a good boy. A good boy," she repeated, "but gullible. Always a little gullible."

"I didn't know..." I said.

"I know you didn't."

"I really think he was trying to help," I said.

"Maybe," she said. "Maybe. But"—she motioned to Ray—"look at my situation. I needed more than trying. I needed consistency. I needed my son."

We sat in silence for a while. I felt betrayed. Eileen said "I tried" a couple of times, urging that she didn't give up on Scotty right away. I knew it was a possibility that Scotty had been lying to me all along, but I burned with shame and anger. Eileen was right. I was gullible. I realized why she looked at me with pity: I'd been had. Nevertheless, I asked her if they might still be willing to come to Scotty's trial. It would help. Maybe Scotty could get clean. Maybe they could reconcile.

She politely declined. She reminded me that the important thing was for Josh Anderson's body to be found. I told her I understood, and I regarded everything that had happened with Scotty with a fresh skepticism. *Does Scotty know where the body is?* I thought. *If he is lying about all this, is he also lying about what happened that night?*

I walked outside with Eileen and helped her lift Ray out of his wheelchair and into the passenger's seat of their old sedan. Eileen walked around the car and opened the driver's-side door. I realized I'd forgotten to ask her something. "Eileen," I said. She stopped. "How did you find me?"

"I called your father. We still had his phone number from the high school basketball roster." She shut the door and got in her car. I stood on the sidewalk in front of my house and watched her drive away into the night.

* * *

Rick was understandably both relieved and frustrated when we met about Scotty's case the next day. He was relieved because when I told him about my meeting with Eileen and Ray, for him it confirmed his belief that Scotty's case was a lost cause. In Rick's mind, one lie was all it took to lose credibility. If Scotty was lying about his relationship with his parents, he was lying about what he remembered from that night. The circumstantial evidence was too great. Scotty killed Josh Anderson. But Rick was also frustrated since he'd done a massive amount of work for a client who'd been untruthful to us.

Shelly was more even-tempered. She thought Scotty's lie was deception by omission. He hadn't mentioned his ongoing drug problem. He'd glossed over the strained relationship with his parents. The omitted facts about his drug use or his parents' attempts to get him clean didn't necessarily mean he was lying about the night in question. I agreed, so I remained conflicted. Plus, I was still obligated to provide him with a good defense, so maybe John had been right all along—whether or not Scotty was telling the truth, it didn't matter.

"What are you going to do?" Shelly asked.

I didn't know. I admitted feeling more trepidation about the Hail Mary defense theory that the Morrison family and my father, with his role on the Board of Supervisors, had conspired to rid the county of Scotty and Josh. Presenting such an argument in court would make me public enemy number one. My father, I'm sure, would no longer speak to me. John always preached emotional dispassion as a fundamental tenant of defense-attorney work, and I didn't disagree, but sometimes it's better to believe your client, even if he's lying, and even if you're both wrong.

I asked Rick about the alibis. Where had members of the Morrison family been on the night of Josh's disappearance? Rick gave me a stern look of disapproval, as though he weren't going to tell me.

"Just because he lied to his parents doesn't mean we should stop investigating the case," I said. "I still want to know."

Rick frowned. "Fine," he said. He looked down at a sheet of notes on his lap. "The weekend of March 12, Ralph Morrison and Sue were out of town. Cole Morrison and his family were with them. I had multiple independent parties place them at the family cabin on the shores of Lake Almanor. That's over seventy miles away."

I nodded.

"They had a quiet night with family, and that checked out."

"What about Paul?" I asked.

"He wouldn't speak to me."

"Could you get anyone to place him?"

"No."

That's why Rick didn't want to tell me the alibis. Paul Morrison didn't have one.

* * *

When I visited Scotty, he acted as though lying to me about his relationship with his parents was no big deal. We were in the interview room of the jail with the fluorescent light beaming down on us, and his placid expression never changed. As I recounted his mother's version of events, he sat calmly with his hands folded, wearing the same hangdog expression he always had. He just sat and listened as I recounted what Eileen had told me—about the drugs, about kicking him out, and about the lying.

"That's right," he said. "She's right."

I threw up my hands. "And you didn't think to mention

this to me?"

"What difference does it make?"

"What difference? Well, how about, for one, I'm your attorney. I told you to tell me the truth, and you didn't. That should count for something."

"All right. I'm sorry," he said.

"Anything else you wanna come clean about?"

"No."

"Well, how am I supposed to take this? You lying to me like that?"

"First of all, I didn't lie. And second, it doesn't mean I did what they say I did."

He was technically right, but it wasn't good enough. I looked into his eyes, searching for a hint of truth. He looked back at me with disdain. "Think of the most shameful thing you've ever done," he said. "Do you tell everyone about it right away? Do you always tell it exactly how it is?"

No. I didn't. I hadn't told anyone about why I'd lost my job with the navy. Not my family, not my friends, and certainly no one from Chico. The only people who knew were the dark-haired beauty who had ruined my career, my commanding officer, and my executive officer, who had decided I should resign. I didn't know what else to say, and I started to pack my things.

"Think about whether or not you want to testify." I got up. "On Monday we start jury selection."

Maybe it didn't matter if Scotty was lying. Maybe it never really mattered. I remembered John's words. In the end, I had my truth, and Scotty had his. Another truth, and the only truth that mattered, was what the twelve members of the jury believed after the trial of *The People of Butte County v. Scotty Watts*. That was the truth that mattered for Scotty's guilt or innocence. The real truth, what had actually happened that night, wouldn't come out until much later.

THIRTY-SEVEN

"Voir dire": the Latin name for the process where attorneys from both sides question those poor, miserable members of the community who've been called to jury duty. During and after the questioning, the attorneys argue about which good citizens are best suited to deliver an unbiased and fair verdict.

An entire cottage industry thrives on the commonly accepted belief that cases are won or lost in jury selection. Scientists, psychologists, mind readers, hypnotists—everyone short of voodoo artists claim to possess the formula for selecting a winning jury. Countless research articles, treatises, and books are devoted to voir dire. John and I both believed that most of this paid advice was based on pseudo-science garbage since no one is a mind reader and it's impossible to determine what a prospective juror is thinking. But John and I were also among those who believed that selecting a favorable jury was crucial to success at trial. In reconciling the two, we landed on resignation. Of all the fancy mind-reading techniques or mathematical formulas used to select the perfect jury, there was one overlooked factor that was more important than anything else, and the one thing entirely beyond anyone's control: luck. In jury selection, you just have to get lucky.

John used to say that jury pools in Butte County were split

into two camps: 1) the dumb and uninformed and 2) those with hardened opinions who wouldn't change their minds even if offered duffel bags of cash to do so.

"Most people have their minds made up, and they don't want anyone to change it," John would say. "It's the same dig-your-heels-in approach to politics. People believe what they want to believe." John could be downright derisive of the common citizen, saying things like "Selecting a jury is like planning a cocktail party you'd never want to attend. You need to pick jury members that are boring, uniformed, and easily persuaded. You want them to have malleable minds willing to bend and fit the narrative you choose. You want the people that cry in movies and vote for politicians because their rhetoric invokes passion and enthusiasm, not because it makes any sense."

"That doesn't exactly narrow it down," I'd tell him, knowing he'd take the bait.

"Why do you think jury selection is so hard?" he'd say.

* * *

The morning of the first day of Scotty's trial, I skipped breakfast and took Arthur for a long walk. My brain buzzed with a restless energy. My hands were cold and clammy as I drove to the courthouse. John rode in the passenger's seat, and we went over the jury-selection theories we'd been over a hundred times. Jury selection wasn't all luck, after all, and doing the best I could for Scotty meant eliminating the worst of the bad jurors—the most prejudiced, the most law-and-order focused, the most prosecution-leaning.

When we arrived, I went to see Scotty in the holding cell adjacent to the courtroom. I jostled my way through the door, juggling my briefcase with the suit I'd rented for Scotty to wear during the trial. I passed him the hanger of clothes. "Should fit all right," I said. "You can change into it before we go inside."

He nodded. "Thanks."

John leaned against the wall in the corner of the room,

examining his cuticles. There was a long tense moment of silence before I spoke again. The room buzzed with electricity. Perhaps it was Scotty's pathetic hangdog expression or the pit in my stomach I got when considering our chances, but I felt like I was marching him to the electric chair. Suddenly I wanted to stop the whole process. I wanted to say something or, better yet, do something, so I did. The words just tumbled out.

"It's not too late to plea," I said. I didn't know if it would actually be possible, but I panicked.

"Are you serious?" he said.

"I just want to remind you that you can change your mind. It would probably require pleading guilty to first-degree, but we could negotiate a lower sentence, and you wouldn't face life without the possibility of parole."

John couldn't help but chime in. "No! Why would you say that?" He threw up his arms. "It's the eve of the trial! Don't tell him that! What are you doing?"

I waved him off like he was an annoying insect circling my head.

Scotty was calm. He shook his head. "No. I don't want to plea."

"Okay. Have you thought any more about whether or not you want to testify?" I asked him.

"I don't know."

"Okay."

"What do you think?"

"I don't know," I said.

We sat in silence for another long moment until there was no more time to kill. We didn't have to decide on Scotty testifying until the prosecution rested its case. We could punt the issue once again and decide later. Shelly popped her head in the room and told me they were ready.

* * *

Before walking into Courtroom 4 of the Butte County

Courthouse, I was conflicted and nervous. I was conflicted to represent Scotty knowing that he'd lied. Eileen Watts's visit to my house had shaken me. I was nervous because in the seven months since Scotty's arrest, I'd added only two more trials to my résumé. Despite all my preparation; the pretrial witness interviews with experts, law enforcement, and Eleanor Jackson; the countless visits to the scene; the brainstorming of theories; and the meeting with Eileen and Ray, I had a sick feeling in my stomach that going to trial was a huge mistake. Perhaps I hadn't reached out to Watermelon Belly enough. Maybe I hadn't followed the right theories of the case. Maybe I'd done something wrong that I hadn't even considered. This would be my first murder trial, and I felt unprepared.

It was 8:30 a.m. on Monday, October 17, 2016. Courtroom 4 was a sea of hungry, tired, glassy-eyed Butte County residents. There were men in camouflage baseball hats, plaid shirts, and Wrangler jeans with big silver belt buckles. Men in khaki pants with plain, ill-fitting dress shirts. Women in plain jeans or workout clothes, their hair in ponytails. A woman with gray hair that looked to be made of straw wore a dark-blue print T-shirt with a picture of wolves howling at the moon. These were my eligible attendees for the cocktail party. My job was to pick the most boring and dumbest of them all. The room was still. I heard a few nervous murmurs. The creaking of wood from someone shifting in their seat. A cough. A sniffle.

John and I sat at counsel's table. The bailiff ushered Scotty in. I was relieved to see that the suit fit okay, and other than his slightly crooked tie, he looked like a man heading into a job interview. Emma and a young male prosecutor I'd never seen before sat across the aisle.

I glanced behind us to the gallery. Mike Sullivan sat in the back. Beat reporters I recognized from the Sacramento Bee and Orange County news outlets had laptops propped open and notepads at the ready. The bailiff called out, "All rise." We all stood, and out walked Judge Leonard Waitskin.

Judge Waitskin looked like the top hat–wearing Monopoly

man, complete with white hair, a shiny bald head, and spectacles. His inflectionless delivery had no effect on the preliminary hearing or pretrial motion hearings, but knowing he'd be the judge for Scotty's trial had worried me, if only because his voice could be an effective lullaby for a meth addict at a rave party. He was meticulous, disciplined, and fit. He was legendary for his daily 5:00 a.m. four-mile runs through Bidwell Park. Attorneys would joke that you could see his pale thin bony legs taking tiny strides for miles. If there was a rule written down somewhere, Judge Waitskin would follow it. He had devoted his entire life to serving on the bench, and he was perhaps the most rule-following dullard I'd ever known.

"Good morning, ladies and gentlemen. I am Judge Waitskin, and I will be presiding over this matter. I want to welcome you to jury service. Participation as a juror is the most critical, significant hands-on experience in our democracy." An elderly man in the third row was fast asleep. His rumbling snores grew louder with each breath. Judge Waitskin went on, oblivious. "Thomas Jefferson thought it was more significant than the right to vote. It has been described as being the only public service that still has the power to elevate an ordinary citizen. It requires the highest level of human natures, the part that is thoughtful, intelligent, empathetic, and fair. It lets us step out of our everyday lives to listen to the facts; to refuse to judge by appearance, charm, or influence; and to understand the rules and apply them fairly."

Judge Waitskin pushed his spectacles down his nose and peered over them, pausing here for dramatic emphasis. "Ladies and gentlemen," he said, "you are the justice system."

Oh God, I thought. Here we go.

He introduced the court staff: his bailiff, the court clerk, and the court reporter, who frantically tapped away on the stenotype machine in front of her. Waitskin droned on, explaining the jury-selection process until finally he filled the jury box with eighteen prospective jurors.

Voir dire began with the judge's standard nine questions. Things like "How long have you lived in the community?"

"What is your occupation?" "Do you know anyone involved in the case?" "Have you ever served on a jury before?" "Have you or a close family member ever been convicted of a crime?" "Do you or a close family member work in law enforcement?" "Do you understand the burden of proof in a criminal case?"

Emma and I took turns volleying off amplifying questions about people's experiences with law enforcement, their position on marijuana use, their obedience to the judge's instructions regarding the law. Slowly and methodically Emma and I whittled the pool down one by one. The woman with the gray straw hair and the wolf shirt answered the questions in a low, timid murmur. I wanted her on the panel because she had the unkempt appearance of a flower child from the '60s.

A squat Hispanic man with tanned, leathery skin gave terse, boring answers. A friendly Asian American man who worked as an accountant and had lived in Chico for fifteen years seemed eminently reasonable. I thought he might be neutral.

I was out of preemptory challenges when a man in Wrangler jeans and a silver belt buckle was called up to the jury box.

"No farmers," John whispered in my ear.

"Yes, John. I know," I whispered back.

"Who are you talking to?" Scotty asked.

"No one," I said.

The man on the panel could have been Paul Morrison's brother. He looked like the man I'd seen riding atop the combine on my way to the courthouse. He had high cheekbones and narrow eyes.

I stood up to question Belt Buckle.

* * *

By late afternoon, the cast of characters was complete. We had our jury panel. Wolf Shirt; Asian Accountant; Leather Skin; and despite everything I could do to argue his prejudice, or incompetence, or bias, Judge Waitskin would not let me remove Belt Buckle. We had our twelve jurors. Our alternates were selected, and the rest of the crowd was sent home. By the time it was over, my white dress shirt was damp with sweat. My hands didn't stop shaking until long after I arrived home. The strange, silent relationship you have with jurors over the course of a trial is like a romantic infatuation. You want their approval, their acceptance, and ultimately their favor, but from a distance, they remain a mystery. We had our twelve jurors. We went home for the day, and Scotty's trial would start the next day.

THIRTY-EIGHT

That night, Arthur and I set out for a run just as dusk fell. The last crescent of the sun peered over the amber-colored hills of Butte County. Heading east on Honey Run Road, the road meandered along parallel to Butte Creek. We ran away from town, and just as we turned out of the driveway, I saw John standing across the street on the porch of a neighbor's house, wearing that stupid three-piece suit he never took off. He waved and smiled at me. *What the hell is he doing?* I thought.

"The bandanna!" he shouted.

Yes, I know, John. The bandanna. We'll put it in evidence. I'll make the argument. The bandanna is important. I ran on, feeling the rhythmic muscular strain with each step. The glassy obsidian water babbled next to us. We ran for a half mile until I saw John again, standing by the water's edge to my right.

"The water," he said.

All right. The water. Sure. Scotty and Josh, they angered the Morrisons. Scotty was framed. I get it. Thanks, John. I don't need to go over basic facts. I need to clear my head.

I kept running. The sun ducked behind the hills. Its afterglow illuminated everything in an orange shade. I listened to the rhythm of my breath. Arthur ran happily alongside me, panting. Sweat formed on my brow. John appeared across the street. He stood upright like a soldier on the edge of the road. He smiled and waved. He looked like he was mocking me. His mouth stayed frozen in a big condescending smile. I heard his voice say, "The farmers," but his mouth didn't move. My skin crawled. He just kept smiling and waving the whole time, but I heard his voice. The farmers. He'd definitely said, "The farmers," but he hadn't actually spoken the words.

Yes, John. The farmers. I get it. That's the theory of the case. Jesus. Leave me alone. I'll see you tomorrow.

The color disappeared from the sky and cast a metallic glow over everything. The night air turned frigid. Arthur and I arrived at Honey Run Bridge, an old wooden covered bridge running across Butte Creek. As we ran by the entrance, I saw the silhouette shadow of a man shrouded under the bridge's wood frame. I made out the faint shine of brown leather dress shoes and the outline of wavy dark hair. John stepped into the light. His lips were pursed like a father expressing disappointment. "The lot," I heard him say as we passed, but his lips didn't move. He just stared, an icy expression on his face. Did he say that? Or did I hear it?

"The lot," I heard his voice say again, but his face stayed frozen. I slowed my pace a little as the disbelief registered and then quickened it out of fear. Guided only by moonlight, objects were cast in a ghastly shade of gray now. I jogged on, trying to determine if any of this was real.

I think I should stop talking to John, I decided. But he was helpful. I had to talk to someone. No. He is a distraction. I shouldn't speak to him anymore.

I continued on but couldn't regain my rhythm. I jogged. I stopped. I jogged. I stopped. I jogged until finally I thought, Screw this. That's enough exercise. I'd been running for a good half hour away from town. I'm going home. I turned around.

When I turned back toward home, I shouted in horror. John's face was inches from mine. His grotesque smile stretched unnaturally wide, exposing a mouth of hundreds of teeth. I brushed past him as quickly as I could, leaving him standing there with unblinking eyes frozen in a thousand-yard stare, smiling at nothing. "Fuck you!" I shouted behind me. Why did he have to scare me like that?

We jogged on. Arthur looked up at me while running.

"What's wrong?" Arthur asked.

"Nothing," I said.

My muscles were tired. My lungs ached. I ran back along the road toward home.

A quiet stillness came over the night. It was dark now. In the distance I saw a figure standing in the middle of the road. We got closer. John, the frozen statue with his thousand-yard stare again. "The wind," he said. I ran closer to where he stood in the street.

"Get out of the street," I said to him. As I got closer, his eyes started to bulge out of his skull. His eyelids stretched wider and wider. Retina veins streaked red across the pure white of his eyeball. He didn't blink or flinch. My heart pounded in my chest. "The rain," I heard him say. Yes. Okay. The bandanna, the water, the farmers, the lot, the wind, the rain. I get it. Jesus Christ, John. You're scaring me.

"We're almost there," I said to Arthur. He panted and ran with me.

"The tracks," I heard John's voice echo in my head. I swiveled my head to locate him as I ran. There was only darkness. "The tracks," his voice said again. The night was black. I heard Arthur's breathing but could determine only his outline in the night. His coat was an even darker shade of night. I ran faster through the darkness, sprinting for home.

"Kelly," I heard John's voice say. I swiveled my head again, but he was nowhere to be found. Suddenly John repeated all the words at once, firing them off in rapid succession: "The bandanna, the water, the farmers, the lot, the wind, the rain, the tracks. Kelly."

I sprinted faster through the darkness. I heard John's voice say again, "The bandanna, the water, the farmers, the lot, the wind, the rain, the tracks. Kelly."

I could hear Arthur panting hard, straining to keep up. I hoped we were close to home. I saw my mailbox through the darkness. Faint. John's voice echoed in my head again, "The bandanna, the water, the farmers, the lot, the wind, the rain, the tracks. Kelly."

"Fuck you! Go away!" I yelled.

He repeated again, faster and faster, "The bandanna, the water, the farmers, the lot, the wind, the rain, the tracks. Kelly. The bandanna, the water, the farmers, the lot, the wind, the rain, the tracks. Kelly."

I was at a dead sprint now. My lungs burned. I saw home. It was there in the distance. Closer now.

The bandanna, the water, the farmers, the lot, the wind, the rain, the tracks. Kelly.

"Goddamn it! Shut up!" I shouted. I turned the corner into my driveway. I saw a figure standing on my front steps, illuminated only by porchlight. I had a momentary panic that it was John again, but I saw the Tesla parked in the driveway. Will. It's Will. Thank God. He was holding a bottle of whiskey. Thank God. Anyone but John.

"I heard your trial starts tomorrow. Figured you could use a drink."

I bent down and breathed in the cold night air. I had been sprinting, I realized. I looked up at Will and said hello.

"What the hell are you yelling about?" he asked.

"Nothing," I said.

"Geez, you really could use a drink," he said. "Are you all right? You're pale as hell."

"Yeah. Fine," I said. "Just going for a run."

* * *

I filled up Arthur's water bowl for him and took a long hot shower. Will sat on the couch sipping a Sierra Nevada Pale Ale. We watched some sports and talked about the events of the day. We talked about the trial, and I admitted to him how nervous I was for it all. He reminded me that Scotty was guilty, so it wasn't going to be my fault if I lost the case. It was Scotty's fault for not taking the deal.

Later that night as I lay in bed, a vision of John's grotesque smile and bugged-out eyes came back to me. His voice in my head started echoing once again.

The bandanna, the water, the farmers, the lot, the wind, the rain, the tracks. Kelly. Why is he harassing me? What is the point of all this? But I couldn't fall asleep. I kept thinking about those words. Something was bothering me about them since all the words made sense—all the words except one.

The bandanna—the third blood type found on the bandanna, proving there was someone else involved.

The water—Morrison Family Farms and the local farmers, worried that Scotty and Josh had been using water they weren't entitled to.

The farmers—the people with the motive to get rid of Scotty and Josh.

The lot—the burned-down house next door to Scotty's cabin.

The wind—howling so hard that night that Scotty would've barely been able to hear himself think.

The rain—falling just enough earlier that day to have created mud.

The tracks—the tire tracks proving someone else was there.

It all made sense. Each word had its place in the narrative. Each word except one. A name: Kelly. What did Kelly have to do with this? Where did she fit?

THIRTY-NINE

"Home is where the heart is."

"There's no place like home."

"Home is the place where, when you have to go there, they have to take you in."

* * *

Some people never leave their hometowns. They reside in one place their entire lives, and they never feel bitter, stifled, resentful, or scornful toward the place that raised them. They implicitly stamp their approval for that place by never leaving, and staying home is their pronouncement that "right here is *good enough*." I don't know that affinity because I've never experienced it. That lack of feeling leaves me with a sense of guilt since I know deep down that Chico is unworthy of my disdain.

There's a lot of proverbial phrases about home, but the line from Robert Frost's poem "The Death of the Hired Man" is the best: "Home is the place where, when you go there, they have to take you in." The poem is about a physically injured man who returns to a farm to ask for his job back even though he could have called on his wealthy brother. The husband and wife owners of the farm debate what they should do since the man left them during a time of great need. The problem is solved, so to speak, when the man dies.

I've been thinking a lot about that poem lately. Specifically the relationship between home and my present state of happiness. If home is the place where you can always return with the knowledge that you'll be cared for and loved, that place should make you happy. But to find happiness, the feeling of acceptance must be reciprocated. I never felt like Chico was *good enough*, and maybe that's because I never thought I was good enough either. Happiness, it seems, is regarding something important in life that's willing to take you in, whether it does so with indifference, love, passion, or strife, and finding comfort in the fact that it is *good enough*. So what if the people take you in but you're still unhappy? What then?

* * *

Judge Waitskin spent all morning lulling the jury to sleep with jury instructions. He was almost finished when I glanced to the back of the room and picked out John, who had a smug smile on his face. Fine by me that he stayed back there since I didn't much want him around anyway, given the events of last night. But I did want to ask him about Kelly. So when Judge Waitskin finished reading the jury instructions and court adjourned for a lunch break, I decided to seek him out. The bailiff called out, "All rise!" Judge Waitskin disappeared into his chambers, and members of the gallery filed out. I gathered my papers and jammed them into my briefcase. I pushed through the sea of people, but by the time I exited, John was halfway down the hallway on his way to the exit. I jogged through the hallway after him, weaving through members of the gallery and other attorneys.

"John!" I called out.

He looked back and picked up his pace. I ran faster.

"John! Stop!"

I was closing on him fast when he turned sharply to the

right and disappeared into the men's bathroom. The door swung back in my face when I followed him inside. But he was gone. I was alone with vacant urinals, empty sinks, and the antiseptic smell of bleach. I heard a toilet flush and the rustling of trousers. A bailiff emerged out of the nearest stall, adjusting his pants under the weight of his service weapon.

"Howdy," he said.

I nodded back. He eyed me in the mirror while he washed his hands. I looked under the stalls. Nothing. I stood in the middle of the bathroom. The bailiff finished drying his hands and asked, "Looking for someone?"

"Uh…no."

The bathroom door swung open. I spun around half expecting to see John's face, but a young attorney walked in and gave me a strange look on his way to the urinal.

"Excuse me," I said and walked out.

Rick was waiting there.

"Hey, are you all right?" he asked. "Who're you looking for?"

"Yeah, I'm fine," I told him. "No one."

"Who's John?"

"Never mind. I thought I saw an old friend. I guess I didn't."

"All right," Rick said. "You ready for your opening?"

"Yeah," I said and hurried off to find a quiet place to eat lunch.

* * *

Judge Waitskin addressed the court. "At this time, the lawyers will be permitted to make an opening statement if they choose to do so. An opening statement is not evidence. Neither is it an argument. Counsel are not permitted to argue the case at this point in the proceedings. An opening statement is simply an outline by Counsel of what he or she believes or expects the evidence will show in this trial. Its sole purpose is to assist you in understanding the case as it is presented to you."

"Counsel?" he said, looking at Emma.

"Yes, Your Honor," she said. She rose from her chair and walked to the center of the courtroom, facing the jury. It was a story I knew by heart now, but Wolf Shirt, Asian Accountant, Leather Skin, Belt Buckle, and the rest of the jurors were all hearing it for the first time. It was the first narrative they'd get about the case.

Emma laid out the facts.

"On the evening of Saturday, March 12, a twenty-four-year-old young man named Josh Anderson got in his white Nissan Titan truck and drove from his home in Chico to a cabin in Forest Ranch...

"...the cabin belonged to Mr. Watts, the defendant in this case...

"...they were business partners...

"...a meeting had been set...

"...agreed between seven thirty and eight p.m....

"...Josh arrived at the cabin...

"...you'll hear from a woman named Eleanor Jackson...

"...Ms. Jackson saw Josh's white Nissan Titan truck pull up...

"...saw Josh get out...

"...over the next three hours...

"...horrific murder..."

I saw Wolf Shirt squirm in her chair.

"...disposes of the body..."

Asian Accountant grimaced.

"...sheriff's deputies arrive on scene...

"...early-morning hours of March 13...

"...pool of blood..."

Belt Buckle was stoic.

Emma walked over and stood in front of our table. She pointed her finger at Scotty, jabbing it at him as she spoke. "...Deputy Haskins saw the defendant frantically wiping up that pool of blood...

"...forensic scientist will explain that the blood on the floor belonged to Josh Anderson…

"…a doctor will testify that the amount of blood found, if lost by a person of Josh Anderson's height, weight, and age, would almost certainly result in his death…"

Then Emma went through the investigative steps, listing off the pieces of circumstantial evidence one by one, explaining each of them to the jury.

"…knife on the kitchen counter with Josh Anderson's blood on the blade…

"…truck found outside the defendant's home…

"…defendant's fingerprints on the knife handle…

"…body is still missing to this day…"

I heard a woman's whimpering cry from the gallery. I didn't need to turn around to know that it was Josh Anderson's mother. Scotty's trial was a daily reminder that her son's body was decomposing in the woods somewhere. From the jury box, Wolf Shirt cast a sideways glance in her direction. Emma paused while Mrs. Anderson's whimper echoed off the courtroom walls. Tears flowed down her cheeks. Scotty buried his head in his hands. I nudged him, reminding him to look up with confidence. "Look at nothing in particular," I'd told him. "Don't make expressions," I'd said.

Emma concluded her opening statement. "Ladies and gentlemen," she said, "all this evidence will lead you to only one reasonable conclusion: that the defendant is guilty of murder in the first degree."

Judge Waitskin looked over at me. "Defense?"

I felt a bead of sweat trickle down my chest. My heart beat like a bass drum against my chest.

"Defense?" Judge Waitskin asked again. I felt the eyes of the courtroom on me. I looked helplessly across the aisle at Emma. Scotty tapped my arm.

"Defense. Your opening statement?" Judge Waitskin said.

I took one final glance at my notes laid out on the table and rose out of my chair.

"Yes, Your Honor."

FORTY

"How can you convict someone of murder when there is no victim?" I asked. "The prosecutor said it herself: 'Josh Anderson's body is still missing to this day.' The evidence will show in this case that there is no proof Mr. Anderson is actually dead. There is no victim in this case." I pointed to the big wooden doors at the back of the courtroom. "Josh Anderson could walk right through that door at any moment. And yet the government wants to send my client to jail for the rest of his adult life."

I could hear the news reporters' pens scribbling on their notepads in the back of the room, and I could feel their eyes on me. I described a very different version of what had happened on March 12, one with Scotty and Kelly as the idyllic young couple living in the woods together, enjoying a pleasant Saturday in early March only to have it end in horror.

"...Scotty Watts and his girlfriend, Kelly, rose out of bed midmorning...

"...they took their dog for a walk...

"...it started raining, and they go inside. They work on projects in the garage...

"...dusk falls...

"...Kelly leaves for work...

"...Scotty goes back to the garage to finish up his project...

"...two hours later, he sits down for a bowl of cereal...

"...howling wind...

"...waits for his scheduled meeting with Josh Anderson, his business partner...

"...last thing he remembers is taking a bite of cereal...

"...mind goes blank...

"...never sees Josh Anderson that night...

"...can't remember..."

I moved on to the investigative flaws of the case.

"...no toxicology on the bowl of cereal...

"...waited two days for toxicology on Scotty Watts...

"...no explanation for this...

"...detectives focus on only one suspect..."

Wolf Shirt rolled her eyes. Belt Buckle glared at me.

"...medical experts will testify about something called antegrade amnesia...

"...Eleanor Jackson sees Josh Anderson go inside, but then she goes to bed...

"...doesn't see a third person arrive because she falls asleep...

"...report of shots fired, but the guns in the house were not fired...

"...no gun is found...

"...Eleanor Jackson hears nothing...

"...there are no other witnesses...

"...we'll never know what happened that night...

"...many other explanations...

"...lots of doubt...

"...focus on the standard of proof..."

As I said these words, I doubted my own theory of the case. Nothing I said rang true in my own mind. *It is probably just my own self-doubt,* I told myself. *Keep going.* The jurors' expressions varied between skepticism and contempt, but I had no choice but to plod ahead. I focused on the government's burden of proof, repeating over and over the importance of the jurors adhering to it. "Innocent until proven guilty," I said over and over.

"…my client was not the most popular guy in town, and neither was Josh Anderson…

"…a bloody bandanna found in the woods…

"…a third blood type on that bandanna…

"…you will find that there's just more-than-reasonable doubt in this case…

"…remember the standard…

"…at the end of this trial, after considering all the evidence in this case, I ask that you return a verdict of not guilty."

I looked to the back of the room. John leaned against a pillar. My opening statement had passed like a dream. I immediately forgot anything I had said beyond those few bullet points. It was as though I'd blacked out during it and woke up during the next phase of the trial.

* * *

Emma called Deputy Haskins to the stand, a fresh-faced deputy with seven years' experience in the Butte County Sheriff's Department. He was thirty-three years old, but as the bailiff swore him in, he looked like he was about twelve.

He told the jury about how he had been on patrol the night of March 12, 2016. "Responsible for the northeast quadrant of Butte County," he said. Sometime after midnight, he and his partner, Deputy Alejandro Sanchez, had responded to a call of shots fired. They arrived at Scotty's cabin. The front door was partially open. He called out to determine who was inside. Hearing nothing, he called out again. No answer. He drew his service weapon and moved to the front door. He pushed it open.

"What did you see when you pushed the door open?" Emma asked.

Haskins fidgeted in his seat. "Mr. Watts was on his hands and knees, kneeling in a pool of blood. Covered in it. He was scrubbing really fast in circles, around and around, with a big wad of paper towels in his hand."

Wolf Shirt raised her eyebrows. Belt Buckle looked bored. Asian Accountant looked at the ground. *What are they thinking?* I wondered.

Emma asked Haskins to identify exactly who the man was he had seen that day, and he unfurled a long slender bony finger and pointed it straight out at Scotty. The eyes of the court turned to him.

"Let the record reflect that Deputy Haskins has identified the defendant," Emma said.

"The record will so reflect," Judge Waitskin said.

"How would you characterize his expression?" Emma asked.

"He was pretty...like...panicked...frantic."

I objected on grounds of speculation, knowing I would lose it. But I hoped the objection would discredit Haskins's testimony in the jury's mind, if only just a little. They wouldn't know why I was objecting or if, in fact, Emma's questioning was improper. Waitskin overruled it, and Emma continued on. "What happened next?"

"The defendant didn't see us at first. I think a board creaked or something, and he looked up. There was a long moment where nobody said anything, and we all just looked at each other. I was too shocked to say anything. I had my weapon drawn, and it was trained on him, but I didn't know what to do. There was blood everywhere."

"Not the typical call for your patrol in Butte County?"

"Right."

"You were scared?"

"Yeah."

Emma asked him what happened next.

"Sanchez told Mr. Watts to put his hands up."

"Did he?" Emma asked.

"He did. He put them up slowly."

Haskins had asked Scotty if there was anyone else in the house. They asked where all the blood had come from. Scotty wasn't read his Miranda rights until much later, and while I considered trying to exclude these statements, I decided against it since, from the very beginning, Scotty's account of what had happened was consistent. He either said he didn't know what had happened or didn't remember. The more of that on the record, the more likely the jury was to believe him.

"Then we called for backup," Haskins said.

Detective Nate Cruz had arrived on scene. At dawn Haskins was told to go home and get some rest. His direct examination was over. Emma sat, and it was my turn. I grabbed a notepad off counsel's table and strode toward the witness stand firing off questions.

"You responded to a shots-fired call, correct?"

"Yes."

"But you didn't actually hear shots fired, did you?" I asked.

"No."

"That information came from dispatch, correct?"

"Yes."

"No other witnesses heard gunshots?"

"No."

"No neighbors heard shots?"

"No."

"No other officers?"

"No."

"Let's shift gears. You testified that when you saw Mr. Watts kneeling in the pool of blood, he looked panicked, correct?" I asked Haskins.

"Yes."

"You said he looked frantic?"

"Yes."

"But you didn't know what he was actually thinking, did you?"

"No."

"Do you think it's possible he was also confused?"

"No."

The number-one rule of cross-examining a witness is to never ask a question you don't know the answer to, and I'd just violated it. My face got hot, and my neck tie seemed to tighten. I pulled at the knot a little to loosen it, fumbling with my notebook.

"Really? You don't think it's possible Mr. Watts was confused?"

"No."

"Why is that?" I was compounding the problem. My vision blurred and shook. Suddenly I couldn't think.

"Because he didn't look confused. He looked frantic," Haskins said.

"Okay. Assuming he was frantic, would you agree that if you unexpectedly lost consciousness in the middle of eating dinner and woke up in a pool of blood hours later, your expression might also be described as frantic?"

"I suppose."

"Would you agree that what looks like panic to you might look different to someone else?"

"Maybe. But he looked panicked to me."

I was making it worse.

"And a reasonable reaction would be to clean up the mess, thinking that it's your own blood you've woken up in?"

"I suppose so," Haskins said, "but I would have called the police or the hospital."

My mind went blank. Haskins, the very first witness of the trial, was making me look like an idiot. I limped through the remainder of the cross-examination, landing a few more light blows, but I felt as dumb and naïve as at my first day of law school. I had no more questions. *That didn't go well*, I thought after confirming with Judge Waitskin that my questioning of the young deputy was over. As I retook my seat, the courtroom was silent.

Then I heard a loud clap from the back of the room. Pause. Then another. Pause. Then another. Clap...clap...clap, with long beats in between. It was John, clapping slowly with a stupid smirk on his face. *Fuck you, John,* I thought.

* * *

From the time eighty-five-year-old Eleanor Jackson was

called to the stand to when she was actually sworn in and seated, it must have been two or three minutes. She shuffled down the aisle, nudged open the knee-high door leading to the well of the courtroom, and gingerly worked her arthritic frame up the small wooden steps before taking a seat. She wore a summer dress and walked with a wooden cane but used it only to steady her balance. For eighty-five years old, she was still the picture of health.

Emma and Ms. Jackson sounded like old friends discussing a fond memory, smiling sweetly at each other with each question and answer. Ms. Jackson provided the jury with some background about herself. She was from Georgia and had lived in Forest Ranch for "almost two decades now." Then Emma walked her through all the standard health-competency questions she needed to ask to establish that Ms. Jackson's testimony was reliable. Her vision was "great," her hearing was "very good with the hearing aids in," and her overall health was "excellent for someone her age."

Ms. Jackson had seen Josh's truck just before dusk. Yes, she was sure it was Josh's truck since she'd seen it before, many times. He'd have plants or gardening tools in the back of the truck. That night he was alone. He almost always came alone. No, she hadn't seen anyone else with him. Sure, there could have been someone else in the car, "but I doubt it," she said.

"Why is that?" Emma asked.

"Because he used that little clicker to lock his car. I don't think he would've locked someone inside," she said with a laugh. Then she had gone to bed. It was around eight o'clock.

My turn for cross-examination arrived. First, I showed her a blown-up picture Rick had taken while standing on her porch looking toward Scotty's cabin. She agreed that the trees partially obscured her view. She admitted that she couldn't see Scotty's driveway perfectly. Then I reminded her that since it was dusk when Josh had supposedly arrived, the lighting wasn't great. She agreed.

I asked clarifying questions.

"Exactly how long after the person you believe was Josh

Anderson went inside the cabin did you go to bed?"

"Oh, almost immediately," she said.

"Is it possible that the person getting out of the white truck wasn't Josh Anderson?"

"I suppose anything is possible, but I'm quite confident, honey."

It was at about this moment that my mind started to wander. I started daydreaming about that night, as though all this testimony was transporting me to the scene of it all. My imagination took over.

"A third person could have been inside prior to you seeing that white truck pull up?" I asked Ms. Jackson. I thought about the vacant lot next door to Scotty's. I wished I'd found those tire tracks sooner.

"I didn't see anyone. But that's possible."

I imagined the third person inside the house. Paul Morrison? Ralph? Someone else?

"You don't know what happened in that cabin once that person went inside?" I asked.

"No," she said.

I imagined Josh walking through the door and seeing a nameless, faceless person standing in the darkness of Scotty's kitchen.

"Did you hear any screaming from inside the cabin?"

"No."

Scotty doesn't remember anything, so the third person must have already been there. Right?

"Calling for help?"

"No."

Why not?

"Did you hear the sound of a gunshot?"

"No."

"At any point in the evening?"

"No."

I imagined Josh looking down at Scotty, lying unconscious on his kitchen floor.

I looked to the back of the courtroom for John but

couldn't find him. I suddenly remembered the book he had given me. *The Conscience of a Lawyer.* I had a strange, detached sensation that I should look at it again. Why had I thought about the book at that moment?

The rest of the cross-examination is blurry, and soon I heard Judge Waitskin's voice. "Counsel?" he said. He had been trying to get my attention. I wondered for how long. "Do you have any further questions?"

I snapped to. I picked up my notebook and started walking back toward counsel's table.

"No, Your Honor," I said. "No further questions."

FORTY-ONE

Getting accused of a crime you didn't commit is a palpable fear that everyone can relate to. You're in the wrong place at the wrong time, and you go from innocent to being in grave danger based solely on bad luck. The problem with being a defense attorney is that everyone proclaims their innocence. Even when an overwhelming mountain of evidence supports a client's guilt, the client will complain that they didn't do anything wrong. There must have been some mistake. Or even if they admit to the underlying crime, something provoked them, or their life circumstances drove them to it, or they weren't given the same chances as the next guy. But feeling victimized doesn't excuse illegal conduct, and the law agrees with me. And it's easy to play the victim. Just look at me.

* * *

Eleanor Jackson's testimony was the last time I considered Scotty's guilt or innocence during the trial. I was too busy, and I didn't have time to worry about it. My personal life had also faded into the background. My father hadn't talked to me since I questioned him about the Board of Supervisors' minutes. I had decided to avoid Will's obnoxious optimism, so I wasn't speaking to him. Lacey Price had drifted from my view. After what Will had told me about her, perhaps I knew her much less than I thought. I figured I would never be able to reconcile the feeling of falling in love with how I saw her then. Too much time had passed, and too much had happened. Even Arthur got less attention. I walked and fed him each morning and each evening, but for the most part, I was alone with the demands of proving Scotty Watts's innocence. The trial marched on. Each day on my drive to the courthouse, I saw the "Justice for Josh" billboard displayed off the highway, and each day I saw an identical companion billboard beside the road near my exit. Bill Dubois was putting the pressure on. But judging from his demeanor in Courtroom 4, Sullivan didn't seem too bothered. He was in and out of the gallery to watch Emma, and I lost the pulse of how legitimate Dubois's challenge was.

Emma called Deputy Alejandro Sanchez, Haskins's partner, to the stand. He corroborated Haskins's testimony. She called Sheriff Trumble, who testified regarding his supervision over the case, including the search for Josh's body. He testified about the day I had called to notify him about the 49ers bandanna in the woods. Emma called Detective Cruz, who testified to the truck found in front of Scotty's cabin, the knife on the kitchen counter, the search for Josh's body, and his conclusion that Scotty was a murderer.

By the end of the week, Emma had started calling expert witnesses. Testimony from experts—usually medical doctors, forensic scientists, blood-spatter experts, and so on—is notorious for putting juries to sleep, and the forensic scientist, doctor, and medical examiner who testified in Scotty's trial were no different. These people testify in court frequently and are often paid handsomely. Because of their experience, they are keen to parsing language and avoiding lawyerly traps. They know better than to deal in certainties. They listen carefully to exactly what question is asked and respond with only the specificity that the answer requires. All this makes their testimony extremely boring.

A balding, spectacled forensic scientist explained how they had compared the blood found on Scotty's floor with a known DNA sample provided by Josh Anderson's family. In explaining the match, he said something like "We could determine with a 99.9 percent probability that the blood found on the floor belonged to Josh Anderson…and that is rounded to a tenth decimal since the probability is actually higher."

A matronly emergency-room doctor testified that "the established estimate of two liters of blood loss would almost certainly result in the loss of life for someone of the victim's size."

"Just to be clear," I asked her on cross-examination, "if we assume this is, in fact, Josh Anderson's blood, and if we accept that two liters of the blood mixture collected off the floor of the cabin belong to Josh Anderson, you still cannot be totally certain that two liters of blood loss would result in loss of life, correct?"

"That is correct," she said. "Almost certainly, but not definitively."

"Just to reiterate, the two liters of blood belonging to Josh Anderson is the high estimate, correct?" I asked her.

"Yes."

"So you cannot say with absolute certainty that Josh Anderson is dead, correct?"

"That's correct."

Arguing semantics with expert witnesses can often leave jury members scratching their heads.

Very little about Emma's case put me on my heels, but there was one thing. Something happened during my cross-examination of Detective Cruz. I was walking around the well of the courtroom holding the evidence bag containing the bloody San Francisco 49ers bandanna. Emma had already elicited from Detective Cruz that a third blood type had been found on it, but I wanted to highlight it for the jury.

"You just testified that a third blood type was found on this bandanna, correct?" I asked him, holding the bag up for the jury to see.

"Yes," Detective Cruz answered.

"Can you describe the findings of the blood analysis in a little more detail?"

"Sure. As I said, three DNA strains were found. One matching with a high degree of statistical accuracy to the alleged suspect, one to the victim, and one to an unidentified human person."

"That third type, it was identified as human blood?"

"Yes. Blood can be distinguished as either human or nonhuman. In other words, belonging to an animal. Diluted slightly more than the others, but this was human blood."

"I'm sorry?"

Diluted? Did he just say "diluted"?

I looked to John, who stood at his post in the back of the room. He smiled, and when he did, it infuriated me.

Detective Cruz didn't say anything.

"Diluted?" I asked the detective.

"Yes," he said. "The concentration of the third blood type was weaker than the other two. The forensic experts identified how much weaker in parts per million."

What? The third blood type was diluted? I burned with shame. *How did I not catch this before trial?*

I looked to the jury box, to Wolf Shirt, Belt Buckle, and Leather Skin. They didn't seem to think too much of it. They shifted their eyes from Detective Cruz to me and back to Detective Cruz, waiting for us. I looked to Emma. She scribbled notes, her head down. She wasn't paying attention. She must have already known. I didn't know what to ask next. I had no follow-up. I didn't even know if this fact helped or hurt the case. I couldn't think. I wanted to probe deeper but feared the uncertainty.

"Was there any indication what caused the dilution?" I asked.

"No. Water probably," Detective Cruz said. "Could be sweat. Rain. It could have been rained on. Could be a lot of things."

Suddenly, from the back of the courtroom, John shouted,

"Move on!" I paused and looked back at him. I saw rows of eyes looking up at me—blank faces, like cardboard cutouts of people, sitting in the gallery. Only John seemed to be animated. "Move on!" he shouted again.

My concentration was broken. I seethed with rage. *John, shouting things out in the middle of my cross-exam. Forget it,* I thought. Maybe John was right. Maybe this was best to ignore. Maybe it didn't matter at all.

I asked Detective Cruz about running the third blood type through the criminal databases, establishing that there were no matches.

"So the third blood type belonged to a human with no criminal record, correct?"

"That's correct."

I established that the toxicology report on Scotty had been delayed and that Detective Cruz never did one on the bowl of cereal that was left on the table. I was planting as many seeds of doubt as I could. Then I asked about the Morrisons.

"Did you interview Paul Morrison?"

I heard a dull murmur from the gallery and the scribbling of pens on notebooks.

"No."

"Why not?"

"Why would we? He wasn't a suspect."

Emma objected based on relevance. I argued that the question would lay the foundation for me to challenge motive. Waitskin overruled her objection, and I continued.

"Did you interview Ralph Morrison?"

"No."

"Were you aware that Ralph Morrison made complaints to the district attorney and to the county Board of Supervisors about Mr. Watts and Mr. Anderson's agricultural practices?"

"No. I was not aware."

I heard another murmur from the gallery.

Before I sat, I caught a glimpse of Shelly and Rick sitting in the gallery. They glared at me and then tried to hide their faces in their hands. They were ashamed, but I didn't care. I had to make the argument, for Scotty.

* * *

By the end of the week, Emma had almost rested her case, and Judge Waitskin dismissed us for the weekend.

On Saturday I went to the office to make final preparations for my witnesses and closing argument. When I arrived, the door to John's office was open, and when I peered around the corner, he was reclining in his chair reading. It was a cold October morning, yet he had the fan on. It buzzed, whirring and oscillating.

"Why is your fan on?" I asked. "It's freezing."

Keeping his eyes on the book in front of him, he flipped a page, and a pleasant smile came across his face like he'd read something especially true.

"Fine, whatever," I said. I left him alone and returned to my office.

An hour later, I darkened his doorway once again.

"How do you think the trial is going?" I asked. I was nervous. I wanted some help. I wanted someone to talk to. He looked up for a moment and smiled at me but then went immediately back to reading without acknowledging what I had said.

"Ignoring me again, huh?" I asked. He didn't respond. "God, you're an asshole sometimes."

Later that afternoon, at around four, I heard our front door chime. It was Shelly. She'd forgotten a birthday card for her daughter at the office and had come to pick it up.

"What're you doing here?" she asked. "It's Saturday."

"Just looking over a few more things before next week."

"Go home," she said. "At this point you're doing more harm than good."

"Okay," I said. I walked her to the door. When I got out to the hallway, I saw that John's door was closed. When I checked it after Shelly had gone, it was locked.

* * *

On Sunday night, Arthur and I went for a long walk. I made him dinner, and we watched *Sunday Night Football* together. I threw a tennis ball across the living room for him until finally he lay on top of it, trapping it with his paws and chewing vigorously at it. I walked over and sat on the floor next to him. I patted him on the head. "You're a good boy," I told him. "I love you."

He stopped chewing the tennis ball for a moment and looked up at me.

"I wonder what Lacey's doing?" he said.

I smiled at him and kissed him on the head. I nuzzled my face close to him. "Me too, buddy. Me too."

He went back to gutting the tennis ball with his sharp teeth.

FORTY-TWO

The next day, I had a daydream in the middle of trial, and it was so real, it felt like a memory. A Butte County sheriff's deputy was driving along Deer Creek Highway, and as he drives past Forest Ranch to the northeast edge of the county, he spots something along the road. He's so far down the highway that he's past Butte Meadows, almost to Lake Almanor. He thinks what he sees is an article of clothing or maybe just a piece of trash. Something tells him to take a look, and he parks his car and walks through a meadow to a mossy tree. When he arrives at the thing he thinks he saw, he realizes it was just the moss growing on a fallen tree. It wasn't anything at all. He looks back to his cruiser parked along the road. The cruiser is a speck in the distance. He begins to turn back, but something compels him to stop and think. Something tells him to walk farther. He doesn't know what it is, but he does. He walks deep into the forest. This time, without knowing or being able to explain why, he walks right to a spot in the woods where a red Chico State sweatshirt with holes in it has been eaten away by weather and bugs. Inside the sweatshirt is what's left of a decomposing body that has been eaten away by maggots, wolves, vultures, snakes, ants, and other forest creatures over months and months. The air has rotted the flesh. Intestines have been boiled, chilled, and fried by the elements. He turns back toward his cruiser to call dispatch. Josh Anderson has been found. And then I woke up.

* * *

"Counsel?" Judge Waitskin asked. I snapped to attention. "You may present your case." I stood up.

Rick was my first witness. We discussed all the preliminary investigative steps he'd taken in the case. How he'd reviewed Detective Cruz's report, how he spoke to Ms. Jackson and other witnesses, how he took pictures of the scene. Finally we arrived at the complaints made against Scotty and Josh. Yes, complaints had been made, he told the jury. Complaints had been made to both the Board of Supervisors and the district attorney. That's when he had met Mary Buyske, and he explained to the jury who she was. He explained what he had found from reviewing the Board of Supervisors' meeting minutes.

Yes, he was surprised that Detective Cruz did not interview any of the Morrisons, and yes, he would have interviewed them. Yes, he would have done the investigation differently.

What was his opinion on the lack of a timely toxicology report?

"It is my professional opinion that not doing the toxicology report on the defendant or the food the defendant was eating prior to losing consciousness was grossly negligent," he said.

"Could there have been a third person in the cabin that night?" I asked.

"Absolutely. There most certainly could have been a third person in Scotty Watts's cabin the night of March 12, 2016."

My father wasn't in court for any of Scotty's trial. Neither was Paul Morrison, Ralph Morrison, nor any of the other Morrisons, but I guarantee that every last one of them knew exactly what was going on.

I called Mary Buyske to the stand. She introduced herself. She told the jury how long she'd worked at the Board of

Supervisors and how long she'd lived in Chico. I asked if she was aware of Scotty applying for a zoning permit to open a business.

"Yes."

"How?"

"Through my job as the secretary for the Board of Supervisors. I remember him coming in to discuss it."

"What happened with his application?"

"He was denied."

"Do you remember how many times he applied?"

"Five."

"How do you know?"

"Because I remember."

"How confident are you?"

"Very confident. One hundred percent certain."

"Do you remember if anyone else spoke at those hearings?"

"Yes."

"Who?"

"Ralph Morrison was there."

"How many times?"

"Every time. All five of the hearings."

"Ms. Buyske," I asked, "without telling us what he said, can you tell us what Ralph Morrison's interest might have been?" Emma objected on speculation, but Judge Waitskin overruled her. I must have caught him sleeping. The objection should have been sustained. Ms. Buyske inhaled and held her breath for a moment.

"Mr. Morrison—Ralph—had filed complaints that Mr. Watts was violating county ordinance 23601.3, which is the unlawful cultivation of marijuana in excess of six plants. Mr. Morrison had a discussion with the board regarding each of those violations, requesting the board deny Mr. Watts's zoning permit and enforce the ordinance."

I'd entered the meeting minutes into evidence, and I walked Mary Buyske through her own notes. Throughout her testimony, she spoke softly and patiently waited for my questions. She looked at her lap while answering, like the truth contained in her iron-clad memory embarrassed her.

I had one final question. I knew she wouldn't be able to answer it, both because she didn't know the answer and because I wasn't allowed to ask the question. But the question had to be asked since it was also the reason her testimony was so important.

"Ms. Buyske," I said, "are you aware that Ralph Morrison's son Paul is Mr. Watts's neighbor?"

Before Ms. Buyske could answer, Emma stood and shouted the objection I had anticipated. Without waiting for a ruling, I told Judge Waitskin I'd withdraw it, and I sat.

My next witness was a gray-haired Cal Berkeley professor. She testified to antegrade amnesia, and with Rick's testimony, it implicitly suggested the possibility that Scotty had been drugged. Yet the only thing her testimony established was that there was more uncertainty. We'd never know if Scotty was drugged since the toxicology report hadn't been done in time. The substantive aspects of my case took little time and went off with little surprise.

* * *

Kelly's hair was up in a ponytail. She wore no makeup and a drab beige pantsuit. *Good,* I thought. *She followed my instructions.* I had wanted her to dress like she had an interview at a nunnery, but even that wasn't enough. All eyes fixated on her as she walked to the witness stand. No amount of dressing down could hide her radiance.

I felt a sense of shame and guilt for subjecting Kelly to Scotty's court proceedings. She cast a sideways glance at Scotty as the bailiff swore her in. Before trial, I'd told her not to look in his direction, but when she saw him sitting there, her eyes immediately started to water. She held back her tears.

She told the jury she was dating Scotty and that they had met while working at O'Haras.

"Did Scotty say why he needed to work at O'Haras?"

"He needed money to send to his mother. His father had

just been diagnosed with MS."

"How long have you been dating?"

"A little over four years."

"Have you ever seen Scotty be violent?"

She wiped a tear from her eye.

"No," she said. "He barely ever raised his voice. He was so gentle with me. And with Arthur." She fought back the tears. Arthur was their dog, she reminded the jury.

"In all the time that you've known Scotty, do you think he's capable of anything like what the prosecution is claiming happened in this case?" I asked.

Kelly wiped a faint line of bleeding mascara off her face. "Scotty is the sweetest person I've ever known. I never thought another person could be that kind and gentle until I met him. I know he's made some mistakes in his life, and some of the things he does might not be acceptable to some people, but I know he'd never harm another person. I know that for sure."

Like water breaking through a dam, suddenly Kelly couldn't hold it together. Her shoulders heaved in big sobs. She buried her head in her hands and whimpered. She plucked a couple of tissues from the tissue box in front of her and wiped her nose. For almost a full minute, we just sat with her and watched her cry. The courtroom was silent except for her loud sobs. When she looked up, her eyes were red and swollen.

Scotty looked at Kelly with a desperate helplessness. He tried to remain stoic, but his eyes were flooded with tears.

* * *

By the time I reached the end of my witness list, I wasn't sure if it was going to make a difference whether Scotty testified, and that's what I told him. It was late in the afternoon. Proceedings had concluded for the day. We sat in the private holding cell adjacent to the courtroom. Since Kelly's testimony, Scotty's face had been a ghastly shade of pale green.

"Just wish I didn't have to put her through this," he said. "Any of it."

"I know. But we needed her—"

"I know. Since my parents weren't here." He hung his head. "I know," he said again.

"Do you want to testify?" I asked him.

"I don't know," he said. "I'm not sure I care anymore. I just want this to be over."

I nodded. "I understand."

FORTY-THREE

Thursday, October 23, 2016.

When we met the next morning, Scotty decided he wanted to take the stand. He looked me in the eye and told me that he at least wanted to tell his side, even if there wasn't much to tell. I agreed. Even if he truly didn't remember, there was no harm in him repeating it for the jury to hear. He stood in the witness box and raised his right hand while the bailiff swore him in.

The facts of his testimony mattered less than whether the jury believed him.

I walked him through all the facts he and I had been over a million times, like how he had met Josh, what he and Kelly did that day, and what he thought when he woke up in a pool of blood. I had him describe the confusion he had felt. As he described that part—waking up in a pool of blood and not knowing how he got there—I glanced over at the jury box. Asian Accountant looked heartbroken. Belt Buckle looked dismayed. Wolf Shirt looked shocked. Leather Skin looked overwhelmed. Or maybe they were all incredulous. Or annoyed. Or angry. Who knows. I was reading these strangers' faces and trying to impart meaning on them. In reality, those assessments were just guesses from one man's perspective.

John stood by my side as I questioned Scotty. His presence

was more an annoyance than anything, and he hovered over my shoulder without offering encouragement, criticism, or advice. It was like someone watching you type.

On cross-examination, Emma laid out all the damning circumstantial evidence, knowing Scotty wouldn't have answers. Yes, he had been in business with Josh. Yes, they had a meeting that night. Yes, they sometimes disagreed on things. Yes, the knife on the counter was his. Yes, the truck down the road was Josh's. No, he didn't have an explanation for it. No, he didn't remember. Emma pointed out all the issues with Scotty's account of the events, but she couldn't nail him down since, regarding the pertinent details, Scotty held firm to his constant refrain of "I don't know" or "I don't remember." There was no way to catch him in a lie if he didn't commit to anything.

There was one question I didn't ask during Scotty's testimony, and that's because I didn't want to know the answer. Or rather, I knew what his answer might be, but I didn't want to hear Scotty say it. But Emma did. I don't know why she asked it because I don't know if it helped her. Maybe she was feeling like her case wasn't very strong. Maybe she was just exasperated from getting so little information from him. Who knows. At the end of her cross-examination, she dropped her pen on the notepad in front of her and looked over at the jury. "Mr. Watts," she said, "did you kill Josh Anderson?"

Scotty paused.

Judge Waitskin shifted in his chair.

I leaned in.

Scotty stared off into the distance, like he truly was trying to remember.

"Mr. Watts?" Emma asked.

He looked up at her. "I...I...I don't know."

* * *

It had been over seven months since Deputies Haskins and Sanchez had found Scotty on the living room floor of his cabin covered in blood. Scotty wasn't the only one who wanted the trial to be over. I was exhausted. I thought John might recognize that fact and leave me alone. Maybe he would notice I'd been stressed out, I'd been working hard, and that I needed a break. I was wrong. Things got worse.

At 9:34 a.m. the next day, Emma delivered her closing argument. She started by describing the various degrees of murder that Judge Waitskin would later instruct the jury on.

"Murder one requires premeditation. Planning. Laying in wait. Second-degree murder requires no premeditation. Just an intent to kill. Voluntary manslaughter requires grievous bodily harm or the intent to kill with some 'mitigating factor,' like provocation. For instance, the victim slept with the defendant's wife. After we complete our closing arguments, the judge will explain all this to you in detail, and you will be tasked with rendering a verdict…"

She recounted all the circumstantial evidence that had made me so hesitant to take this case to trial in the first place: the blood, the knife, the truck, Eleanor Jackson.

Suddenly John appeared out of nowhere, sitting next to me at counsel's table.

"Almost done!" he shouted in my ear. I jumped. The sound of my chair grating on the tile floor bounced against the walls.

Scotty leaned over to me. "What was that?"

"Sorry. Yes. I'm fine," I said. I glared at John. "What do you want?" I whispered.

"Just checking on you, buddy," John said. "You're doing great." He smiled and gave me a thumbs-up.

Emma continued, "…he lured Josh Anderson to his cabin…

"…had the motive to kill him…"

"She's pretty good, isn't she?" John asked.

"…intended to kill him…

"…committed the act…

"…a multicounty search involving nearly every law enforcement agency…

"…sophisticated disposal of the body…"

"She makes some good points," John said.

"After considering all that evidence, I am asking that you find the defendant guilty of murder in the first degree," Emma concluded.

Twelve sets of eyes shifted in my direction.

When I got up to deliver my closing argument, John got up with me. "What are you doing?" I said. "Sit! Down!"

Scotty leaned over to whisper something to me, but I was already too far away.

John didn't sit, but he threw up his arms in an appeasing gesture. "I'm just here to help," he said. "Knock 'em dead!" He stood off to the side.

"Ladies and gentlemen of the jury," I said, "remember, no body was recovered in this case."

He moved closer.

"This case is about doubt. It's about whether you're comfortable reaching a guilty verdict despite the fact that"—I pointed at the back of the courtroom—"the supposed victim could walk right through that door at any moment."

"Could he, though?" John asked, lurking over my shoulder.

"The lack of a victim isn't the only thing wrong with the prosecution's case. Think about all the doubt. Think about the possibility that there was a third person in that cabin."

"Remember that book I gave you?" John asked. I ignored him.

"It's not my job to prove that there was a third person in that cabin," I told the jury.

"Yes, it is," John said. "Look at it again. The book."

"The burden of proof is on the state. It's also not my job to identify who that third person might have been."

"I think you know who it was," John said.

"Or to explain exactly what happened," I said.

"You're getting warmer!" John said.

"That's the government's job," I said.

I walked in front of John to block his view and hopefully shut him up.

"But instead of doing so, instead of the government

explaining the presence of that third blood type on the red bandanna found in the woods, investigating leads as to who else might have been in the cabin with Scotty and Josh, or considering the possibility that there is some other explanation for Josh Anderson's disappearance, the government fixated on only what was right in front of them: the scared, frightened, confused young man who woke up to a macabre scene you wouldn't wish on your worst enemy."

I pointed at Scotty, who slumped in his chair. "Scotty Watts woke up to a nightmare, a living nightmare lasting seven months long."

"I like this version," John said.

"Stop it!" I shouted. The eyes of the courtroom that were already on me changed. Everyone sat up straight. I looked around, confused for a moment, realizing what I'd just done.

"All right. Fine, fine," John said. He shrugged and walked back to counsel's table and sat.

Judge Waitskin peered down at me from the bench. "I'm sorry? Counsel, is there a problem?"

"O-objection," I stammered. I looked at Emma. She looked like she'd seen a ghost.

"You're objecting to your own argument?" Judge Waitskin asked.

"No, Your Honor. I'm sorry," I said.

"Very well. Please continue." Judge Waitskin looked very concerned.

I tried to recover.

"Eleanor Jackson could not tell you if there was another person with Josh Anderson when he got out of the truck," I reminded the jury. "She never heard a gunshot, and she never heard a struggle or screaming for help. You can focus on what she saw. Or you can think about what she didn't see. What she couldn't have seen.

"It's no secret that Scotty Watts and Josh Anderson were engaged in an unpopular business. It's no secret that they had some enemies."

I picked up a stack of papers from the table.

"I'm not here to cast aspersions or prove someone other than Scotty Watts killed Josh Anderson."

I waved the stack of papers in the air.

"But there was at least one other constituency that did not like what they were doing up there in Forest Ranch. We know that from Ms. Buyske's testimony. We know that from Ralph Morrison's presence at the Board of Supervisors' meetings. We know that there is at least one other explanation for what might have happened in that cabin on that night."

"This is pretty aggressive!" John shouted.

"So when you think about rendering a verdict in this case, when you think about that standard of proof—*beyond a reasonable doubt*—think about Eleanor Jackson's testimony, think about the fact that we still do not have a victim, think about the third blood type on that bandanna found in the woods by the cabin, and think about how Scotty's girlfriend described him. 'He's the sweetest person I've ever known,' is what she said about that man right there." I pointed over to Scotty. He looked down.

"Think about the things that don't add up. Stack up all that evidence and the questions it raises in your head, and you will find that you're not even close to beyond a reasonable doubt in this case. If you have doubt about Scotty Watts's guilt, your doubt is more than reasonable; it's logical. It's normal.

"Ladies and gentlemen of the jury, there is only one reasonable verdict to reach in this case, and that is to find Scotty Watts not guilty."

John rose to his feet and started clapping. He was the only person standing, and his slow clapping was the only sound I heard. My face felt hot. I walked back to counsel's table.

Clap. Clap. Clap.

As I passed him, I whispered through gritted teeth, "Sit. Down."

John kept clapping. He wouldn't stop.

"I thought that was pretty good," he said. "Very compelling." He thought for a moment and then said, "I'm gonna get a snack." He paused, waiting for my answer, but I ignored him. "Do you want a snack?"

I slumped in my chair. I was sapped of all energy.

"What the hell was that?" Scotty whispered. "What's wrong with you?"

I ignored him. Suddenly noises sounded far away, as if I were underwater trying to hear the world on the surface. I was oblivious to anything Judge Waitskin said, any rebuttal argument Emma made, or anything else that was going on. I was still underwater when Judge Waitskin read the instructions to the jury and the bailiff called out, "All rise!"

Blurry shapes of people stood. I stood with them and watched the jury file out. The trial was over.

FORTY-FOUR

There was no way of knowing how long jury deliberations would take, I explained to Scotty, but he would still perk up every time I visited him in his holding cell, hoping I had some news. No matter how many ways he asked when we might hear something, my answer was always the same: "Could be an hour, could be two weeks. No idea." I needed something to distract me, so I had Shelly deliver a stack of files to me at the courthouse. It didn't work. Every time I sat to work, I would just stare at the pages as though they were blank. I could think of nothing but Scotty's case and the impending verdict.

Thursday and Friday passed unceremoniously. I paced around the courthouse. Men and women wearing suits came in and out of the hallways for hearings. I hid in vacant rooms pretending to look over new cases. I reviewed Scotty's file, knowing how silly and futile it was, looking for things I had missed and mistakes I had made. I caught concerned sideways glances from Shelly and Rick. On Friday afternoon, Judge Waitskin called the jury into the courtroom. The jury still wasn't close to an answer, and he dismissed us for the weekend.

The next day, I saw Eileen and Ray Watts. I was pushing my cart along the back of the grocery store, considering cuts of meat, when I glanced down one of the aisles. Eileen was examining the nutritional contents of a box of cereal. Ray was in his wheelchair next to her with his head slumped off to the side, drool hanging from his fishhooked mouth. I froze. Ray's eyes darted up at me, and he groaned. Eileen regarded me with that same pitiful smile she had always regarded me with. It made me feel like a child. I hated it. She pushed Ray up the aisle toward me.

"Hello," she said.

"Hi," I said. I told her Scotty's trial was over. "We're waiting for the verdict."

"Oh." She paused for a moment, thinking, and then said, "I heard what you did…the things you said about your father and about the Board of Supervisors. I wish you wouldn't have done that. You didn't have to make all that up."

"I know," I said. But I hadn't made it up. Any of it. I'd only planted a theory in the jury's minds. I'd given them an alternative version of the truth. That was all.

"Is your father angry with you?" she asked.

"I'm sure he is. I haven't talked to him."

Then I told her something I'd been wanting to tell her for a long time. "You know, Scotty is really sorry."

"It was another boy's life…Apologies don't cut it when you do something like that."

"Not that. He's sorry for letting you down. You and Ray," I told them. "I don't know whether or not he killed Josh, but I know he's sorry for what happened to his family. He tells me all the time."

A tear fell from Ray's unblinking eye. Eileen's lip quivered. A woman with a cart half-full of groceries and with a small child in the basket pushed past us. "Excuse me," the woman said. Eileen nudged Ray's wheelchair out of the way to let the woman pass. I watched the woman push the cart down the aisle while Eileen thought about what to say.

Finally she said, "I'm sorry too."

* * *

Monday was another treacherous day of waiting. We had no more matters to take up, which meant more waiting around and more watching people come and go. I couldn't concentrate on other cases. I didn't know what to do with myself. On Tuesday I was preparing myself for much of the same, but at 3:30 p.m., Shelly knocked on the door, opened it, and said, "Verdict." I threw papers and files into my briefcase and rushed out.

We reassembled in Courtroom 4. Judge Waitskin took a seat in his big leather chair. I was suddenly keenly aware of everyone in the gallery. Kelly was in the front row next to Shelly. Mr. and Mrs. Anderson sat next to three young people with the manicured gloss of the Orange County nouveau riche. I hadn't noticed them before. They must have been Josh's cousins, siblings, or classmates. Mike Sullivan was in the back with his arms crossed, trying to separate himself from the horde of reporters crammed in the pews. And of course, there was John. He leaned against the back wall, plucking potato chips from a tinfoil bag and popping them in his mouth. He was chewing so loudly, I could hear the crunching of the chips. Crunch, crunch, crunch. No Eileen Watts. No Ray. Still.

The jury—Wolf Shirt, Belt Buckle, Asian Accountant, Leather Skin—looked somber and nervous.

Judge Waitskin addressed the court. "We are reconvening in *People v. Watts*. The record shall reflect that Counsel and the defendant are present. Are we ready to proceed, Counsel?"

"Yes, Your Honor," Emma and I said.

"All twelve jurors are present and properly seated." He looked to Asian Accountant. "Mr. Foreperson, I understand the jury has reached a verdict?"

"Yes, Your Honor. We have," Asian Accountant said.

The bailiff collected the verdict form and delivered it to Judge Waitskin. He examined it and handed it back to the bailiff, and the bailiff took it back to the jury box. This was it. All those months of waiting, all that time wondering and guessing, theorizing and strategizing, and this was it.

"Defendant and Counsel, please rise," Judge Waitskin said.

Scotty and I stood. Crunch, crunch, crunch. *Goddamn John with his chips.*

"Would the foreperson please read the jury's verdict?"

A lifetime passed in the next half second. I could feel a droplet of cold sweat soak into the waistband of my pants. The faint scent of Arthur's matted black hair emanated off my wool suit. I shut my eyes and took a big breath in. Suddenly I smelled…pine trees. A cool breeze of mountain air wafted across my face. The scent of pine filled my lungs. I opened my eyes, and I was in Forest Ranch. It was evening. I was in Scotty's cabin. Scotty was there. Arthur lay happily at his feet. He wore his collar and the 49ers bandanna. It was spotless and clean. Scotty took a bite of cereal. Arthur groaned. Scotty looked down at him.

"Good boy," he said.

Outside, dusk settled over the forest. The wind started to pick up. I watched Scotty take another bite. Arthur yawned. The sky grew dark.

The bandanna, the water, the farmers, the lot, the wind, the rain, the tracks. Kelly.

Suddenly I was outside. I stood in the clearing of the marijuana field at the back of Scotty's property. John was there. We stood side by side, overlooking the canyon. John shut his eyes and breathed in, just like the first time he had brought me here. Except now the field wasn't barren. Behind us, full-grown marijuana plants towered high in neat rows. I looked down one of them. Irrigated water lines dripped slowly onto the plants. Drip. Drip. Drip.

The bandanna, the water, the farmers, the lot, the wind, the rain, the tracks. Kelly.

I was in church, standing in the back as usual. My sister preached from the lectern. She was preaching about David and Bathsheba again. The frozen congregation fixed their attention on her. Ralph Morrison sat next to his wife, Sue. Paul, Lacey, my father—they were all there. Suddenly two heads among the crowd started rotating on shoulders. The heads turned slowly, as if cranked by a mechanical device, knotting their twisted necks. Profiles came into view. Ralph and Paul. Their square jaws. Their dark scruffy beards. Their lips were stretched impossibly wide in grotesque smiles. I darted my eyes between them. I backpedaled toward the door. Their heads kept turning on their shoulders until their deadened eyes were trained on me, with wide mirthless grins on their faces. The rotating stopped. Their bug-eyed gazes bore into my soul. The frozen congregation took no notice. My sister continued to preach. *Jesus.*

The bandanna, the water, the farmers, the lot, the wind, the rain, the tracks. Kelly.

I was back in Scotty's living room. The sky was darker now. I watched him slurp up spoonfuls of cereal. I heard the rumble of Josh Anderson's white Nissan Titan truck. I heard the faint shutting of a car door through the howling wind that shook the sliding-glass doors.

The bandanna, the water, the farmers, the lot, the wind, the rain, the tracks. Kelly.

I stood on Eleanor Jackson's porch. She sat in a rocking chair next to me, rocking back and forth. Her attention was fixed on Josh Anderson. She watched Josh get out of his truck and walk up the stairs to Scotty's cabin. I looked to the right at the vacant lot next to Scotty's. Through the trees I could make something out. A car? A blue car? Or was it green? Or gray? I couldn't tell. Something was there. Just ahead of the car, I saw a figure moving through the trees. I could see it. It looked like something, or someone, making its way from the car, through the trees, and toward Scotty's cabin. It was barely perceptible through the thick pines.

The bandanna, the water, the farmers, the lot, the wind, the rain, the tracks. Kelly.

O'Haras Bar. Downtown. The smell of stale beer and piss. It was late. I was drunk. I could barely stand. I held a half-empty cocktail. People circled around me. College kids danced. Laughed. Flirted. Loud sounds of revelry. I stood motionless. I saw Will. He stood at the bar trying to order a drink. He leaned over the counter waving his credit card. Kelly stood opposite him, shaking her head. She took a step back. The scene moved in slow motion. She backed away from Will. She looked over at me. Her eyes were puffy and swollen from crying. Mascara-stained tears ran down her cheeks. She walked toward me. The muffled sounds of the bar grew louder and louder. Kelly kept walking toward me. The sounds of the bar got louder still. The shouting. The music. The glasses clinking. The girls shrieking in delight. Kelly was almost to the end of the bar, and she started to say something to me, but the clinking of glass and chatter were deafening. I shut my eyes.

When I opened them, I was back in court.

"Guilty."

The word rang out in my head, and it took me a long moment to attach meaning to it. Asian Accountant spoke the words clear and confident. "We the jury find the defendant guilty of murder in the second degree."

Guilty. Murder. Second degree, I said in my head. *Guilty of murder in the second degree.*

I pictured Scotty as the twelve-year-old kid playing catch in my backyard. I pictured him wearing the 49ers hat his father had bought for him, wearing it every day. *Guilty. Murder. Second degree. Guilty. Murder. Second degree,* I thought to myself over and over.

The words had just come out, short and blunt. Guilty. *Scotty was guilty of murder in the second degree.* I suppose I expected more preamble. It was the outcome I had both expected and even foreseen, yet it still seemed like a dream. A murmur of voices rumbled from the gallery. Reporters rushed out of their seats and out the back of the courtroom toward the television crews waiting outside. I heard a loud sob. It was Mrs. Anderson crying tears of relief. I looked at Scotty. He had the same expressionless gaze as when I had first met him, like he had known it was all inevitable. Like he'd been waiting patiently for this sword of Damocles. John walked out of the courtroom. I heard more crying, but it was different from Mrs. Anderson's. It was soft desperate sobs. I turned around and saw Kelly taking small gasping breaths. Her shoulders shook. She cried quietly into a tissue. It was the heartbroken, helpless cry of shattered hope. Shelly rubbed her back. Judge Waitskin recited the last few lines of his trial script, thanking the jury for their service.

I turned back to the gallery again. Kelly's head was bowed. She looked at the ground in front of her. Tears fell from her cheeks onto the tile floor. She looked up for a moment and met my gaze, but the pools of water in her eyes were so heavy that I doubt she could've seen anything at all.

FORTY-FIVE

Weeks went by. They weren't memorable; they just passed.

The election happened. Donald Trump was elected president. My dad retained his Board of Supervisors seat. He had run unopposed. Mike Sullivan soundly defeated Bill Dubois and was reseated as the district attorney. Josh Anderson's body was still missing, but the people of Chico had got their conviction. Dubois put up the toughest fight Sullivan had seen in twenty-five years, yet he still lost by a wide margin. The municipal judges all ran unopposed and retained their seats, including Judge Waitskin. Aaron Rodgers and the Green Bay Packers were 4–5 headed into a week 11 matchup against a tough Tennessee Titans team, and people around town were worried they might miss the playoffs for the first time since 2008.

After the trial, Will and I started hanging out again. *Screw it,* I thought. *I don't have anything to live for.* We'd meet for drinks on the weekends and for happy hours during the week, and I'd drink until I forgot who I was. If I was drunk enough, I'd agree to go to O'Haras, but if Kelly was working, I would just sit at the end of the bar and mope. Will would yell at me and tell me to go home. Our basketball league started up again, and I agreed to play. *What difference does it make?* I thought. Time moved on.

* * *

Scotty's sentencing hearing was on Tuesday, November 22, two days before Thanksgiving. Now that he was a convicted felon, he didn't have the privilege of dressing as an accused man during court proceedings, and he was back to wearing his orange jumpsuit. I had Shelly return the suit I had rented for him. He faced a minimum of fifteen years in prison, with the possibility of life.

I've always thought a sentencing hearing and a funeral are similar, being that they are both perfunctory and dour affairs. The obligation and formality of both events have no real resolution. They're either the confirmation or announcement of some very bad news. I thought back to my mother's funeral. I missed her so much.

The probation officer recommended a sentence of no less than twenty-five years, weighing Scotty's prior criminal history with the severity of the crime.

I argued for leniency, of course, on the basis that Scotty felt remorse for what he had done, even though we'd just spent two weeks steadfastly arguing his innocence. This is one of the perverse legal fictions we must all embrace. You argue for your innocence and then turn around and apologize.

Scotty's lack of character evidence didn't help him at sentencing. I'd tracked down an aunt and uncle who lived in Nevada. They hadn't spoken to Scotty in fifteen years, but they agreed to write a letter on his behalf. I somehow convinced our high school basketball coach to write a letter. The owner of O'Haras and the lead manager each wrote letters. Kelly must have convinced them to do it. They wrote about how reliable and hardworking Scotty was as an employee. There was another letter from Scotty's chemistry professor at Butte Junior College. It noted his "satisfactory" performance and remarked how Scotty had caused "no problems or disruptions" in class. He noted how Scotty had earned "a well-deserved B." Not exactly lofty praise. I almost didn't include it. The letters all seemed like eulogies for the living—a few final nice words about a person soon to be forgotten.

When ordering the sentence, Judge Waitskin could consider only the evidence in front of him, but I knew he would take unconscious note of the letters that were not present—those of Eileen and Ray Watts. Everyone knew Scotty was estranged from his parents; Butte County was too small a place to avoid it.

Emma's sentencing argument was short. She highlighted the main points of the probation officer's report and agreed with the recommendation. She had got her conviction, her boss had been reelected, and spiking the football would have been in poor taste.

Judge Waitskin's ruling was as unceremonious as when Asian Accountant had delivered the verdict. He listened to our arguments, considered the evidence we submitted, but offered little explanation as to how much he considered any one piece. He simply cleared his throat and said, "Given the defendant's past criminal behavior, as well as the heinous nature of this crime, I'm ordering a sentence of three hundred and twenty-four months to be served concurrently."

Three hundred and twenty-four months. Twenty-seven years. If Scotty served the full term, he wouldn't be eligible for parole until his sixtieth birthday. Scotty didn't seem to care or acknowledge the harshness, but I suppose years on a criminal sentence seem relevant only if the total number is small. All his adult life was gone. When I heard the words, I let my head fall into my hands. Judge Waitskin adjourned court, and two beefy corrections officers started ushering Scotty out in handcuffs. I told him I'd come see him as soon as I could.

"No need," he said.

Kelly and I sat on a wood bench in the courthouse hallway. She dabbed at the corners of her eyes with a tissue. I rubbed her back.

"I'm so sorry," I told her. "I'm so, so sorry."

Kelly hadn't reacted much when the sentence was issued.

Tears rolled down her cheeks, but her face was a placid calm. I think she'd already cried out most of the emotion her body could manage. She appeared too exhausted for anything more. We sat for a long time without speaking. Finally she asked, "What are we gonna do about Arthur?"

I actually hadn't thought about it, and I shrugged when she asked me. I think I'd had Arthur for so long, I'd forgotten he wasn't my dog.

"Would you mind keeping him?" she asked.

"Sure," I said, but I was oddly relieved.

"It's too painful. I love him so much, but I don't think I could have him around. It would remind me of Scotty too much," she said.

"Yes, of course," I said.

"You don't mind?"

"Not at all. I'm actually sort of glad," I said, then felt bad for saying it. "Sorry."

She laughed. "It's okay. He's great, isn't he?"

I nodded.

"I'd still like to visit him sometimes, if that's okay."

I nodded. "Sure. Of course that's okay."

* * *

Shelly watched me come and go like the concerned parent of a moody teenager. She was kind enough not to comment on my work product. I was mailing it in. My pleadings had misspellings, cited unpublished cases, and were generally a mess. I made minimal edits to the templates we used. I'd miss obvious errors. She'd catch my mistakes and be patient with me.

I hadn't spoken to my father since before the trial. I had stopped going to church. I explained to my sister why it was a bad idea for me to be there since I knew Ralph and Paul Morrison were probably furious, and perhaps no one more than our father. I didn't want to cause a scene.

I hadn't seen John since the day of the verdict over a

month before. Then, on a Sunday night in mid-December, just before dusk fell and the sky turned gray, Arthur and I walked in from the backyard. We'd been playing fetch, and John was standing in the middle of the living room.

"Still haven't figured it out, huh?" he asked.

I ignored him. After Scotty was found guilty, I didn't care what stupid advice he had. It wasn't going to help anyone now. If John wanted to be helpful, he should have done it sooner. I filled Arthur's water bowl and grabbed a beer out of the fridge. I opened it and took a big swig.

"I left you something on the dresser in your room," he said. "You should have a look."

I sat on the couch and turned on the TV.

"Okay," he said. "I'm gonna get going."

I petted Arthur's head, and the next time I looked up, John was gone.

Later that night, I was brushing my teeth before bed when I walked into my bedroom. On the dresser was the green leather-bound book John had told me about. I read the title again: *The Conscience of a Lawyer*. I leafed through it, wondering why he kept thrusting this book into my life. The last time he had tried to get me to read it, he said something was highlighted, but it wasn't. But this time as I leafed through it, I found a few pages with paragraphs highlighted in a dull yellow, like it had been done many months before. I sat on the edge of the bed and read them to myself. As I read them, I heard John's voice in my head.

> The lawyer, as a lawyer, is no sweet kind loving moralizer. He assumes he is needed and that no one comes to see him to pass the time of day. He is a Prober (issue spotter) an analyzer, a planner, a decision-maker, a compromiser, eventually a scrapper, a man with a strange devotion to his client. Beautifully strange, or so it seems to the man-in-trouble; ugly strange to the untroubled on looker…

This Man-in-trouble is…you and I, and our neighbor, at the right moment. The lawyer, some lawyer, is there for each of us, with a lack of discrimination among clients and causes so disgusting to Authorities among clients, and causes so disgusting to Authoritarians of every stripe and stature.

A substantial part of the major criticism of the lawyer—his presumed indifference to truth—is rooted in fundamental misconception of the lawyer's mission. The lawyer does not exist to spread the word of truth and goodness to the ends of the earth. Somewhat more limited, the lawyer's mission is the nonetheless awesome task of trying to make a reality of equality before the law. If your "truth" or mine get dented some in the process, it is only because we deal here with something less than the Kingdom of God, and something more than one truth.

In the back of the book, John had written a note. "At the end of every criminal trial, there will be a lot of unanswered questions," the note read. "The unanswered questions arise from, and ultimately cause, both confusion and doubt. People fill in the gaps with their own truth, and justice is the truth that people can live with.

"Good Luck, —J."

I couldn't fall asleep that night. I tossed and turned, thinking about those words, listening to Arthur snoring from his doggy bed. By midnight I resolved on what was bothering me. Whatever version of the truth Scotty Watts's trial had uncovered wasn't the truth I could live with. I knew that another truth was out there.

FORTY-SIX

There's a reason why lawyers often work in teams. While working alone, it's very easy to become fixated on one defense theory at the expense of another equally valid theory that may be more successful at trial. It's hard to consider all the theories that will exculpate your client or know which one to choose. The things I missed about Scotty's case, I did so subconsciously, of course, and if I'd have known where to look at the time, I would have looked there. So maybe you'll find the mistakes I made obvious or think I'm stupid, but that's trial work; it makes you lose sight of what's right in front of you. It's easy to lose perspective when you're alone.

* * *

It was Tuesday night. Will and I were lacing up our shoes for our men's-league game. He was still annoyed with me because I was fixated on Scotty's case. The sounds of basketballs caroming off rims, dribbling, the squeaking of sneakers, and jovial chatting of young men echoed off the walls.

"It's the right result," Will said. "Scotty was guilty all along. It's not your fault he went down like that."

"I suppose so."

He picked up a basketball and shot it. "He could've taken a deal, and he didn't."

"I guess we'll never know."

"Yes. Exactly. So move on."

"Still sad," I said.

Will nodded. "Maybe. But it's not your fault."

We were down five points in the third quarter. I set a screen for our point guard at the top of the key, and he dribbled off the screen and pulled up for a jump shot. I ran toward the hoop, following the flight of the ball with my eyes, angling in for the rebound. That's when things went dark. When I woke up, I was lying on my back by the padded baseline wall with a blonde-haired woman in a dark-blue uniform shining a small flashlight in my eyes.

"Hey," she said. "There he is."

"Huh?" I asked.

"You got hit pretty bad," she said. "What's the last thing you remember?"

"Playing in the game. Going in for a rebound. I don't know. After that, I don't know," I said.

Her military–crew cut paramedic coworker hovered over her shoulder with a worried look on his face. The bright lights of the gym made my head hurt. I stayed lying on my back on the hardwood floor for a few minutes while they looked me over. They decided I didn't need a stretcher and got me to my feet. I wobbled a little and blinked again and again, trying to clear my vision while they helped me to the sideline. Someone handed me a bag of ice that I put on my head.

"Shit, man," Will said. "You all right?" He put his hand on my shoulder. "You got hit pretty good."

I touched the back of my head, and my fingertips came away painted in red. I saw that droplets of blood were scattered on the baseline where I'd been lying.

"Don't worry. You don't need staples," the blonde paramedic said. "It's a small cut and will heal on its own. There's just a lot of blood up there, that's all."

"What happened?" I asked.

Will jumped in. "Some wiry asshole came flying in from out of nowhere and cracked his elbow on your noggin, bro. That's what happened."

"How long was I out?"

"Like two minutes."

"You could have been out much longer," the blonde-haired paramedic said. "You have a slight concussion. But you really should see a doctor to make sure you're okay."

Will drove me to the ER. The ice pack I'd been holding to my skull was almost totally melted by the time a nurse appeared in the doorway and called out my name. I waited another thirty minutes in an examination room until a freckled woman in a white lab coat walked in. I had a concussion, she explained, which there wasn't much I could do for other than take it easy. Head injuries needed time. "Time and rest," she said. She could do a CAT scan, but that almost certainly wasn't necessary. She told me I could go home. I called Shelly and told her I wouldn't be coming in the next day.

All morning a cold, wet rain fell from the sky, and I alternated between sitting and lying on my couch. Arthur would walk over and lick my fingers or nuzzle his head into me. In the afternoon, as the rain pelted the roof and the sides of my little house in fat drops, I drifted off to sleep while lying on my back. When I woke up an hour later, the rain had stopped, but water dripped slowly from the gutter and the trees.

"I can't believe you weren't out for longer." John was standing there, next to Arthur, who was half-asleep in his doggy bed. John seemed to have a way of appearing just when I was thinking about Scotty's case, and when he arrived at that moment, the parallels that I'm sure are obvious to you— between hitting my head and Scotty hitting his—suddenly appeared obvious to me. I realized that the jury hadn't heard much testimony about the bump found on Scotty's head, and that he could have been knocked out by a blow to the head just as easily as by a drug. It was simply a path I hadn't taken.

Scotty's head injury was something I had given little attention to and provided scant evidence of at trial. I'd subconsciously chosen to ignore it. I figured he had suffered the head injury when he fell from his chair, that he hit his head on the ground or the kitchen table. I tried to remember. Maybe I'd considered that he suffered the blow to his head during a struggle and just dismissed that notion for lack of evidence, or maybe I just glossed over it altogether. I couldn't remember. Instead, I had chosen to focus my energy on the failure by law enforcement to do a toxicology report and left the head injury mostly alone.

"How long was Scotty out before the sheriff's deputies found him?" I asked John. He shrugged. I pictured the drops of blood running down off my head and dotting the baseline of the gym. I recalled Scotty's blood mixed into the pool of Josh Anderson's.

"Do you see now?" John asked.

"I need to talk to Kelly," I said, reaching for my phone. I called her and asked if we could meet.

Driving to O'Haras in my rusty green Honda, I felt like all the thoughts that had been swirling in my head over the last few months were coming together. I thought back to the night I went out with Will. It was the night when we had met the handsome couple and taken tequila shots. The night we went to the narrow bar and saw Paul and Cole Morrison. I thought about the familiar stranger I saw staring back at me through the mirrored window. The night of heavy boozing had left me with only vague memories and blurry recollections. We had gone to O'Haras. I remembered that familiar smell of stale beer and piss. I was barely able to stand. But there was that one image I couldn't forget: Will leaning over the bar and waving his credit card at Kelly.

What was going on there? Just a pushy guy ordering a drink?

Kelly had stood opposite him, shaking her head and backing up. *What was that look in her eyes? Was it fear?*

I saw it all much clearer now than during or immediately after the event. The pieces started gluing together in my head.

"Kelly!" I burst out. John was in the passenger's seat, and I turned to him. "That's what you meant by Kelly! That's why you brought her up. That's what you were trying to tell me!"

John smiled wide and tilted his head back. He gazed out the window. "Beautiful day today," he said.

"Why, though?" I asked him. "Why that night?"

"The rain stopped," he said.

"Don't be an asshole!" I said. I parked my car outside and rushed in. I'd forgotten I was in sweatpants and ignored the funny looks when I burst into O'Haras.

"Kelly!" I said.

"What can I do for you?" she asked.

I asked if she remembered that night, reminding her it had been just before Scotty's trial began. She did, vaguely. I asked her if she knew or remembered Will.

"Of course. You guys know him from high school. Scotty mentioned it before. Plus, I'd seen him around."

I asked if she thought there was anything weird about it.

"The only thing weird about it was that it happened all the time. He comes in here just about every weekend. He's always pretty wasted. Always pushy."

That sounded like Will, all right. I asked her if Will's behavior seemed obsessive or creepy.

"Yeah, but I get that a lot," she said.

I thanked her and turned for the exit. My mind still raced. My brain buzzed like I was responding to an emergency.

"Is that it?" Kelly asked.

"Yeah, thanks!" I said, rushing out the door.

"Wait! How's Arthur?" I heard her ask, but I'd already walked out into the sunlight. I was practically to my car.

John rode with me on the drive back to my house. "What're you thinking?" he asked.

"When Scotty's file landed on my desk, who did I first call?"

"Will."

"And what did Will say?"

"'Scotty Watts…Good luck with that one.'"

"Exactly. And he's constantly coming in Kelly's bar," I said.

"So what?"

"And he's a misogynist pervert."

"Aren't we all?"

"No, we're not, John. Jesus."

Scotty's teenage life had been the envy of us all. He had attention, celebrity, girls, and status. The roles were reversed now, in a way, except Will was living Scotty's teenage life as an adult. Will had the glossy exterior of what a teenage boy might want, but the moments between his empty pleasures and vapid relationships must have been dreadful. Scotty, on the other hand, once again had something Will didn't. He had Kelly. He had love. Will had only a rotating harem of women he loathed. I floored the accelerator toward home.

"Over the last seven months, every time I talked to Will about Scotty's case, he'd try to convince me Scotty should plead guilty," I told John. "Every time I brought Scotty's case up to him, he'd convince me Scotty was doomed."

"Wasn't he?" John asked.

"The case wasn't *that* bad," I said. "There wasn't even a victim!"

"The jury missed that memo," John said. "You lost the case, remember?"

I seethed.

Will had seemed confident from the beginning that Josh Anderson's body would be found, but was that just posturing? Had he actually known all along that the body was so well hidden, so well buried, that it would never be found? He was constantly lobbying for a swift, painless resolution of Scotty's case. But why? Because it would tie a bow on things. If he was the murderer, having someone take the fall for Josh's death would tie up loose ends.

"But why would Will murder Josh Anderson?" John asked. "If Will was so jealous of Scotty, why bring Josh into it? What was the point of that?"

"I don't know. Yet."

"Maybe you should lie back down. You know, head injuries can be—"

"Shut up," I told him. "I'm figuring this out."

We came to a skid in the gravel driveway. I hopped out of the car. "Arthur!" I shouted. He bolted out the front door and jumped in my back seat. We left the driveway and headed east on the highway toward Forest Ranch.

John pointed to the back seat. "What's he here for?" he asked.

"I don't know, John. I think better with him. What's it to you? Leave him out of this." I thought about Will. "The obsessiveness. The opulence. The misogyny," I said as we drove. "Of course it was Will. Will did this."

"You still haven't explained why he killed Josh. Or why he disappeared him. Or whatever."

"When I found that bandanna in the woods, who did I call?" I asked.

"Will," John said.

"What did he say?"

"Leave it."

"Right. 'Don't do anything,' he said."

"Okay," John said.

"He was adamant. Remember? The bandanna was the one piece of evidence he couldn't tie a bow on," I said. "That was the one piece of evidence that got away from him." I looked in the rearview mirror at Arthur, who was resting in the back seat. "All because of you, buddy. Good boy!"

"You still haven't answered, Why Josh?" John said.

"Stop asking me that."

"It has to be answered," John said.

"I know, I know," I told him.

"Where are we going?" John asked.

"To answer it! Now shut up."

We crested over the horizon of Deer Creek Highway, and pine trees started popping up out of the dry bush beside the road. We were almost to Scotty's cabin.

FORTY-SEVEN

I parked at the spot of the tire tracks. Or rather, the spot where the tire tracks had once been since they were barely distinguishable now, the weather having worn them away.

"He parked here," I said, my brain still operating in emergency mode.

What was he doing here? What was he doing here?

"He'd been coming here!" I said. "He'd been watching Scotty and Kelly. He'd been watching them because he was jealous! Obsessive!"

We got out of my car.

"He snuck through the woods," I said as we walked through the trees toward Scotty's cabin.

"This is a lot of speculation," John said.

"Shut up."

The cabin looked serene and peaceful. There was a For Sale sign in Scotty's driveway. The crime scene tape was gone. We walked into the clearing and up the back steps.

"He walked up these steps." We stood on the back deck, and I peered inside through the sliding-glass door. The cabin was empty.

"He was drunk. He'd been watching them for months, and his frustration and rage had been building. The wind was howling, so Scotty couldn't hear. His back was to him." I reached for the door. "The door was already open." I slid the door open and took a step inside. "In a fit of jealous rage, standing over Scotty, his anger built and built, and he clubbed Scotty on the back of the head."

"With what?" John said.

"With a rock! With a rock he picked up in the forest."

"Ever stop to consider where you are getting this?" John asked. "Nice story, but you're going to need facts."

"Scotty was unconscious on the floor," I said. "A moment later, Will hears Josh Anderson's truck pull up."

"I think you know where you're getting this," John said.

"When he hears the truck, he panics. Will doesn't know about the meeting. He didn't know Josh was on his way." I moved to the kitchen counter and then behind the front door. "Will hears Josh walking up the front steps. He sees Scotty bleeding on the floor. He grabs a knife, hides behind the door. He doesn't know what to do. Josh appears in the doorway and sees Scotty passed out, bleeding from the head. Josh turns and sees Will. Will knows he's going to get caught. He panics. There's a struggle, and Will slices the blade across Josh's neck, killing him. Now Will's screwed. He has no choice but to dispose of Josh's body and frame Scotty for the murder."

"Oddly specific and oddly detailed, don't you think?" John said.

"You brought me here, John! You're the one instigating all this shit! So shut up!"

"Fine, fine," he said.

I went back to narrating the scene, trying to piece the rest together. "Will makes sure to wipe down his prints. He puts Scotty's prints on everything he can and makes it look like Scotty did it all. He ties up all loose ends. He's a lawyer. He knows how to get away with it."

"What's the fact that proves this wild theory?" John asked.

I was breathing hard. My heart pounded in my chest. I walked back to the kitchen table near the sliding-glass door.

"You know the fact, John," I said. "You know the piece of

evidence. And we're going to get it out of the evidence locker and test it." But when I turned to John, he was gone. Arthur was too.

The sun had gone down long ago, and the night was getting dark and cold. I walked back down the steps and found Arthur waiting for me, lying on the cold, bare ground with concern in his eyes.

"Where's John?" I asked.

"I don't know," Arthur said. "Let's go home."

"Okay," I said.

* * *

Rick was not happy to see me when I brought two sealed ziplock bags to his office a week later. I'd already been in his office for a half hour answering questions like "Are you okay?" and "Are you sure you're getting enough sleep?" He kept asking about how things had been going since the trial, and it felt like forever for me to convince him that everything was fine. "Shelly is worried about you," he said.

"That's very nice of her," I said.

He pointed to the ziplock bags. "So what the hell is this?"

One bag contained an old half-full plastic water bottle, and one contained a sweaty basketball jersey.

"DNA samples," I told him.

"What do you want me to do with these? Please do not tell me this is for the Watts case," Rick said.

"Hear me out."

"No."

"I need them tested against the bandanna."

"No."

"Please. Just have the guys at the lab test these samples against the bandanna and see if they're a match."

Rick sighed and leaned back in his chair. "What have you been doing the last month?"

"It doesn't matter. I've barely spent any time on this at all. I'm just asking for this one thing."

He thought about it. "You have two alternate suspects you're chasing after?"

"No. Same person." I held up the water bottle and jersey. "These should match. I'm just giving you two samples to make it easier."

The jersey and water bottle had been easy enough to get, of course. The previous Tuesday at our men's-league game, I had slipped the water bottle directly into a large ziplock bag I'd hidden in my backpack. I made sure only Will had used the bottle and I didn't contaminate it during the transfer. I also "accidentally" grabbed his jersey, which, of course, I'd then told him I'd misplaced.

"Whose DNA is this?" Rick asked.

"It doesn't matter," I told him. "Please. I'm asking for a big favor. I just want to see if they match. I won't ask for anything else. I promise. This is the last thing I'll do on this case."

"I'm not worried about the favor. You know I'll do a favor for you anytime. I'm worried about you getting all spun up over a case that's dead and buried."

"Please."

"This is insane."

"Rick. Please."

He grabbed the ziplock bags. "I'll do it. But this is it. The last thing I do on this. And you owe me."

* * *

It was the holiday season, so it took almost three weeks to get the lab results back. I spent the holidays floating around in a blur. I felt the presence of other people, like Shelly at the office or my sister and father on Christmas Day, but they felt like ghosts or apparitions. John and Arthur were the only people who felt real. My father doted over my sister's new baby, but I felt absent from it all. I always thought the charm of the holidays went away after my mother died, and I felt underwater again, observing the world around me as though it were all taking place on the surface.

New Year's I spent with John and Arthur. We holed up in my house on Honey Run Road. I hung lights around the house. John made eggnog. Arthur wore a funny hat. We drank a lot of booze and watched the ball drop. Will had invited me to a party, but I declined. I'd been avoiding him as much as I could. I sat outside on my porch at midnight and looked up at the night sky. The stars were bright. I wondered what Lacey Price was up to. I wondered if she was back with Paul, or what she might be doing for New Year's. She was probably at a fun party with a lot of fun people, I figured.

It was three days later that Rick walked into my office like he'd seen a ghost.

"How did you know?" he asked.

I felt a rush of blood to my brain. An electric charge ran through the room, and I jolted forward in my seat. "They matched?"

"Whose DNA was that?"

"You're not going to believe me."

"How did you know?"

"I'm not sure you're going to believe that story either."

"You better start telling me what's going on, right now." He was almost angry.

"Calm down," I said.

Shelly hovered in my doorway. I told them about hitting my head in the basketball game, Will's strange behavior about the case, and how I had pieced it all together.

"He was always kind of bombastic, but why would he be jealous of a drug dealer exiled to a cabin in the woods?" Shelly asked.

"Who's also estranged from his family?" Rick asked.

"Because Scotty had Kelly. He was jealous of their love," I told them.

Rick and Shelly exchanged a look that made me uncomfortable. It felt like they were sharing a secret that was about me, right in front of me.

"That's impossible," Shelly said. "It's impossible that you would figure that out on your own."

Then John's voice called out, "Well, not impossible." I hadn't seen him walk in, but he must have been standing in my office all along. He was leaning against the wall.

"That makes no sense," Rick said. "What's the motive? Why would Will do any of this?"

"Jealousy!" I told them. "That night I was out with Scotty, I saw how he looked at Kelly. It was an obsessive look."

"I still don't understand," Shelly said.

"Me neither," Rick said.

"Maybe we never will," I told them. "But I'm going to start drafting a motion for a new trial. Will one of you please call Sheriff Trumble?"

Shelly walked back to her desk and mumbled something I didn't hear.

Rick tapped a couple of buttons on his phone and walked back into the hallway. "Hey, Sheriff," he said. "You're not going to believe this."

FORTY-EIGHT

I wasn't there when Will was arrested, but I heard about it. It was early one Saturday morning when the sheriffs busted in his door and found him naked in bed with a twenty-three-year-old yoga instructor. He was indignant. He protested his innocence, just like they all do, and declared he had nothing to do with Josh's disappearance.

"This is insane!" he shouted. "What evidence do you have? I'm being framed!" Sheriff Trumble presented him with the evidence. He showed him the report of the third blood type found on the bandanna and the DNA match from the jersey and water bottle. It wasn't a slam-dunk case, but neither was Scotty's. How Will's blood might have got on that bandanna without him murdering Josh Anderson would be up to his lawyer to explain. He'd need an alibi, and he didn't have one. The night of Josh Anderson's disappearance, he'd been at home, alone.

Scotty would be getting out of jail hopefully in the next year. Appeals take time. Even with the new evidence, motions had to be filed, and arguments had to be made. The last time I visited him, tears started to well in his eyes almost immediately.

"I don't know what to say," he said. Then he said, "Thank you."

He told me how he was already busy piecing his life back together. He'd told Kelly to hold off on selling the cabin. He wanted to find another way to make the numbers work and start a family with her there. He reached out to Eileen and Ray, and they responded. The relationship was still very strained, but it felt good to have both his parents talking to him again. They planned to start the relationship over. Everyone seemed forgiving and willing to let the past be in the past.

"The docs don't think my dad will live much longer," he said, and I assured him that I would do everything I could to get him out of jail as soon as possible.

"But I'm handing the appeals process off to someone else," I said. I explained to him that I was moving away. I'd talked with Watermelon Belly and wanted someone else to work the panel-attorney position. He was sad at first that I wouldn't be seeing him, but the focus was on getting out of jail. He told me how much it would mean to him to spend time with Ray.

"I just want to spend as much time as I can with him before he goes. End on a good note, you know?" he said.

I told him I understood.

When I went to see Kelly, she thanked me too. I worried she might ask for Arthur back, now that Scotty would be getting out, but she told me they'd talked about it and said, "You know, Scotty and I love Arthur more than anything in the world, but we also see how much he means to you. So if you want to keep him, we're willing to let you."

I felt selfish and relieved and overjoyed all at once.

"Scotty said you earned his companionship. And I agreed," she told me.

I told her that it meant a lot to me since "I never thought I'd get a best friend out of the deal."

Kelly and I talked about how hard the last year had been. I remarked that I was so nervous the first time I came to O'Haras to talk to her.

She looked at me funny.

"What?" I asked.

"That wasn't the first time you came in here," she said.

"What do you mean? Yeah, it was."

A man shouted from the end of the bar, "Here we go! Now we're putting it together." It was John, sipping on a beer alone.

"You'd been coming here for months," Kelly said. "We'd just never met." She laughed a little. "You were always pretty wasted. This must have been your last stop before home. I figured you didn't remember, so I never brought it up. I didn't want to embarrass you." She winked at me.

"Really? How long?"

"How long what?"

"How long had I been coming in here?"

"Once every couple of weeks. You'd just stand in the corner usually," she said. "You seemed pretty shy. And I was right."

"Oh…" I said.

"It's no big deal. You weren't like that creep Will Norris."

John patted me on the shoulder on his way out the door. "You're close," he said. "You're starting to get it."

I felt like everyone was keeping a secret from me again.

* * *

When I called Watermelon Belly to tell him I wanted to be removed from the panel of defense attorneys, he growled at me, "Are you sure?"

"Yes, I'm sure."

"What are you gonna do?"

"I don't know. Something else."

"Well, we're gonna miss you. You did a great job with that Watts case. Crazy case, that one."

"Yeah, it was." Words of praise from him sounded so foreign, they made me uncomfortable. We made a plan for me to wrap up the rest of my cases by summertime to ease the transition of my replacement.

* * *

I went to visit Will that July just before I moved away. He was in the Butte County jail awaiting trial. I wasn't sure if he'd be willing to talk, but the guards escorted me back, and I sat in the chair next to the telephone and waited for him to appear. I'd heard he wasn't going to accept a plea. With the forensic evidence of the bloody bandanna and no alibi, this seemed like a bad move. The only thing that would be hard to show was motive. Hard, but not impossible.

He walked into the waiting room and sat across from me. He looked terrible. His normally smooth skin was lacerated with fresh red scratches and scars. One eye was swollen almost entirely shut. His hair was cut short, but clumps were missing from his scalp. He must have been taking a beating in there. For a long moment we just stared at each other. I'd never seen so much rage in a person's eyes, and I could see the person who might have had some vindictive jealousy against Scotty and reacted in fear and panic by killing Josh.

"What do you want?" he asked. I started to speak, but he cut me off, saying, "I don't know how you did this, but you are going to rot in hell for it."

"Will—"

"You piece of shit," he said.

There was a long pause, and I wondered if he was going to let me get a word in. He seemed like he was done, so I spoke. "I just think that…you know…Josh Anderson…"

He leaned back in his chair, like he was trying to distance himself from the anger bubbling in him.

"Josh's body is still out there. You could tell the family where it is. I'm sure they would appreciate it."

He leaned toward me. "I don't know why or how this is happening, but you should know that when I get out of here, I promise you, you will pay for this. I know you're responsible, and when I find you, you're going to wish you were dead."

He slammed his fist on the table in front of him and jerked out of his chair, turning his back on me. He waited by the door until a buzzer sounded and the guard opened it. Then he disappeared down the hallway forever.

FORTY-NINE

The night before I moved away, the panel attorneys took me out to dinner. In the time I'd been a defense attorney in Butte County, each of us had worked autonomously, so I didn't know any of them particularly well, and it was a bit strange celebrating with mere acquaintances. But John was there, so I felt comforted, and I figured if there was ever a time to celebrate, it was now, since I was leaving Chico for a fresh start.

We went from one bar to another. We went to dinner, then to another bar. The conversation was filled with trite banter and empty platitudes. I sucked down hard liquor drinks with an earnest focus, trying to bludgeon the awkwardness of interacting with strangers whose mock affinity made me nauseated.

I may have been comforted by John's presence, but I was annoyed by his behavior. He was hovering in my ear all night. As I chatted with my colleagues about the uncertainty of my plans and the wild resolution of *The People of Butte County v. Scotty Watts*, he murmured cryptic comments like "How did you figure it all out without actually figuring it out?" and "This isn't quite the end, is it?"

"Shut up," I'd tell him.

"Who are you talking to?" a colleague would ask.

"No one."

At the end of the night, as John and I rode in an Uber home, John started reciting passages from that book he loved and had given me. I was drunk.

"The lawyer's mission is the nonetheless awesome task of trying to make a reality of equality before the law. If your 'truth' or mine get dented some in the process, it is only because we deal here with something less than the Kingdom of God, and something more than one truth."

I started laughing. "Shut up, John."

"Did you say something?" the Uber driver asked.

"Sorry for my friend. He's stupid."

"Who?"

"Never mind."

The Uber driver stopped in my driveway. John and I got out. I went inside, grabbed a bottle of whiskey, and took it out to the front porch, and John and I sat there drinking it.

"Maybe it was just bad timing," I said.

I thought about the years that had passed—getting kicked out of the navy, being disillusioned with love, and feeling like I was without close friends, as well as my strained relationship with my family, my mother's deterioration, and John's death. I looked around at the mostly empty street. Trees were everywhere. It was so calm.

"Chico is a beautiful place," I said. "I really love it here." It all started to make me sad.

"I think you're missing the point," John said.

"What's that supposed to mean?"

"Never mind."

I looked up at the night sky—a million points of light against an infinite darkness.

"Don't get anything like this in the city," I said.

Pretty soon we'd finished the whiskey, and I stumbled in through the garage. I'd been packing earlier that day, and I'd forgotten to close the garage door. Chico is the kind of place where you can do that. Boxes packed with my belongings were stacked and scattered all over the garage. I stumbled between my rusty green Honda, and when I reached out my hand, a box toppled over.

"Careful!" John called out.

I made it to the door leading into the house, but when I reached for the handle, I lost my balance and fell into my trash can. I went tumbling over and sprawled out onto the ground.

"Told you," John said.

I looked at the ceiling and laughed at my clumsiness. I groaned at him and then shouted, "Shut up, John!"

John seemed much more sober now.

"Are you ready to face it?" he asked.

"Face what?" I said. "Stop talking like that!"

I lifted my heavy head. My trash can lay on its side, and I saw something wedged in the corner nook behind where it had been. I rolled onto my side and looked closer. It was a white T-shirt, stained red with blood.

"There it is," John said.

I remembered right away where that T-shirt was from. It was the T-shirt I had loaned Will from the men's league game when he got a bloody nose. I'd let him borrow it to sop up his blood. I thought I'd thrown it away. I must have overshot the trash can, and it'd been there the whole time.

"Whoops," I said to John. I lay back again and laughed.

"With startling accuracy did you recount Will's murder of Josh Anderson," John said.

"So what?" I said. "I figured it out."

"Mostly, but not yet," John said.

A panic welled up in me. The room started to close in. My heart raced. Then my vision shook. I got up and grabbed the T-shirt.

I went from lying on my garage floor to being back in court in the middle of Scotty's trial. I was cross-examining Detective Cruz.

"Diluted?" I asked.

"Yes. Diluted," Detective Cruz said.

I was in the forest, holding the bloody T-shirt in my hands. The shirt was wet, and I held it over the bandanna, wringing it out with surgical precision, creating fine droplets that fell on the red fabric of a bandanna covered in San Francisco 49ers logos. Drip, drip, drip. Drops of light-red blood falling in the forest night air, landing and absorbing into the fabric. Diluted ever so slightly more than the other bloodstains.

Back in the garage, John stood before me, smiling. "It took you long enough," he said. Then he said casually, "At least all that envy and rage turned into remorse at some point. You've really got some issues, though."

"Shut up!" I shouted.

"You just transferred the blame is all," he said. "Must have been the guilt you felt."

Then I wasn't in the garage anymore. I was back to the night of Emily's rejection. It had rained that day. I was drinking a bottle of whiskey and looking up at the stars. Then I was getting in my car and driving to Forest Ranch. Then I was sitting in my car, parked in the vacant lot beside Scotty's cabin, watching Scotty and Kelly. It was a familiar routine I'd erased from my mind. I looked over at John sitting in the passenger's seat.

"Remember when I died?" John asked. "It's harder to account for your time when you're alone. You have no one to share the experience with."

I was back in the garage. I wiped sweat from my brow and felt the chill of the nighttime air. My heart dropped to my stomach, my head felt empty, yet my mind raced. I opened the driver's-side door to my car and popped open the trunk. I looked closely at the fabric of the empty trunk. Staring back at me were splotches in the gray-black fabric of the trunk, darker and outlined by a faint hint of red.

"No. No, no, no," I repeated, looking at John for answers.

"Yes," John said. "You're getting it."

Horrified, I stumbled back into the driveway, tripped, and fell on my backside. I didn't want the trunk to be open. I didn't want to hear John's voice anymore. But I had to know. I had to confirm it. I got up, shut the trunk, and snatched a hammer off the garage workbench. I ran out the side door of the garage to the back of the house. I stood before the metal barrel drum, looked down at its sealed lid, and looked to John once more.

"Don't open it," he said.

My face contorted like someone was wrenching knots into my skin. A well of emotion bubbled up. I started sobbing, a release of emotion I'd never known.

"You don't need to open it," John said. He eased closer and reached out a gentle hand. I ignored him.

I jammed the claw end of the hammer into the lid of the metal barrel drum and leaned on it. The rust of the barrel's lid groaned under the weight of the lever, but the claw slipped, and I fell back onto the wet ground. I cried harder.

"It can't be," I said.

"Yes, it can," John said. "You've got it now. It's okay."

I dug the claw in again and tried once more to wrench the barrel open.

"Shut up! Stop it!" I yelled. I was furious at him.

The hammer slipped again, and I fell back onto the grass, wet with dew. I needed something stronger—a crowbar maybe. I raced back to the side door of the garage. As I turned the corner, I tripped over something—a moving box—and watched the ground rush up at my face. Then things went dark.

* * *

I woke up the next morning to a metallic odor flooding my senses. I lifted my head and felt drips of viscous blood fall from my cheek, pooling into the puddle below. My mouth was dry. From where I lay, I could see the trashcan standing upright in its usual spot in the corner nook. I reached out and nudged it slightly, but pulled my hand away and rolled onto my back, groaning from my aching body. My temples throbbed. My vision was blurry.

Suddenly, John's face appeared inches from mine, so close that I could feel the heat of his breath on my skin. He leaned in, eye-to-eye with me, and tilted his head, regarding me with a curious look, like I was a strange creature he'd just discovered. Then he smiled wide – the lip-stretching, hundred-toothed, horrific grin of a demented lunatic. The walls of the room shook violently behind his face.

"Do you remember now?" he asked.

ACKNOWLEDGMENTS

Thank you to my good friend Joe. Without your friendship and support over the last decade, I could not have completed this book.

Thank you to Dan and Brendan for your close readings of early drafts and thoughtful feedback. You were instrumental in helping me get to the finished product. Your unwavering friendship over the years means the world to me, and I can't thank you gentleman enough.

Thank you to my beta readers who provided careful feedback - Laura E., Collin R., and Hitchko. All of your suggestions were extremely valuable and your enthusiasm kept me going when I wanted to give up.

I want to thank all of my friends who put me up while I was traveling, listened to my excited rants, and either showed or feigned interest in my completion of this project. I don't know what I did to deserve the good friends I have, but without you I'd be lost. Thank you.

To Elise, thank you for believing in me and supporting what I'm trying to do, and for your expert marketing guidance. My life is so much better with you in it. I love you.

Finally, thank you to my mother for always being supportive and encouraging of my desire to tell stories.